SHOCK TREATMENT
GENE CAFFREY

Published by

Automat.Press

//automat.press

Austin, Texas USA

Design and layout by

Jeff Vorzimmer

¡caliente!design

//caliente.design

Austin, Texas USA

Shock Treatment ©2015 by Eugene I. Caffrey

ISBN: 9781517790332

Automat Catalog #A001

V5.1

0 9 8 7 6 5 4 3 2

THURSDAY, FRIDAY
October 20, 21

Chapter 1

Owen pulled his Highlander off City Avenue, conceding to himself that it was just dumb luck he'd made the appointment for late in the day. It had taken him hours to get moving. He'd hoped the forced activity would nudge him out of his funk, yet he'd cursed himself all day for agreeing to Rick's request in the first place. Not that it was *that* big of a deal. But he dragged around a lengthening chain of uncompleted tasks for his own pathetic life. Why should he add links for a girl he didn't even know?

Because she was probably Rick's new girlfriend, is why. And Rick had stood by him as he swooned into his blue mood.

The brick facades of the Chelsea Arms complex flushed in the brilliant October sun and the oaks scattered about the grounds had started to shed their leaves. Three hatless Hispanics were raking them as Owen curved up the drive. Wind had picked up and the young men were struggling to keep their leaf piles from dancing away. The one nearest the drive, wearing a Sixers jacket, directed him to the management office.

The gray-haired receptionist expected him but asked that he wait for the manager to return from checking a bad dryer in one of the laundry rooms. She introduced herself as Rose and offered coffee. Owen refused and took a seat in a stiff chair against the wall, as far away as he could get in the small room. Annoyingly, Rose seemed to have nothing else to do but make conversation. She twisted a finger through her long hair as she spoke.

"It was a shame about Virginia. We were shocked. Such a sweet young thing. Were you related?"

1

"No. Her sister is a friend of a friend. He asked me to help wind up her affairs." Owen picked up a magazine from the small table beside him, hoping Rose didn't ask any more questions. He was out of practice making small talk. Besides, all he knew was that Virginia Steele had been killed in an auto accident in South Jersey and her twin sister Barbara worked in New York with Rick. Rick said she was too distraught to tend to what Owen had come in the last few years to call the details of death. And maybe she was. She and the dead girl were twins, after all. And, okay, all other family lived in Iowa. But probably, Rick just wanted to give him something to do and get him out of the house. Poor Rick. Always trying to help.

Rose ignored his intense concentration on the movie magazine in front of him.

"You know, we have lots of young people here, being so close to the university and all. Easy to see most of them driving stupid enough to get themselves killed. But it's hard to believe Virginia would do that."

Owen looked up but said nothing. On the phone that very morning, the guy at the body shop where the girl's wrecked Honda had been towed told him she'd been either reckless or careless. He hadn't asked why he thought so, and he hadn't really cared. So he stared at Rose for a second, bit his lip, and then buried his head back in the magazine.

After a few minutes of welcome silence, the office door opened and a pudgy forty-something with a round face and dark drooping mustache stamped in. He was wearing an old-fashioned grey cotton sweat suit and black sneakers. The man looked like a walrus and Owen wondered how long it might take to get that blubbery himself. He'd put on weight steadily since returning to Philadelphia in May and now wore a lot of old sweats himself. At that moment, an oversized safety pin was closing the waist of his too-small khakis. He was hoping the sport coat he wore for the big outing hid that makeshift solution to his wardrobe problem.

After quick introductions and Owen's awkward acceptance of sympathies over the girl's death, the walrus-manager proposed a friendly termination of Ms. Steele's lease, provided Owen would empty and clean the "unit" within two weeks. Owen thought that sounded fine but asked to see the apartment. The manager nodded.

"Sure, Mr. Delaney. Rose has an extra set of keys. You can keep them until the unit's empty. Rose'll show you her apartment."

The manager shook Owen's hand and went into his office. He was the first person Owen had touched since Rick had dropped by his house in August and hugged him after their long soulful talk.

• • •

The girl's third-floor walk-up had a nice view of the grounds. A strong light, filtered slightly by the trees outside, streamed through the windows and gave a warm luster to the hardwood floors. Owen took shallow breaths as he poked around for a quick tour while rap music boomed from down the hall.

The place was small but uncluttered. To Owen, whose housekeeping had turned to shit, the girl's neatness stung like a thump in the chest: bed snugly made, dishes all put away, clothes hung with military order, bathroom spotless, no piles of newspapers or magazines. He had to agree with Rose. Hard to imagine the girl who lived here as your typical careless driver.

The sparsely furnished apartment was remarkable also for its lack of decoration or personal effects. On a plain wooden desk squeezed into a corner of the bedroom sat a few books, a large calendar pad and a picture of a young woman he took to be Barbara, the twin in New York dating Rick. A laptop computer in its canvas case rested against the wall near the desk. But that was about it. Nothing hanging on the walls or setting elsewhere on the furniture. Not even a TV. Rick had told him to send all personal items to Barbara in New York and then give away the clothes and furniture to charity. Owen could see that even for him, the job wouldn't be too difficult. He took a deeper breath and wandered around again for a closer inspection.

In the bathroom, the medicine cabinet was packed with treatments for everything from allergies to burns, colds, infections and diarrhea. The girl was prepared for anything.

In the bedroom, a triangular patch of bright sunlight glared off the calendar pad on her desk. The calendar held one large tear-off page for each month, each day indicated with a box big enough to list the day's appointments. In tiny writing, the girl had carefully noted her monthly schedule. Owen guessed that, like him, the girl didn't own one of those smart phones that does everything for you.

Owen opened the shallow center drawer of her desk: pens, yellow legal pads, a roll of stamps, some envelopes, and a nearly empty address book. All very orderly. In the neatly labeled files in the file drawer, he found both her auto insurance and—sister Barbara would be pleased—a small life insurance policy naming her as beneficiary. He wrote the auto-insurance policy number and the claims department phone number on a page from one of the yellow pads, folded it with exaggerated precision, as the fastidious dead girl might have done, and put it in the breast pocket of his sport coat.

He reached across the desk for the photo he assumed to be Barbara. She was about his age, late twenties, pretty, with a wholesome yet wistful look and long, wavy auburn hair and smiling green eyes. Owen guessed sensitive and intelligent. Lucky Rick.

The picture reminded him of a girl from Connecticut he'd met in Lisbon during his travel period after college. He'd read her his poems and wallowed in young love for two intense weeks before she had to return home. He hadn't thought about her for a couple of years, and now the memory of those adventurous months traveling abroad hurt. His life had taken some disturbing twists since then and he longed to get back to being the old Owen, even if that guy had been overly serious and, probably, too sensitive.

But maybe he was not entirely dead. Seeing the picture of Barbara, for whom he'd turned off the TV and gotten out of the house, upgraded his day from the typical gray and foggy to the merely overcast. Owen wondered if he'd ever meet her. But he then remembered his pact with Rick not to poach each other's girls. He assumed it was still in effect.

He folded his arms across his chest and sighed. Pointless to spend any more time in the apartment. Concluding that it would only take a large van to move the girl's furniture and not more than a few small boxes for the personal items, Owen locked up the apartment and left about five.

On the way out, he stopped at the bank of mailboxes in the lobby and opened the one marked *Steele*. Very little there: junk-mail, electric bill and a small pink envelope, hand-addressed to Virginia Steele, with a return name and address of "*M. McNeil, PO Box 1141, Rancocas, NJ.*" Owen opened the envelope and read the note inside.

Virginia,

I am pretty sure we were spotted today. I'm scared. You should be too. My cell phone has died. But don't call me on the office phone. And no emails. Just write me at my post office box until I get a new phone.

Marian

The note was dated October 15. Last Saturday. The day of the accident.

There were no chairs in the empty lobby so Owen went outside and sat on the steps to read the note again. It fluttered in the wind and the glare of the setting sun made its faint feminine script difficult to read. But he went through it twice.

It sounded desperate. The girl's accident must have occurred just after her meeting with McNeil. Maybe she'd been panicked, not reckless.

Owen had a wild imagination. People had kidded him about it for as long as he could remember and it had always been a great source of entertainment for his friends who, for such a serious soul, had at one time been plentiful. Those flights of fantasy had been more or less grounded since he'd fallen into his funk except, of course, for Colgrove revenge plots. And he liked it better with his imagination subdued. No wasted effort on fantasies that often verged on the paranoid. So he tried to suppress the images that popped into his head as he stared at the pink paper flapping in his hand: an indistinct figure spying on the two girls seeing . . . what? Their stealing dresses from an upscale boutique? Their lying in bed together? Dealing drugs?

Owen desperately wanted to get his life back together and didn't want any complications as he struggled to do that. This Virginia Steele thing was supposed to be a simple step in the process. He'd even taken a shower before leaving home. But he hoped he wasn't getting into some messy situation that might be more than his fragile psyche could handle. He tore the note into small strips and wondered around looking for a trashcan.

After sprinkling the shredded note into a dumpster behind the girl's building, Owen took a while to find his car. He hadn't paid attention when Rose walked him to the apartment. When he finally found it, he got in and stared blankly at the dashboard for a moment before winding his way back down to the rush hour surge on City Avenue.

Crawling along with the stop-and-go traffic, he found himself for the first time thinking about the dead girl as a real person. He now had a picture of her—she undoubtedly looked just like Barbara—and, from the condition of her apartment, he assumed she was intelligent and compulsive. Probably good at her job as a paralegal at Fletcher & Rhoades. He sighed. A faint wave of sympathy made him squirm in his seat. And, despite his resolve to ignore it, he found himself puzzled again by that note. No clue what it meant.

He squashed an image of Virginia passionately kissing McNeil before getting into her Honda for the last time. He didn't want to think about it. And Barbara. No point in thinking about her either, pretty as she was. Would he ever meet her? Probably only at Rick's wedding.

Owen could feel his juices begin to flow and that bothered him. He had grown comfortable as a slug. Part of him wanted to stay a slug. His stomach felt heavy.

All this wild thinking reminded him of his high school cross-country days. He remembered running down steep hills, afraid of falling but unable to slow down. He'd often been tempted to sit on his butt and skid to a stop. Unlike the fearless Rick Jennings who'd played football. Rick had once described squeezing through the line on what was supposed to be a short run from his halfback position. As Rick told the story, once he'd seen daylight beyond the line, he'd asked himself "Why not just keep going?" and took off for a long, broken field touchdown.

Pulling into his driveway, Owen decided not to answer Rick's call if the phone rang that evening. If the phone rang it would have to be Rick. He was the only one who ever called. Everyone else had drifted away. Rick always called about eight, so, in theory, Owen would know who it was and pick up the phone. But Owen didn't want to talk. He wanted to sit and skid to a stop. Rick had plenty of friends. Let someone else do the favor.

• • •

The house phone rang at eight on the dot as Owen was finishing his second bologna sandwich. He ignored it. A few minutes later, his ancient cell phone rang and it occurred to him once again that it was pretty stupid having both a landline and a cell phone, since he rarely used either. He ignored the cell phone as well.

His stomach turned at the thought of telling Rick he couldn't handle even the limited favor he'd agreed to do. He left his unfinished sandwich on the kitchen table, slouched to the sofa in the big room off the kitchen and sulked, eyes glazed and mind wandering as the TV rolled on all evening. His mother had always referred to that big room as the family room even though the family was rarely there together. Hank had had a hectic business and civic life and played golf a lot so he was rarely home. For the millionth time Owen wondered why he'd ended up being an only child. Hank had a gung-ho temperament like Rick's dad—and the Jennings had six kids. Maybe there'd been something wrong with Hank or his mom or maybe they liked being only children themselves and thought he'd like it too. Or maybe it had to do with Colgrove. But that would have to mean that Hank knew.

When the TV news ended, Owen went up the back stairs to his bedroom, switched his TV on to Sports Center, kicked off his shoes, undid the safety pin at his waist, and stretched out on his bed with a couple of pillows propping up his head. From that position he could watch TV without straining. He could also see a total of six empty pizza boxes, two empty cartons from Shanghai Garden, and most of the clothes he had worn for the past week. He promised himself that the next day would be more productive. Get himself over that hump. When he began to drift off, he muted the TV and tried to keep watching the day's sports highlights. But he was soon asleep. In his clothes again.

Chapter 2

The morning after his visit to Virginia Steele's apartment, Owen woke early but, despite his best efforts, he couldn't get himself back to sleep as usual. Conflicting impulses were engaged in a street fight somewhere inside him, and he was trying unsuccessfully to slink past it in the dark. He got out of bed and showered, congratulating himself on his second shower in two days.

In the kitchen he made himself coffee and toast and sat at the round oak table. The soft morning light angled across the yard and passed its arm through the big kitchen window. Outside, fallen leaves swirled about the lawn. Owen remembered that the weather guy on TV had mentioned a front on the way.

The Delaney property spread out for half a football field, much bigger than even the other impressive properties in the neighborhood. Muscular maples, dropping their red and brown leaves in the wind, ringed the lawn and gardens which, unfortunately, were no longer as manicured as when Hank supervised their care. He wished he could still take a proprietary pleasure in the beautiful grounds. But he just couldn't.

Owen had slipped into his sluggish "woe-is-me" existence after his mother died the previous November, just a day after telling him about Colgrove. He'd never told anyone else about him and had tried without success to repress all thoughts of the man since he'd gone to meet him last Christmas. His funk had deepened after that horrible visit. He managed to graduate law school—but just barely. Hadn't even bothered to sniff around for a job. And when classes

10

ended in May, he packed up and came back to Philly to hibernate alone in his house in the upscale Chestnut Hill neighborhood.

He'd grown up in that oversized stone monstrosity. Inherited it from his mom along with a small fortune in stocks and cash. He could afford to remain a recluse for as long as he liked. And he had been doing just that. Although he told himself each night that he should get himself moving again the next morning, he simply couldn't get himself over the hump.

How many breakfasts had he eaten at that table over the years? Thousands? Mostly alone or with his mom. Hank had always hustled off to work at dawn. Odd, he couldn't remember ever calling him anything but "Hank". Never "Daddy" or "Dad" or "Pop." His mom had always referred to him as Hank and he'd picked that up from her. Looking back, it seemed a clear sign. Even so, he'd been happy. More or less. Of course, in those days, the leaves were always raked up and dirty dishes weren't stacked at the kitchen sink.

He missed the morning paper and wanted to kick himself for letting his mom's subscription expire. And why hadn't he bothered to call and re-subscribe himself? What a useless shit he'd turned out to be.

In self-defense, he decided to take some action. Any action. He got up to check if Rick had left a message when he'd called the previous evening. There was nothing on the landline. But the cell phone had a long one.

"Sorry I missed you, Odee . . ." Rick almost always called him Odee. Owen Delaney . . . OD . . . Odee . . ."But I wanted to suggest something."

Owen thought at first that Rick wanted to add wrinkles to the favor. But it was something different altogether.

11

"When I told Barbara you'd agreed to help out despite your situation, she felt guilty for imposing. I told her I thought getting out would do you good, but she wanted to thank you personally. She asked for your phone number but—hope you don't mind—I suggested we meet in person. I know you could use a little socializing."

Great. Now that he'd decided to beg off doing Barbara's bidding, Owen was no longer so keen on meeting her. Damn Rick's good intentions. Sometimes his enthusiasm just pissed Owen off.

Rick began speaking quickly, probably trying to finish what he had to say before voicemail cut him off.

"It turns out that both Barbara and I and Joanie are free on Sunday. Is it possible that we could get together? I know I haven't mentioned Joanie to you. She's a girl I'm dating whenever I get a chance. But anyway, it would be easier on us if you come up to New York, but maybe we could drive down to Philly. Let me know."

Owen smiled. So Rick and Barbara were *not* an item, as his mom used to call it.

How many days until Sunday? Never sure of the day of the week, every day being just about the same for him, he used the weekly Eagles games as a point of reference and calculated that it was Friday. Maybe he *should* push on. He probably had time to do enough to make Barbara at least a little grateful when they met on Sunday. He'd always liked to please women and it could be the lever he needed to get himself up and out. But he'd have to hurry.

He forced himself to call Fletcher & Rhoades, where Virginia had worked and where he'd have to tend to more post mortem details. He knew the Fletcher & Rhoades number by heart and would remember it forever. Hank had been a partner there and had worked at the firm for twenty-five years before he died. Owen had grown up with the firm as a background to his life and Hank's friends all assumed he'd be working there someday too. But things hadn't turned out that way. Owen had hoped he would never set foot in the place again. Fortunately, the Virginia Steele business would be back office stuff so he might not have to see anyone he knew.

Owen lived in dread that he would meet someone, somewhere, some place, who would realize what a waste he'd become. It had to be obvious, even if the mirror said the only things different were a haggard look to his bright malamute eyes, about seven pounds of junk food around his middle and a perpetual need for a shave and a haircut. And of course, the greasy look to his fine blond hair would shock anyone who knew him. His hair had always been his trademark. Straight and long, like a maestro or a scientist in a 1940s movie. Blond as a Clairol girl's. An angel's hair, spun from light, his mom used to say. All his life, the ladies had felt compelled to stroke or kiss it. Yet he had ceased caring for it or about it. On the other hand, he had at least taken a shower that morning.

When he explained to the Fletcher & Rhoades operator the reason for his call, she switched him to the office of Carter Brock, the firm manager. The woman who answered for Brock put him on hold for an inordinate amount of time before returning to report that Mr. Brock could meet with him at three that afternoon.

Owen then emailed Rick. Sunday would be fine but he hated the idea of driving to New York. He preferred to meet in Philly.

After checking the train schedule and finding he had until one-fifty to catch the Chestnut Hill Local to Center City, he spent the balance of the morning cleaning up the mess in the kitchen and the adjacent family room—just in case. Took two loads in the dishwasher. For only one person who never cooked. Damn, he'd been lazy. Maybe he should hire someone.

He finished up with time to spare and a crazy smile on his face. But dressing for the trip again posed some issues. This time he wore a long sweater to cover the pin in his pants. It covered better than the sport coat. Besides, the informality would be a kind of protest against the old-style law firm etiquette that had always made him so uncomfortable.

• • •

On the train into Center City, once out of the residential neighborhoods, Owen lost himself in the miles of intricate graffiti on the walls of abandoned buildings along the way. If Hank had taken photos during his thousands of commuter runs over the years, he could have made a telling time-lapse of the changes to industrial Philadelphia. Owen knew that, in Hank's early years with Fletcher & Rhoades, the cinder-block warehouses and brick factories along the rail line were well maintained and bustling with activity. But as industrial output in the region had waned, the buildings were shuttered and abandoned. Now, with a vitality that seemed out of place, vines climbed mangled chain-link fences and weeds smothered old loading docks. Windows that once poured light into successful industrial operations were now broken or darkened.

These mothballed warships of the Philadelphia economy were now good only as canvases for the street artists who eventually filled every flat space visible from the train between North Philadelphia and Thirtieth Street Station.

From one perspective, the time lapse of the striking mural would almost be beautiful, as the graffiti increased in color, style, and sheer wall coverage. On the other hand, it was common knowledge that the deterioration of Philly industry had meant job losses, a shrinking tax base, and a more difficult life for everyone. Even for Center City lawyers who, Hank had complained, had to hustle for business that had been there for easy picking a generation before. His mother had often said that the slumping of the Philadelphia economy and the changes in the firm had been the real causes of Hank's heart attack.

In Center City a fine piercing rain fell. Owen had forgotten that the incoming front was supposed to bring some precipitation on Friday afternoon. Within minutes his wet wool sweater began to smell like a puppy.

The Fletcher & Rhoades offices were only a few blocks from Suburban Station and as Owen hurried along he thought of Hank. How many times had he quickstepped over the same wide sidewalks in the early morning light to his roost atop the Harcroft Building? Often toting two briefcases. Hank had always wanted Owen to be lawyer. Just like he'd always wanted Owen to play those competitive ball sports at which Hank himself had been so good. But though Owen avidly followed most sports, he sucked at playing them and hated even to try. He didn't want the lawyer's life either, particularly one like Hank's.

Though Hank eventually gave up on the sports, he'd never stopped pushing for the law, even when the college-aged Owen (with his mom's secret encouragement) dreamed of something more exciting. He had tentatively fixed on the idea of a life as a poet or novelist, maybe by way of an academic career. But Hank was relentless. He recruited some of his partners to put the hard sell on Owen as well. They gave him summer jobs in the mailroom, invited him to important courtroom presentations, and even had him sit in on the closings of major corporate transactions in their impressive paneled conference rooms.

Owen had respectfully resisted the pressure and managed to buy time with a one-year travel adventure after college, which he was stretching to two when Hank had his massive heart attack and died suddenly.

Back home, remorseful that he and Hank hadn't resolved their differences, Owen felt he owed something to Hank. Out of a kind of love and loyalty that he now realized had been misguided, he'd enrolled in law school in New York City the fall after Hank died. Throughout law school he'd questioned that decision; but damn those Rick Jennings pep talks, he'd plodded through. Until Colgrove, of course. At that point, he told himself, he owed nothin' to nobody. He would not be a lawyer and all the lawyers in the Harcroft Building would not be able to put Humpty Dumpty, Esquire together again.

Owen pushed through the heavy glass doors to the Harcroft lobby then stopped to dry his hair with his handkerchief. He took much longer than he needed. His heart rate had quickened as the familiar squeak of his rubber soles on the marble floor reminded him that he might end up in a packed elevator. More than one bright summer morning had been ruined by an attack of his claustrophobia when an aggressive crowd shoehorned into his elevator, squeezing him into a corner for a panicked ride up to his job in the mailroom. And if those crazy fears about the elevator weren't enough, the anticipation of entering Fletcher & Rhoades again made his stomach flip. He'd always felt out of place in the hard driving atmosphere of the firm and in his current funk, should he meet any of Hank's old partners, he'd feel as if he had been accused of a crime of which he was totally innocent and completely ignorant. Even the fantasy of a grateful Barbara did nothing to undo the knot in his gut. Yet he managed to squeak his way to the bank of elevators and wait for a lull in the lobby crowds for an empty car.

The current offices of the firm occupied the building's top eight floors. The reception areas on each floor were done up in what his mom had called a "Williamsburg" style when she had helped with the décor. They were formal and imposing, but lighter than the heavy leather reception areas in the firm's old offices near Broad and Chestnut. Carter Brock had his office on the top floor along with the most senior partners, making it unlikely that Owen could avoid seeing people he knew.

According to Hank, the firm had no manager when he'd started there. The job of tending to the firm's business details fell to a rotating partner who hated the assignment because he'd have to give up some of his beloved practice to do it. But as the firm grew and firm management became more complex, Fletcher & Rhoades went the way of all big firms and hired a professional manager to oversee everything from strategic planning to marketing, from productivity evaluations of the firm's lawyers to space requirements, from insurance to hiring and firing non-legal personnel. Managers like Carter Brock were important and got a top-floor office.

Owen's breath quickened when the receptionist told him Mr. Brock was running late and he realized he'd have to spend time in the very public waiting area. He sat in a wing chair in the corner. To pass the time, but more importantly, to avoid possible contact with any of Hank's buddies who might walk through, he grabbed a large, three-ringed binder from the table next to him and, like a near-sighted old man, held it close at eye level, shielding his face and as much of his hair as he could. He wished he had a hat.

The binder contained information about the firm and its lawyers. Skimming through it he recognized many faces, most of which had a self-important look that he couldn't imagine himself ever projecting. Even the women. Even Margaret Taylor, the hot-shot anti-trust lawyer who, already well into her forties, had one summer afternoon stopped by the mailroom just to ask if she could touch his hair. Over the years, many older women had done similar things and, ridiculous as it might seem, he'd come to think of his hair as exerting a powerful force field that affected everyone who looked at him. It was an odd, sometimes scary and sometimes annoying phenomenon. Scary, say, when it gave tough guys the impulse to pick on him, more likely than not calling him a queer, and annoying when older women treated him like a five-year-old. But, even aside from its appeal to women his own age, the force field did have its pluses. Like the time in Greece when a middle-aged woman had seductively beckoned "Blondie" up to her room when she saw him walking on the street below her window.

As he paged through the firm binder, he didn't recognize any of the younger faces. The new guys all looked to him like earnest ass-kissers, maybe even eager Nazi privates in a World War II movie. As usual, he made gentler judgments about the new young women.

He stopped to read the page about Carter Brock, who looked a little different from the rest. Like a friendly owl, with a pleasant round face, round glasses, and close-cropped graying hair that frizzed up at the edges, he must have been in his mid-fifties.

Georgetown Law, a couple of years at Sterling and Moss —Rick's firm in New York—and then a Wharton MBA. Spent twenty years with a consulting group specializing in law firm management and strategic planning. Joined Fletcher & Rhoades about five years ago, just before Hank died.

At three-ten, Brock bounced into the reception area in shirtsleeves—a big no-no in the early days of Hank's career—and greeted Owen with an outstretched hand. "Nice to meet you, Owen. I knew your dad a bit. I joined the firm only a few months before he passed. He was highly regarded around here."

"Yes. Thank you." Owen didn't remember telling Brock's secretary that his father had worked at the firm. But maybe he'd said something about it. Whatever.

Trim and fit, Brock moved with an athletic stride that Owen would never have imagined from the photo of the studious-looking lawyer in the firm PR book. He gripped Owen's hand firmly and did not let go as he spoke. "Very sad about Virginia Steele. She hadn't been here very long and I didn't know her, but the lawyers she worked with all say she always did a wonderful job. Careful and thorough."

Brock's hand finally released Owen's but then moved to his shoulder. "Let me bring you to her work space. It's down on the fourteenth floor with the real estate paralegals."

To his surprise, despite all the touching, Brock didn't set off any alarms in Owen. Probably because he had no history with him through Hank.

As they approached the elevator, Owen heard his name called from down the hall.

John Frazier waggled his hand in the air, signaling Owen and Brock to wait as he rushed through a conversation with a younger man, also in shirtsleeves. Frazier, now about seventy-five, wore the full legal uniform. No shirtsleeves for him. Old school in every way. Prominent Philadelphia family connected to all the important manufacturing fortunes of the area, New England prep school, and, despite only "gentleman Cs" at Penn undergrad and law school, desired by all the white-shoe law firms when he came on the market. He was a pillar of the legal community during Owen's childhood, active in the bar association and member of any number of blue ribbon panels and charitable boards in the city. Tall and lean, he still had good bones and a patrician air. And even Owen could see that his dark pinstriped suit fit him perfectly.

When he finished his conversation, Frazier approached them. "Owen, after you are done on the fourteenth floor, come back up and see me. I want to catch up. I have no appointments this afternoon, so just ask the receptionist to buzz me."

"Will do, Mr. Frazier."

Owen wondered how Frazier knew his business at the firm.

On the fourteenth floor Brock introduced Owen to the paralegal who worked in the cubicle next to Virginia's and suggested that, after collecting Virginia's personal effects, Owen return upstairs where they could review any relevant matters from Virginia's employment file.

Virginia's workmate, a mousy girl with a munchkin voice, about twenty-five, had little to say when Owen asked about Virginia.

"I really didn't know her that well. I've only been here four months. We were both new." She spoke to the floor, then directed her gaze over Owen's left shoulder. "We did a little work together.

She was very professional and thorough. And smart." Then she turned her head well to Owen's right. "She seemed a bit on edge for a week or so before her accident. But maybe that was just my imagination."

"Any idea what might have been bothering her?" That note from Marian McNeil continued to nag at Owen.

"Oh, no. We never talked about personal things." Her eyes were now cast down toward her flat-heeled shoes.

Owen shrugged and began examining Virginia's workspace. Like her apartment, the cubicle was almost barren: a few yellow pads, some blank purchase and sale agreements for residential real estate, and a copy of the Philadelphia Zoning Code. No work papers of any sort and nothing of a personal nature other than another photo of Barbara. He picked it up to take with him.

"I always thought it was a little odd that she kept a picture of herself on her desk." The mousy girl snuck a sideways glance at the picture as she spoke.

Owen almost laughed out loud when he realized that the photo that had so infatuated him the previous day could easily have been someone other than Virginia's twin. Maybe even her friend that McNeil woman. He had wished it to be Barbara, so he'd believed that. But unless Virginia had indeed surrounded herself with her own photos, the pictures had to be Barbara. Owen decided that, if Virginia hadn't told the girl she had a twin, he wouldn't mention it either.

The girl took Owen to the closet where the paralegals kept their personal items and he retrieved a pair of sneakers, an umbrella, a purse, and an overcoat that belonged to Virginia.

With his arms full, he made his way to the elevator and back up to the twentieth floor where he was shown to Carter Brock's corner office.

Brock had a slim file open on his desk, which he closed as Owen entered.

"Have a seat, Owen. I've just finished reviewing Virginia's file and talked to bookkeeping. It turns out she does have a partial pay and a little accrued vacation due. But that'll be direct deposited on our next payday so there's nothing we need to do about it now."

He slid the file aside and leaned back in his chair. Owen noticed the family photos on the credenza behind his desk. Skiing and beach scenes. Looked like happy times. Owen's house in Chestnut Hill had remarkably few family photos on display. He felt a tightness in his throat.

Lacing his hands behind his head, Brock went on. "I wish we could have been more proactive in all this. We haven't even sent a sympathy card."

Owen wondered what a big firm like Fletcher & Rhoades typically did when a lower level employee died. Flowers and cards from the firm, sure. But Brock seemed to expect even more from himself. If Owen didn't find Brock so likeable, he might have concluded that he was witnessing a little act put on for his benefit.

Lost in his reverie, Owen missed some of Brock's energetic narrative.

". . . a sister in New York as her emergency contact. I called the number. A hotel, but she'd moved and left no forwarding information. The police who called our switchboard Saturday when they found our business cards in Virginia's car had reached the sister. Don't know how they got the number. But they'd misplaced it by the time I called for it on Monday. Hadn't been for that police call, it would've been like Virginia disappeared into a black hole."

Brock raised his hands in exasperation as he finished his story. "The medical examiner said he turned the body over to a New Jersey funeral home for cremation. The funeral home would give us no information other than the remains had been sent to Iowa.

"I hate the thought that we're just standing on the sidelines here. How did you know Virginia, Owen?"

Owen tensed at the question. Unsure of Brock's sincerity and wary of all things Fletcher & Rhoades, Owen decided on minimal disclosure. His voice was throaty when he answered. "I didn't. A friend of mine in New York is a friend of the family. He asked me to help them out. I don't know the family at all."

Brock perked up. "Would you ask your friend for some contact information, Owen? I truly dislike doing nothing in these circumstances."

Owen said "sure" but had no intention of following through. He wanted to have as little contact with the firm as possible. And he didn't think either Barbara or her family in Iowa would be disappointed that they hadn't received a sympathy card from Virginia's employer.

"That's great," sighed Brock. "Now, what did you find downstairs?"

"Nothing much." Owen showed Brock what he had.

Brock came around the desk to inspect Virginia's things. He raised his eyebrows as he poked through them. "No files? I guess someone has gone through her things already."

Owen wanted to be helpful. "No. No files anywhere downstairs. And none in her apartment either. I've been there already."

Brock nodded. "Well, there shouldn't have been any files in her apartment. We have a strict rule that no files can be taken from the office by non-lawyers." He backed two steps towards his door.

"I guess that's it, Owen. Nice meeting you." He waited for Owen to get up and gather Virginia's things. "If you are going to see John Frazier, the receptionist will direct you."

As Owen reached the office door, Brock added "And don't forget that contact information. Please."

The receptionist called Frazier on the intercom and then directed Owen to his office. Owen took a while to get there, having first asked for a plastic bag for Virginia's things—which had to be fetched from the nineteenth floor supply closet—and then having stopped in the men's room. As he approached the office, midway down a hall of plush blue carpet, Owen recalled that, years ago, in the firm's old offices, Frazier had a huge corner office in which his gigantic desk and tons of awards and mementos fit comfortably. Frazier had not been one of the partners Hank had recruited in his campaign to make a lawyer out of Owen, so Owen had never been to his current office. And when he peeked in the open door, its small size surprised him. But at least it was still on the top floor.

Frazier sat at his desk, back to Owen, facing the window. His slack posture made Owen wonder if he was asleep. Owen remembered Hank complaining about older lawyers at the firm who had so little to do they actually napped on the job. But that seemed unlikely in Frazier's case. He cleared his throat and Frazier turned, waved him in and pointed to the chair facing him across his old boxcar of a desk. It took up almost the entire width of the office. Owen's mom would have counseled against placing it in such a small space.

Frazier blinked his eyes a few times before he spoke. Damn. Maybe he had been asleep.

"Well, Owen, did you get everything done with Carter?"

"Yes. Not much to do, actually."

"Good. I am glad someone showed up. We have heard nothing from that poor girl's family since the accident. I've been worried and asked Carter to let me know if anyone contacted us. It surprised us to learn you would be coming. How did you know Virginia?"

Fully awake now, Frazier leaned forward at his desk, looking directly at Owen. Owen was struck by his handsome appearance, even in his mid-seventies. Full head of wavy gray hair, which he wore long enough for curls to lap the edges of his crisp white collar. No glasses. Broad forehead and clear blue eyes. Still sparkling teeth and strong, perfectly balanced features with a ruddy tint—from years of riding with the hounds, Owen assumed. No wonder that according to Hank, Frazier had been called Prince John when he was a young lawyer in the firm.

Owen took a few seconds to remember Frazier's question. He had not only been captivated by Frazier's appearance close up, but had also stumbled over Frazier's concern about Virginia. He found it hard to see Prince John being worried about the family of a lowly paralegal who had barely started her career with the firm.

After only a few missed beats, he regained his bearings and gave Frazier the same answer he'd given Carter Brock. "I didn't actually know the girl. I was asked to tend to some details by a friend in New York who knows her sister." For some perverse reason, Owen again held back the information that Virginia's sister was a twin.

Frazier swiveled in his chair to move some papers to a small filing cabinet behind his desk. Owen looked over Frazier's shoulder at the view. The rain had stopped and the fading light softened what would otherwise be a harsh, low-rise landscape of small office and commercial buildings receding into the slums of north Philadelphia. Not as impressive as the views from the front of the building which looked out on City Hall and the downtown area. Not nearly as nice as the view from Carter Brock's office.

Frazier changed the subject when he turned back to face Owen. "And you. What are you up to these days? You should be just about finished law school, no?"

"Actually, I finished this past spring."

"And you're working in New York?"

"No." Owen didn't want to go into great detail. "I'm taking a little break, living in the house in Chestnut Hill. Not quite sure that I want to practice law."

Frazier nodded. "Understandable, Owen. Had I known years ago what the practice of law would turn out to be, I might have chosen something else for myself as well. Although it was a great life for a while."

He leaned forward again and spoke in a lower voice. "When I started with the firm, and even when your dad started, we had a true profession." His eyes narrowed slightly and he turned his head to the side, holding that pose for a few seconds before facing Owen again. "We were men of honor and respectability. The firm encouraged us to put time into the community, for the good of both the firm and the community."

He paused and neatened up some papers on his desk, furrowing his brow slightly, as though he was debating whether or not to share an important secret. But he continued. "We worked civilized hours and never had to fight with clients about our bills. But today, with the region's economy having slipped so far, the law is just another cutthroat business."

Almost whispering now, he leaned further forward. "Believe me, Owen, it *can* be cutthroat. Hire young studs and fillies to work as many hours as you can squeeze out of them. Bill clients for their hours at three times what the kids are worth. What the hell, let the clients pay for their training."

Prince John sounded more like a disgruntled employee than a prince. "And even as a partner, you are expected to bill for an unconscionable number of hours. It's no wonder lawyers pad their time. And no wonder that clients refuse to pay."

Frazier's bitterness shocked Owen. Not just the words. He had heard those complaints before, from Hank sometimes, and from guys in law school trying to show off their sophistication. But the tone. The changes Frazier described made him more than sad. They made him angry. The veins in his already ruddy face became more noticeable, almost blue. His whispered rant had turned into a teeth clenched hiss and he finished with a tiny speck of spittle in the corner of his mouth.

And then the tirade was over. He resumed his princely demeanor.

"You know, Owen, I'm going to be part of a symposium at the Union League next week on the changes in the practice of law. Tuesday at four. Why don't you come? There will be old lawyers like me and new, efficient types like Carter Brock—who doesn't even have to practice law or bring in a single client to make a decent living at this firm. It might help you make up your mind about what you want to do."

Owen didn't think he needed any help. His mind had been made up when he met with Colgrove. But Prince John's invitation flattered him, and after experiencing the angry prince, Owen's gut said to humor him.

"Sounds interesting. I just might come." That made two white lies in a matter of minutes, counting his false promise to get Barbara's contact information to Brock.

A light tap on the open door caught their attention. The lawyer in shirtsleeves who had earlier been speaking to Frazier in the hall poked his head into the room. Mid-forties, short, balding, with coarse, lumpy features—almost dumb looking—he carried himself with a kind of street-smart swagger. His sweet cologne overpowered the little room.

Frazier looked up. "Phil. Come in. Let me introduce Owen Delaney. I have known him since he was a boy when his dad worked here. Owen has just finished law school."

"Scrounging for a job?" Phil's smile showed bad teeth and, Owen thought, bad manners.

Before Owen could respond, Frazier interrupted. "Phil. Don't be so quick to assume everyone is grasping for your rung on the ladder. Owen is actually here on a work of mercy, on behalf of Virginia Steele's family."

Frazer lifted his eyes toward the ceiling and opened his palms to the heavens, a father exasperated with his wise-assed son. "Owen, this is Phil Gordon, one of our aggressive new partners. Phil is in the real estate department."

"Pleasure," said Owen, and immediately turned back to Frazier. He started to roll his eyes but then saw that Frazier was looking up at Gordon. Owen waited.

"John. Don't want to interrupt. But we have to talk about that Solebury Township deal today. Something has come up. When you're finished."

Gordon's manner did not reflect the traditional deference to a senior partner that Owen would have expected. Frazier apparently failed to notice. "Fine, Phil. I will call on you when Owen and I are done."

"Good. And good luck to you, Owen." Gordon hurried down the hall.

Owen and Frazier continued their small talk for a while, remembering the "old days" as though Owen were a senior himself. The quantum increase in Owen's human contact for the day finally began to take its toll. He checked his watch and faked surprise at the hour. "Gee. It's four-fifty. I need to hurry for my train."

"Of course, Owen." Frazier stood. "Hope to see you at the Union League Tuesday."

"I'll try to be there." Owen picked up the bag of Virginia Steele's things and gave Frazier a short-armed handshake. He walked alone down the hall toward the elevators, musing that Hank would be alarmed that John Frazier had abandoned the old-school rule about escorting guests to and from their visits to a lawyer's private office.

• • •

Owen emerged on the street with a little swagger for having come through his visit to the firm unscathed—not that he had conjured up a clear idea of what those boogie men were supposed to do to him. But he welcomed even a pea sized bit of new self-confidence and was contemplating crossing the Parkway for a beer in the corner pub when Phil Gordon appeared at his side from nowhere, still in shirtsleeves, Styrofoam cup in hand.

"Hello again, Owen. Just stepped out for my favorite brew from down the block. Don't like the coffee the firm makes." He took a sip. "By the way, how did you know Virginia Steele and her family?"

Now, Brock had already asked that question. And so had Frazier. Coming from them it had seemed understandable and reasonable. But coming from Phil Gordon, the question felt prying, maybe even sinister. Owen told himself to quiet his imagination. The question seemed offensive only because Gordon's himself was a little offensive. Nevertheless, Owen was tempted to tell Gordon to mind his own business. He resisted the temptation, but did stiffen.

"I didn't. A family friend asked me to help out since I live in Philadelphia."

Gordon rounded his mouth and nodded. "Oh. So you don't know much more about her than we do?"

"No. I don't." Owen looked down on the shorter Gordon and smiled, hoping his attitude conveyed a trace of disdain.

Gordon's bantam rooster pose sagged, and Owen walked away without another word, leaving Gordon squinting, sucking on his lip, and holding his cup in an outstretched hand like a panhandler asking for spare change.

Chapter 3

Returning home about five-forty-five after his visit to Fletcher & Rhoades, Owen found an email from Rick agreeing to bring Barbara and Joanie to Philly on Sunday in the early afternoon. After months of studiously avoiding human contact, the modest success of the day had him all fluttery over the visit. His mind raced with the details. How should he dress? Should he have something for them to eat? Then it occurred to him that they might not be planning to come to his house. Rick's parents lived just three houses down the block from Owen and they could just as easily meet there.

If they came to his house, they'd be the only people to enter his house since that night in August when Rick knocked at the back door after visiting his parents. And Rick, that night, had been his only visitor since Owen had moved back to Philly in May.

Rick had come to see his parents after passing the New York bar and, not having heard from Owen since May, he'd popped in without phoning first. He later said that a call would have been futile since his dozens of prior calls had gone unanswered.

Hearing the knock at his back door, Owen had hesitated before getting up from the TV. But with it still light outside, he'd seen Rick's car in the drive and shuffled through the kitchen to face the music. When he opened the door, Rick's mouth fell open.

"Jesus! Odee, what happened to you?"

"Whadaya mean?" Owen had mumbled flatly.

Rick had then walked uninvited into the kitchen. Looking around, he winced at the stacks of dirty dishes and bags of trash. "What a mess! What have you been doing to yourself?"

"Nothing. I'm just tired."

Rick moved quickly through the kitchen into the family room, grabbed the remote, turned off the TV, and plopped himself into one of the big armchairs.

"Too tired to return my phone calls? Too tired to send an email? Too tired to take out the trash or get a haircut? You look like Albert Einstein. Damn it, Odee, you're not tired. You're clinically depressed."

Owen had felt dizzy. While at some level not far from the surface, Owen had made the same diagnosis, it had taken Rick's saying the words out loud to get him to admit his condition to himself. Sitting down on an ottoman facing Rick, elbows on his knees, he lowered his head to his hands.

"Yes, I know, Rick."

"Well, what are we going to do about it, Odee?"

They talked for an hour.

Owen had always liked talking to Rick. They'd known each other for most of their lives but Rick, two years younger, had permanently latched on to Owen in early high school when they both worked on the student literary journal. Rick's dad felt the journal wasted his son's time. He wanted Rick to spend more time on sports. But Rick, a superb jock like everyone else in his family, also liked hanging out with all the poetry nerds who acknowledged Owen to be their brightest star.

The group would lounge for hours in the cramped office of the journal talking books and movies and psychoanalyzing each other.

They particularly enjoyed analyzing Owen's claustrophobia, a hot topic after his embarrassing panic attack in the crowded back seat of Bob Doherty's two-door Ford. Most of the young Freuds in the group offered exotic, ever-changing explanations for the problem. But Rick never did. He just made sure he always saved his idol a seat up front.

When Owen enrolled in law school after his European travels, Rick, who had just finished college, entered with the same first-year class. In law school their relationship changed. A natural at the law, Rick had played the big brother, coaching Owen through his coursework and encouraging him to fight his ambivalence about the career path he was on.

That night in August they had talked about everything that had fed Owen's depression—no career, no parents—but Owen's chest tightened every time he was tempted to tell Rick about Colgrove. So Rick knew only part of the story and his well-meaning resolve to keep in closer touch with his friend missed the mark by a wide margin.

Looking back on that August evening, Owen again recognized Rick as a good soul. He had done the right thing agreeing to help Rick help Barbara. Even if it was a major hassle. And even if Barbara didn't fall in love with him on Sunday.

But Owen's stomach rolled when it occurred to him that ever thoughtful Rick, remembering the pigsty Owen had been living in, did indeed plan to bring the girls to his parents. That would mean he'd have to face Rick's parents. He rubbed his palms down his pants legs, then hurried to Hank's office and emailed Rick that his house would be much cleaner than the last time he visited and he'd expect him and the girls between one and two. He then turned on the TV and watched ESPN until it was time for the eleven o'clock Philly news.

Halfway through the news, he became upset at a young reporter's bugging a tearful mother whose toddler had been badly injured by a hit and run driver. So he muted the TV and lay back on the well-cushioned sofa that his mom had always described as the focal point of the family room. He intended to put the sound back on for the Tonight Show, but he drifted into a half sleep during which troubling thoughts about the day's visit to Fletcher & Rhoades trickled through his consciousness like the news stream constantly crawling across the bottom of the TV when he watched CNN.

The Fletcher & Rhoades news stream was derailed by the image of a young woman in a car rental commercial who reminded him of Barbara. He sat up, stretched, had a glass of milk in the kitchen and eventually wandered upstairs where he changed for bed like a normal human being and fell asleep imagining a long, heartfelt conversation with that girl in the photo.

SATURDAY
October 22

Chapter 4

After coffee and toast the next morning Owen decided to check out Virginia's car. Those details would make for a more complete report to Barbara when they met the next day. So he called the body shop in South Jersey for directions. The same nasal voice that had said Virginia was reckless answered the call.

"We're just off Route 295 in Mt. Holly. Take the exit for 537 and go east about two miles. We're on the right." He ended with a sneeze that explained his voice.

Owen pulled out of his driveway for south Jersey about nine thirty. He would have preferred a more sporty car than his mom's old Highlander, and he could easily afford one. That huge inheritance was at least one benefit to being an only child. Hell, he hadn't even taken a dollar out of that damn envelope Colgrove had slid to him across his shiny desk. But he couldn't get himself up for the hassle of shopping and negotiating for new wheels. So, he was still driving a middle-aged woman's car.

The trip across the Delaware River to Mt. Holly took about an hour. Most of his travels into New Jersey had been intermediate steps on his way to New York City, and he was very familiar with the axis of rusty industry that lined the Jersey Turnpike from Philadelphia to the Big Apple. But his infrequent ventures into South Jersey always pleased and half-surprised him: so many rural areas with pretty farms and quaint little towns, many of which had not changed in decades. Not a puddle remained from the previous day's showers, and the morning sun promised one of those luscious Indian

Summer days. The drive moved the needle a bit on Owen's cheer meter.

He had no trouble finding "Chet Odum's Auto Repairs", identified with a faded blue sign on a pole along the highway. Damaged and totally wrecked vehicles filled its yard. He found no one in the office but noticed a pair of legs protruding from under an undamaged BMW in one of the repair bays. He walked over.

"Excuse me," he said to the legs.

He had to wait for a second or two before the rest of the body slid out from under the vehicle on a rolling board that the guy at his neighborhood Sunoco always called his creeper.

"Sorry. Just trying to get some work done on my own car while I had a chance. What can I do for you?" The mechanic remained on the creeper, looking up at Owen.

Owen recognized the nasal voice as the one he'd heard on the telephone; but he was surprised by the clean-shaven face, set off by clear brown eyes and neatly parted black hair. Chet Odum looked more like a capable CPA than an auto mechanic.

"Hi. My name is Owen Delaney. I called this morning about the Honda in the accident that killed the girl last week."

"Oh yeah. I'll show you."

Chet got up off the creeper and led Owen into the yard. There he pointed to an older two-door coupe with a crushed front end and a web of jagged cracks in the windshield on the driver's side.

"Wow." The image of Virginia in that wreck made him feel like he weighed three hundred pounds. His voice was weak. "Do you know how the accident happened?"

"From what the police told me, she drove smack into a huge sycamore when she couldn't negotiate a turn on Harris Road. There were no skid marks, and they wondered if she might have done it on purpose."

Owen peered inside the front seat. "Doesn't look like the airbag opened."

"That's another thing that made the police wonder. Disabled air bag."

Owen did a double take, from the driver's seat to Chet and back to the seat.

"Disabled? I didn't know you could disable an airbag on the driver's side."

"Sure. At least in this model of Honda. Look." Chet shouldered past Owen and bent into the car to look up at the underside of the steering column. He removed a plastic cover from the column and exposed several tiny electric plugs. "See that yellow plug?"

Owen squeezed next to Chet and squinted up at the opening he'd uncovered.

"Yeah. It's not plugged in."

"Exactly. That's for the air bag. It's been disconnected. Some stunt drivers do that so the bag won't open when they spin out or turn sharply. They're already safe enough in their six point harnesses. But I doubt that she used this car for trick driving."

Owen said nothing as he waited for Chet to replace the cover on the steering column. He had not considered suicide.

"Do you think it was a suicide, Chet?"

"Don't know. I know nothing about the girl, her state of mind and all that. I prefer to think of her as just the reckless type."

"How so?" Owen remembered the first phone call with Chet. He hadn't been particularly interested in what Chet had to say then. But he was now.

Chet took a handkerchief from his rear pocket, blew, then sniffled and looked back at Owen.

"Well, this car is nearly eight years old. Any previous owner could have disabled the airbag. But if they did, she'd have ignored the warning light for as long as she had the car."

He stuffed the handkerchief back in his pocket then raised his eyebrows, apparently checking to make sure Owen followed his logic.

"And her seatbelt wouldn't slide far enough to close properly. She hadn't gotten that fixed either." He tilted his head back and held his index finger in the air. "One more thing. She let her brake fluid run out. I always check the brake system when the police tell me there were no skid marks. Her pads were fine; but the fluid had evaporated or leaked out. She should have sensed that happening way before the accident. But she didn't do anything about it."

Chet stopped and threw his shoulders back, then said "I think it was an accident—but one she could easily have prevented."

Owen might have agreed had he not been to Virginia's apartment, so damn neat he almost hated it, and not heard the flattering reviews of her careful work at Fletcher & Rhoades. Suicide, unfortunately, now posed a more likely scenario. His mind turned again to the note from Marian McNeil.

Marian and Virginia must have done something Virginia felt was very wrong. Maybe it wasn't the first time. And driving home from their meeting on the 15th, Virginia killed herself out of shame or maybe the fear that what they had done would become known to others. Maybe she even saw or sensed the same thing Marian had later alluded to in her note.

Despite changing attitudes on the subject, sex with that McNeil woman was the only thing he could think of that might cause such a crisis. But even if that was the case, things still didn't add up. Could Virginia have orchestrated such a technical suicide? Would she have had the know-how to disconnect an airbag or drain her own brake fluid? And why the brake fluid? Why not just disconnect the airbag, leave her seatbelt off and smash into a tree? Could she have wanted it to look like equipment failure?

Owen bit his lip for a few seconds before speaking. "Do you think the police speculation about suicide will affect the insurance claim?"

"No. The cops didn't put anything about it in their report. It was just shop talk." Chet shrugged as he wiped his hands on a rag attached to his belt. "Just make the insurance claim. The adjusters'll only look at the damage and the car is clearly totaled. They're not going to investigate the circumstances too carefully. To them, it'll be just another case of a driver losing control on a sharp turn. I'm sure not going to say anything."

Sweat trickled down Owen's brow and his armpits felt damp. He couldn't tell if it was the strong October sun or his new, pulse-thumping concerns about Virginia.

"Well, thanks Chet. You've been very helpful." Owen walked heavily back to his Highlander. The prospects of an heroic turn at Sunday's meeting with Barbara, during which he would ply her with soothing thoughts about her sister, suddenly dimmed.

• • •

Owen meandered home from Chet Odum's along a route that took him through Center City, Philadelphia, within easy reach of

City Avenue. With one hand on the wheel, he'd used the other to pinch his bottom lip until it was almost sore. The obvious next step, returning to Virginia's apartment, made him a little light headed and he offered himself any number of reasons why it was not really necessary at that time.

Still on the Jersey side of the Ben Franklin Bridge, he noticed a U-Haul dealer with a big sign advertising packing boxes and he gave up the battle. He stopped to buy what he thought he'd need, then drove on with his shoulders pushed back and his jaw set tight, alternatively telling himself he'd just get the packing of Virginia's things over with and be done with the whole matter and then wondering if he might find something in her apartment to answer the questions that had bubbled up.

Owen's breathing grew heavier the moment he entered Virginia's apartment and he went straight for the laptop leaning in the bedroom, yanked it out of its case, and snapped it open on Virginia's desk. Packing could wait. Blocking out the sounds of college students screaming their conversations in the hallway outside—how could Virginia stand the commotion?—he prayed her email was not password protected.

Unfortunately, it was.

He tried everything. Every combination of her name and initials, every combination of her sister's name and initials, the name of her law firm and its initials. Her street address. Initials with her street address. The word "Iowa," even spelled backwards.

Eventually he gave up and began packing Virginia's things.

Her clothes and linens went into boxes he marked *Salvation Army*. The contents of her medicine cabinet went into a box for *Trash*. After about an hour, as he began on the contents of the desk,

41

which he placed in a box marked *Barbara*, his cell phone rang. A rare event in the daytime. He hesitated, but saw it was Rick and answered it, guessing correctly Rick would be calling to confirm the details for their Sunday meeting.

Rick said he'd pick up Barbara and Joanie at about eleven. They were roommates so it would only take one stop. He anticipated being at Owen's before two. Owen should not expect to entertain them. If they were hungry, they'd go out or to his parents'.

Owen barely heard a word after Rick said Barbara and Joanie were roommates. As Rick wound down, Owen interrupted.

"Hey, Rick, I'm at Virginia's apartment right now. Packing up stuff to give to Barbara tomorrow. I wanted to browse Virginia's emails to see if there were any matters I should try to close out down here, but I don't know her password. Any chance you could see if Barbara knows it?"

"I suppose," Rick answered. "But it's Saturday. She's not working. She and Joanie don't have a landline and I don't know her cell. Joanie'll be home at six when she finishes her shift at the hospital. I'll call then and Joanie can ask if Barbara has any clue."

Owen frowned at his watch, realizing he couldn't wait till six, but his pulse quickened when Rick added "Meanwhile, try 'I hate Bruce' with like an 01 or 02 after it. We were joking about passwords one night and Barbara said she and her sister never had any trouble remembering them because their passwords all had to do with unpleasant events in their lives. She used that as an example. I remember wondering which of them had dated Bruce."

"Okay, Rick," said Owen. "See you tomorrow." Owen sat down at the desk in front of Virginia's laptop.

Whether Virginia also hated Bruce or whether she had just copied Barbara didn't matter. Her email screen opened with "ihatebruce03."

Owen scrolled through all Virginia's sent and received emails searching for the name "Marian" or "McNeil." Nothing, though it looked like she had kept an awful lot of stuff going all the way back to her arrival in Philly in the Spring. Even so, there was surprisingly little.

Most of the emails were from Barbara and he read them first. During the spring they came regularly, sometimes more than one a day. Scheduling Barbara's visits to Philadelphia and Virginia's to New York. Barbara realizing that she couldn't afford to live in her working women's hotel much longer and needed to get a roommate. Virginia complaining about the student racket in her building. Barbara, in late July, happy that she had found a place to share with a nurse whose roommate had just gotten married. Virginia asking when Barbara could come down again for a visit. Barbara describing a developing social life in New York. Virginia complaining about not having made many friends. Students in the building driving her crazy. Needed to get a new place when her leased expired.

Barbara's emails thinned out during August and almost ceased by mid-September.

There were also a couple of emails from an Aunt Donna, addressed to both Virginia and Barbara, saying she had been thinking a lot about the two of them as the anniversary of their mom's passing approached. She hoped they were happy and well. Virginia had replied that she missed their time in Des Moines very much and that life in the east was much more hectic and that it was hard being apart from Barbara.

Then Owen noticed emails from a popeye@xxxx.com coming about every two weeks. He opened one at random. Then another. And another. His neck and shoulders tensed as he read what could only be described as on-line stalking. They started shortly after she'd arrived in Philly. Whoever sent them knew all about her. What she looked like and, occasionally, what she had worn that day. Where she lived, even the apartment number, and where she worked. Even that she had come from Iowa and had a sister in New York. Somehow he—Owen assumed it was a he—had gotten her email address, and Virginia had inadvertently let him through her junk mail filter.

The stalker urged her to be careful. She was a beautiful girl in a big city. But he said that he would watch over her. In some of the emails, he told her about himself. He lived alone, loved to cruise around in his van and play basketball in the winter but otherwise made most of his friends online. He sounded creepy; though Owen realized his own recent life could sound just as bad.

Virginia never answered the emails. Nor did she ever mention them to Barbara. They had started well before that mousy co-worker at Fletcher & Rhoades noticed she had been "on edge" at the firm. Although the emails were not themselves overtly threatening, Owen easily conjured up a vision of the stalker sneaking up on Virginia and Marian McNeil when they met on the 15th. Had Virginia been followed by a van when she left that meeting, driven too fast and crashed as a result? No. Couldn't be. Marian's note suggested that, if anyone, she had been the one who'd been followed.

On the other hand, while the rest of the email trail did reflect what might be described as Virginia's growing isolation—or maybe just disappointment with life in Philadelphia—it didn't suggest a suicidal mood either.

He stood up, stretched, and walked over to the bedroom window. Outside, small knots of college kids strolled to and from City Avenue. Black plastic bags bulging with leaves dotted the grounds. The excitement he had felt on arriving at Virginia's apartment had dissipated. Though uncertain what he had expected to find, he had not found it. He went back to packing.

The box for Barbara would be the last one. He'd already set into it the things from Virginia's desk drawers and noticed the address book at the bottom of the box. He reached down for it and flipped it open to "M". Then "Mc". No Marian or McNeil. He dropped it back in the box.

Next, he repacked the laptop in its case and set that in as well. Then he started on the items atop the desk. Barbara's photo. The books. He decided against packing the big calendar. He couldn't imagine Barbara using it even though Virginia did. Who used them now with smart phones so common? But it had a full second years' worth of blank months under the October page and maybe somebody without the latest electronic device might want it. He tore off the October page and noticed the name Marian McNeil printed in the square marked October 15.

That didn't tell him much. The mysterious note was dated the 15th and had referred to a meeting that day. But maybe the use of Marian's last name on the calendar suggested a formal relationship. Something other than sex. Unless the sex "just happened." Still, if their get together was purely social, she'd likely have just written "Marian". Hard to say.

He threw balled-up October in the trash. Then he reopened one of the Salvation Army boxes so he could lay the calendar on top of the sheets and towels already stuffed inside. As he pulled the calendar off the desk, two white papers fluttered from underneath it to the floor. He picked them up.

Photocopies. Pages five and six of a document apparently prepared by Brokers Land Title and Insurance Company, the name appearing in small print at the top of each page. In larger print, the pages were captioned "Judgments and Mortgages" and contained descriptions of, what else, a number of mortgage loans and court judgments. Virginia—at least it seemed like Virginia's printing—had written the name Marian McNeil with a New Jersey phone number in the margin of one of the pages.

He looked for Virginia's phone. No landline. And, come to think of it, no cell phone around either. It dawned on him that, with his mind racing about a possible suicide, he hadn't looked through Virginia's car for any personal items and might have to go back.

He took out his own cell phone and punched in Marian's number. His heart raced as the number rang and he rehearsed his approach. Surely, if they were friends—or *lovers*—Marian would want to know that Virginia had died. Hell, even if they had just met for the first time on the 15th, she shouldn't be offended by his call. He'd explain that he was cleaning out Virginia's apartment, knew she hadn't made many friends during her brief time in Philly, but saw Marian's name among her things. Thought she would want to know, particularly as it seemed that she was the last person to have spent time with Virginia. He could ask how Virginia seemed during that time.

No answer. He let it ring. Ten times. He would call again before the meeting with Barbara and Rick on Sunday.

Owen folded the pages of Judgments and Mortgages into a small square, slipped them in his back pocket, sealed up the Salvation Army box again, locked up the apartment and left, carrying the box for Barbara with him. He had made progress on the tasks Rick had asked of him; but he'd not even begun to answer the questions that were prickling the hairs at the back of his neck.

He realized he had begun to care.

Chapter 5

Between bursts of cleaning that evening after his packing at Virginia's apartment, during which he finished straightening up the kitchen and family room as well as the downstairs bathroom, Owen made several calls to the number he had for Marian. Still no answer.

Then he remembered Marian's note said her cell phone was dead. Either he was calling the number of a phone that didn't work or he was calling a work number. On a hunch that Marian might work at that Brokers Land Title and Insurance Company, Owen went to the computer in Hank's office. At Hank's desk, he turned on the computer and scanned the room as he waited for it to boot up. Neither his mom nor he had touched the room since Hank's fatal heart attack. Leather furniture still spread comfortably on the gray Berber carpet. Same law books in the mahogany shelves. Some of Hank's old correspondence was still sitting on the leather desktop. Though he used the room often enough to surf the web, Owen had done nothing to make it his own and realized he had no plans to do so. Frankly, until this Virginia Steele thing, he had no plans for anything and rarely thought ahead other than to the TV programs he intended to watch.

He Googled "Brokers Land Title" and found five offices in the Philadelphia area. One in Mt. Holly, New Jersey, with the phone number Virginia had written for Marian McNeil. That meant he'd have to wait till Monday morning. And it meant he had to make a decision about what to say to Barbara about Virginia's mysterious death without learning what Marian had to say.

About eight, Rick called to say that Barbara didn't know for sure what Virginia had used as her email password; but she too suggested Owen try "ihatebruce."

Owen sucked on his cheeks. "Yeah. After we spoke this afternoon I tried it and it worked." He sat down and swallowed hard, then said "Are you with Barbara and Joanie right now, Rick?

"No. Believe it or not, it's eight o'clock on a Saturday night and I'm still at work. Why? You want to speak to one of them?"

"No. I just wanted to make sure you could speak freely."

"Speak freely about what, Odee?"

Owen exhaled through his nose. "The guy at the body shop said the police thought Virginia might have been suicidal. No skid marks before she slammed into a big tree. Her air bag was disconnected. The body shop guy himself thought Virginia was just reckless."

Owen quickly summarized Chet Odum's careless/reckless theory, then stopped for breath. "But believe me, Virginia was not the reckless type. I'm afraid suicide is a more likely explanation." Owen paused again and could hear Rick's breathing at the other end. He inhaled and continued.

"I can't believe she messed with her own car to cause the accident, though I can imagine she let things slide before committing the final act. My question is, should we talk to Barbara about it?"

The line was quiet for a moment before Rick spoke. "Oh, boy. Barbara's a tough girl, raised on a farm in Iowa. But I know she feels she let Virginia drift off on her own down there in Philly. They had never been apart before."

Rick blew hard into the phone. Owen could picture his cheeks puffed as he thought. "She got busy up here with work and doing things with Joanie. And she's full of remorse now that she can never make it up to her. That's why she didn't feel up to doing the clean-up work herself. Oh, boy." Rick sighed. "I wouldn't mention it."

"I guess you're right, Rick." Owen stared at his stocking feet. "See ya tomorrow."

He closed his phone slowly, telling himself that Rick was generally right in this kind of thing. But it didn't *seem* right to Owen that such a big thing should be swept under the rug. He hoped he didn't mess up when he met Barbara the next day. He even debated calling Rick back to cancel their plans. After all, Rick didn't need to bring Barbara down to Philly just to thank him. She could do that by phone. And truthfully, despite his infatuation with her photo, he was ambivalent about in meeting her now that her sister's death was raising questions.

Maybe Barbara wanted to come because she, herself, had questions.

Owen went to the kitchen for a Coke and sipped it at the kitchen table until his anxieties passed. Soon, he was again looking forward to Sunday afternoon.

SUNDAY
October 23

Chapter 6

On Sunday morning Owen found himself tingling with an excitement he hadn't felt since his days traveling in Europe. Silly as it seemed, he anticipated the afternoon meeting as if it were a first date with Barbara who, he fantasized, would fall in love with him for all he was doing for her. After a long shower during which he washed his hair twice—and even used some of his mother's old conditioner—he faced the dressing dilemma. No decent pants fit and yet sweatpants might not make the proper impression. Opting for the lesser of two evils, he wore grey sweats and sneakers, with a black turtleneck that he thought set off his hair just right.

After his usual coffee and toast in the kitchen, he rinsed out the coffeepot and put everything else in the dishwasher, beginning to like the way things looked all cleaned up. To pass the time and, honestly, to feel more grown up, he decided to buy some bagels for his guests, just in case. He had not been down to Dellasandro's in a long while and had a craving for the onion bagels he had been buying there since his high school days at Philadelphia Friends. The school, like Dellasandro's, had refused to move from the old Germantown neighborhood despite some pretty rough changes to the area.

He enjoyed the excursion. Bright sunlight and crisp October air. Hardly any traffic on Germantown Avenue. Colorfully dressed black kids with their mothers, making their way to the storefront churches along the avenue as he got down into the tough Germantown section. Few homeless on the street at that hour.

He drove back up into Chestnut Hill practically singing and stopped at a convenience store for cream cheese. He actually told the clerk to have a nice day.

Home again, he put his purchases away and turned on the TV for one of the Sunday news-talk shows. Hadn't watched one in a dog's age. Too much thinking required. He searched for that one moderator he liked, a guy who never let his guests get away with too much spin or evasion and tried to force them to answer the questions he'd asked. Owen found him after a few clicks. But unfortunately he was signing off, thanking his guests for their appearances. After the camera panned the faces of the guests, it fixed on the moderator who added, matter-of-factly, "And I would like to thank Dr. George Colgrove, member of the President's Commission on Competitiveness, who joined us earlier in the show from our affiliate in Lexington. See you all next week."

Owen squeezed his eyes shut and clenched his hands into fists. The evolving joy of his day instantly unwound, like an exciting Eagles kick-off return nullified by a penalty. He forced himself to take a deep breath. It was not the first time that Colgrove had been in the news and been forced into Owen's consciousness. But each time, Owen's breathing became short and fast, his skin tingled and he wished he'd never contacted Colgrove in the first place.

Unfortunately, he could not undo that horrible visit.

It had all started on his mom's deathbed.

With one day left to live, wracked by a virulent cancer and frequently delirious, his mother had pulled Owen close with her frail grasp and whispered "Go see George Colgrove . . . Kentucky Southern University . . . He's your real father."

At first Owen thought she was confused, her quirky mind gone haywire on her deathbed. But, truth be told, he had often wondered about his stark differences from Hank, in both looks and temperament. Hank was dark Irish and intense; Owen, like his mom, was Nordic blond and mellow. Sure, most kids favored one parent or the other. But his case was extreme. He never saw any trace of Hank in himself.

So a few days after Alice's funeral, he had Googled George Colgrove and discovered that he *was indeed* President of Kentucky Southern but had taught at a university in Philadelphia where Alice had worked as a librarian until just before Owen was born. With a tenseness in his stomach, Owen had hand-written Colgrove a note, introducing himself and explaining that his mother had told him, just before she had died, to contact him. Owen left only his email address for a response. Colgrove responded after a week's delay that he would meet with Owen during Christmas break when his schedule would be less hectic.

Owen had traveled south the day after a painfully solitary Christmas and, the next day, sat alone in the reception area of Colgrove's dark, wood-paneled office suite in the President's Hall at the university. After a ten-minute wait, the receptionist led him, lightheaded and shaky with anticipation, through the door of Colgrove's inner office. A man of about sixty-five, with a shock of fine but fading blond hair, grown long and combed straight back, rose to meet him. They stared at each other, each looking at themselves across a canyon of years, before Colgrove directed Owen to a red leather chair in front of his desk and returned to his own seat behind it. He spoke first.

"Owen, do you know why your mother wanted us to meet?"

Owen instinctively ran his right hand through his hair. "I think so. She said you were my real father."

Colgrove had the deep resonant voice of a bishop and spoke with a deliberateness that seemed pretentious to Owen.

"Well, biological father, yes. But Hank Delaney raised you, Owen. I think he has to be considered your real father."

Owen said nothing as he stared at Colgrove and struggled to focus on his explanation about an affair at the university while both he and Alice were married, Alice only recently so. His attention piqued at a dramatic Colgrove pause during which Colgrove stroked his own hair.

"She became pregnant and, in the way of women, said she knew I was the father. When she refused to end the pregnancy, I broke off the relationship." Colgrove's blue eyes fixed directly on Owen.

Owen could feel himself on the verge of tears. But Colgrove didn't notice. He continued without a change in tone or expression, as practiced as if testifying before a congressional committee.

"She promised never to tell anyone about your biological paternity. I am sorry she did not keep her promise."

Owen wanted to spring up, grab Colgrove by his blond mane, and smash his head down on his desk, over and over. The voice in his head screamed "I'm your child, you self-centered bastard." His violent fantasy was interrupted when Colgrove pulled a thick brown envelope from his desk and slid it across to Owen.

"Take this. And please don't contact me again."

With a heavy feeling in his stomach, Owen took the envelope and left, leaving the office door open behind him. He found his way out of the building, staggered to his rental car and flipped the envelope on the seat beside him. He drove in a fog to the airport, telling himself he would open the envelope later.

He'd have to change his return flight, since he hadn't expected to leave so soon. In fact, he'd imagined a warm meeting with Colgrove during which the old man would comfort him about his mother's death, ask him about his life and interests, and ultimately give him a feeling that he belonged to someone. He had actually expected to stay for the rest of the holidays. His disappointment was immense.

To spite Colgrove, he resisted opening the envelope. Nothing Colgrove had to say or give to him would ever be important to him. But flight change made, waiting to board, he gave in to his curiosity and tore open the envelope. It contained two stacks of crisp hundred dollar bills wrapped in ten thousand dollar bands.

Owen stiffened, enraged that Colgrove could dismiss him so easily. Then he began to wonder about Hank. Had Hank been a hero or a tyrant, doing his best for Alice's boy or pushing Owen to be like him to get back at Colgrove. Clenching and unclenching his hands, he condemned Hank for his insensitive vindictiveness. He had no father at all. He wanted his mother. His first impulse was to leave the airport, buy a gun, and shoot himself in the head. Maybe shoot Colgrove first. But he just sat there. In time he began to sob softly, overwhelmed by loss and completely alone.

• • •

The painful recollection of that December day in Kentucky immobilized Owen. An hour later, having forgotten about Rick and the girls, he was still sitting in front of the TV, deaf and dumb, as a pretty brunette business reporter finished up her review of the week's news. Thinking about Colgrove always had that effect on him. Mom and Hank were gone. And his "real" father wanted nothing to do with him. No brothers or sisters. No aunts, uncles or cousins, either. He chided himself for his melodrama. But he couldn't shake the aching chest and the angry flashes of heat always brought on by thoughts of Colgrove. This time, he didn't even try to repress the haunting images of Colgrove's fine head of hair and piercing blue eyes or turn off the sound of his pompous voice grinding away in his mind's ear.

He shook off his stupor only when he heard a car pull up the driveway toward the parking area near the back door. He lumbered through the kitchen and out onto the back porch to greet his visitors. And, in the way the mood of a room full of adults can be lifted when a cuddly infant appears, Owen's mood lifted when he saw Joanie and Barbara. He recognized Barbara immediately from her picture. She was taller than he had imagined, almost his height, and wore a long black peasant skirt, high boots and a beige leather jacket over a white blouse. Elegant. His mother always loved that look.

And Joanie was stunning with short dark hair, fair skin and a lovely athletic figure. From a distance she looked like a young Elizabeth Taylor. As they approached, he could see that Joanie had a striking facial resemblance to Rick. They could be brother and sister. Blue eyes and perfect, happy features. Energy sizzled off them like heat-waves on a highway.

Rick spoke before they had even gotten to the porch steps.

"Hey, Odee. Great to see ya. You're looking very well." Owen had moved to the bottom of the steps where they all stopped to smile at each other.

"Odee, let me introduce Barbara Steele." Rick gestured toward Barbara. "And Joanie Costello." After a round of nice-to-meet-yous and handshakes, Barbara offered the first note.

"What a beautiful house, Owen. And what a lovely neighborhood. Rick tells us you grew up in this house."

"I did. It was little big for a one child family."

Bittersweet images came to mind, of he and his mom reading quietly in the family room with the rest of the six thousand feet unused and deadly silent. "But space has its advantages, I guess."

"I'll say," chirped Joanie. "I grew up with four other kids in a tiny row house in Queens. Can't wait to see the inside."

They filed up the steps, through the kitchen and into the family room. Rick, Barbara and Owen took seats while Joanie poked around. She called back to them. "These rooms are huge. Nice to have space like this, huh, Barb?"

Barbara gave Owen a wide-eyed look, maybe embarrassed by Joanie's enthusiasm. "Our apartment in New York is quite tiny. It's a good thing we're both out working so much." She sat with her hands folded in her lap at the far end of the sofa from Owen's side chair.

Owen nodded, curious about her. "Rick tells me you're from Iowa, Barbara?"

"Yes. My sister and I lived on a farm till we were about thirteen. Then our mom sent us to live with her sister in Des Moines." Though Barbara spoke with a pleasant energy, she sat very still and her hands never moved from her lap.

"Why'd she do that?" Rick asked.

"Well, she told everyone we'd get a better education in the city. We lived in Grimes, in the middle of nowhere." Barbara paused for a second, unfolded her hands then folded them again. "But she really

58

wanted to get us away from our stepfather. She was planning to divorce him." She lowered her eyes towards her hands, but then perked up again. "Oh, by the way Owen, did you ever get my sister's email opened?"

"Yes. 'Ihatebruce03" worked. But I didn't find anything that needed following up." He chose not to mention the on line stalker.

Rick's mouth opened and he lifted his head. "I take it your stepfather was named Bruce"

Barbara did not respond; but Joanie, who had just come back into the room, chimed in. "Yup. And what a bastard he was. Tell them Barb."

Barbara said nothing; but the words rushed out of Joanie.

"He came to work on the farm after Barb's father died and her mom needed help to run the place. He became critical to the operation. Brucie boy was much younger than her mom but he wanted to marry her. Just about blackmailed her into marriage, saying he loved her and would have to leave the farm if she didn't marry him."

Barbara squirmed in her seat. "I don't think Rick and Owen are interested in this, Joan."

Owen held his breath and leaned toward Barbara, but she was still shifting uncomfortably on the sofa. Her hands were tapping on her knees. He sat back in his chair and cleared his throat loudly. "What about some bagels and coffee? Rick, I went down to Dellasandro's this morning for some of those onion bagels we used to get before school."

"Sounds good to me. Let me and Joanie get them ready. I think I remember where everything is."

Rick got up to go to the kitchen but Joanie, eyes wide into her story telling, sat down. "Let me first finish up about Bruce and Barbara's mom. It's fascinating."

Barbara shrugged and flipped a palm at Joanie.

"Once Bruce married her mom," Joanie continued, "he took charge of everything. He was a tyrant. Borrowed money to buy more property and equipment. Hired farm hands. Took a nice farming business and buried it in so much debt it could no longer make money. When he started making eyes at Barb and her sister, her mother had had enough. She moved them out."

Barbara fiddled with a charm bracelet on her wrist then leaned back. "We actually liked living in the city. So much more to do. My mom had planned to move there with us after the divorce. But she became ill and died before the divorce went through."

"Yeah. And when she died, old Bruce got the farm and had all his debt paid off with her life insurance. Their bank had demanded to be the beneficiary." Joan seemed more incensed about the story than Barbara. "The girls got nothing."

Except for the bit about getting nothing, Owen could relate to the story. His throat ached and he felt a powerful urge to move closer to the quiet girl sitting across from him with her hands now back in her lap. Maybe put an arm around her shoulder. But he held still. Then the thought occurred to him that a Virginia suicide could be a delayed reaction to earlier painful episodes in her life. He could feel his pulse accelerate.

"How old were you when your father died?" He leaned toward Barbara again as he asked, afraid he would be digging up one too many memories.

Barbara answered calmly. "We were about eight, I guess. His tractor overturned as he was plowing the only steep hill on our farm. My mom later joked that it was the only steep hill in all of Grimes." She smiled faintly and raised her eyebrows. "Virginia and I had loved living on the farm till then. My mom and dad had been high-school sweethearts and married young. But they put off having children so they could both work and save up to buy a farm. They were happy to have had twins. Made up for lost time." She smiled again before saying "They owned everything free and clear when we were young. No stress. And we all had a happy time." She lifted her hands from her lap and opened her palms toward Owen and Joanie like she was easing a door closed.

Joanie finally got up and joined Rick in the kitchen.

Barbara moved down the sofa, nearer to Owen who remained in his side chair. Her clear green eyes looked directly into Owen's and he had a hard time not turning away.

"Owen, I don't want to forget my reason for coming was to thank you for taking a burden off my shoulders. Virginia and I had been very close all our lives. We went through a lot together." Her breasts rose slightly as she took a deep breath. "We were never apart before these last six months. And I just wasn't as considerate of her feelings as I should've been. After a few months I put less and less effort into maintaining contact and, when she died, I felt so guilty I couldn't face the prospect of closing down her life. When Rick said he'd ask you to do it, I jumped at the chance"

"I'm happy to do it". To Owen's surprise, his perfunctory answer was now the God's honest truth. And he felt a little giddy, like the room was closing in around them and he didn't care. His cheeks were warm.

Barbara had been through a lot—by any rational standard, as much or more than he had himself. Yet she remained steady and direct. She'd even adventured all the way to New York and held down a decent job. Her life had apparently not missed a beat.

She leaned toward Owen. "When Rick told me your story, and that your dad had worked in the same firm as Virginia, I felt very selfish imposing on you. I hope all this has not been too hard on you?" She reached out and touched his hand.

"Not at all. It's helping me get out of a funk I've been in for a while." Again the truth, he realized. And again, a feeling of intense closeness. So close he was tempted to tell her all about that funk, all about Colgrove. But he couldn't yet. And then he remembered Virginia's possible suicide.

Barbara was still leaning toward him, her face uplifted. Resisting the urge to stroke her cheek, he inhaled and slouched back in his chair. The closeness had taken his breath away.

"Tell me about Virginia. What was she like?" He felt he had to say something and that was the first thing that came to mind. But it was a question that had been stewing for the last few days.

Back in the day, Owen had enjoyed conversation because he had been truly interested in other people. It had made him generally liked by others and, probably, what made him want to be a writer of some sort. Even apart from his probing about Virginia's possible suicide, he found now that he was, in fact, curious about her. He crossed his arms and waited.

Barbara moved back a bit on the sofa. "Well, she was nine minutes younger, but sometimes it felt like nine years. I was the big sister. Ginny was never that good at making friends and could be moody at times. She also overreacted to problems."

"Like what?"

"Oh, I don't know." Barbara lowered her head for a few seconds. "Not that our mom's death wasn't a big blow to both of us, but it took her forever to get over it. She became a loner. Until we were both working in Des Moines, I was probably her only friend."

"Then why didn't you stay together when you came east?"

Barbara sighed. "We should have, I guess. But when we told our bosses in Des Moines that we wanted to relocate, Ginny's boss contacted Fletcher and Rhoades, where a law school classmate was a partner. Ginny was more or less hired on her boss's recommendation. Same thing happened to me with Sterling and Moss. So we decided to see what it would be like living apart. New York and Philadelphia seemed close enough." Barbara bit her lip. "It pains me to remember that I sort of welcomed the idea."

"Yeah. I can see that. Maybe take a little pressure off." Owen had always been an attentive listener and had a natural tendency to let people know he was feeling with them. He realized how badly he missed real human contact.

"But why did you leave Des Moines in the first place?"

"It was Ginny's idea, really. She had a falling out with the one close girlfriend she had. A girl at work who was also from Grimes. They had known each other as kids. I never knew what the falling out was about. She wouldn't tell me. Just cried and cried over it for weeks. She finally announced that she wanted to go away and I felt obligated to go with her. I liked my job but had no strong attachments in Des Moines. Now I regret not finding a job in Philadelphia. New York was just not close enough for her."

She stopped and shook her head slightly. "I've been beating myself up about it since Ginny's accident. She was usually a careful driver; but when she got into one of her moods, she could lose concentration. Had we been together, maybe it wouldn't have happened."

All this information made a Virginia suicide seem more likely, though Barbara's remorse shot a quiver trough Owen's gut and he knew he shouldn't discuss it. He reached out to pat her arm and she choked back a sob. He was about to move next to her and give her a hug when Joanie called them in to eat. As they walked the few steps into the kitchen, he gently placed his hand high on her back and gave her neck a soft squeeze. She turned to him and smiled. Rick was right. No reason she had to know about the suicide theory.

The four of them sat at the table over coffee and bagels for almost two hours. Owen enjoyed himself tremendously. Rick and Joan's energy and humor spiced the conversation; and the connection he'd made with Barbara in their private conversation carried through the afternoon. Except maybe for some of his fun chats with his mom, the old table had never been witness to such lightness of spirit. Owen wasn't sure that his fantasy about Barbara falling for him was coming true. But the reverse certainly was.

As the three of them were leaving, Barbara asked Owen for something to write on and then, in a neat hand resembling Virginia's, printed her name, address, cell phone and work phone numbers on the card he had given her. Owen then brought her the box of Virginia's personal belongings that he had collected from her apartment and the bag of items he had brought home from the firm. She thanked him again and gave him a soft kiss on his cheek. It would have felt more special if Joanie hadn't done the same.

MONDAY
October 24

Chapter 7

Owen roused himself like a grownup the following morning and watched the early news until he could call Brokers Title and Insurance Company at nine on the dot.

"Marian McNeil, please."

"I'm sorry. Marian doesn't work here anymore. Can someone else help you?" The crisp female voice sounded wary.

"No. It's a personal matter. Old friend. Do you know how I can reach her?"

"Well, I guess you haven't heard. Marian died in an automobile accident last week."

"Oh. I'm sorry to hear that. Thank you." He replaced the phone gently, like it was wired to a bomb.

Owen suddenly felt cold. He shivered and hugged his chest with his shaking arms. Impossible. What were the odds? Owen sat frozen at Hank's enormous desk where he had made the call. Through the office windows, he could see the front yard and the street beyond. A few commuters were still quickstepping along the sidewalk to the train station up the block. A FedEx delivery was being made to the Crawsons next door. The renovations on the big house across the street were still on hold over a dispute with the neighbors and the place was still an empty mess. And Mrs. Jaron was letting her poodle pee on the azaleas at the end of his driveway. The dumb normality of it all set his ears pounding. His world had changed again.

What was going on? A *double* suicide? Maybe. But probably something worse. If he read Marian McNeil's emails he'd probably find messages from that same on-line stalker? Probably, she'd noticed him snooping around after the meeting with Virginia and confronted him? Enraged him, perhaps.

It was a police matter for sure, but which police? South Jersey? Philadelphia? And what should he tell them? He imagined the exaggerated sighs they'd give him when he filled them in on the online stalker. He was not a very credible narrator. He didn't even have a pair of pants that fit. And he had torn up that note.

He took a deep breath, uncrossed his arms and placed his hands on the desk. Then he snorted delicately and smiled. He was getting carried away. His old friends would've had a good laugh at his racing imagination. And a racing imagination was a good sign of a modest improvement in his disposition. But still. The accidents could be more than a coincidence, particularly given what he'd learned about Virginia's. Maybe he should go back to Chet Odum's. He'd never checked Virginia's car for personal items, so he had a reason to return. But maybe he could get Chet to examine the car more closely for him. If Chet found something, they could go to the police together.

He called the yard and, without giving a reason for his visit, got an okay to come by that morning.

• • •

Back at Chet Odum's yard by ten thirty, he told Chet he needed to inspect the trunk and glove compartment since he'd forgotten that last time.

"You know, I wondered about that after you left." Owen was again impressed with the guy's attention to detail. Chet went on. "Come into the office and get the keys you'll need." His cold seemed better and his voice no longer sounded like someone was pinching his nose.

As they walked to the office, Owen swallowed hard and said "Chet, I'm still puzzled about the accident. I've gotten to know a little about the driver and I don't think she was the reckless type you imagine, though she might have been distracted by something. I'm also concerned someone fiddled with her car to cause the accident. Is that possible?"

Chet didn't even stop walking. "You've seen too many bad movies. It's virtually impossible. That old cut-the-brake-line cliché would never work in real life." Chet quickened his pace, almost yelling over his shoulder as he put an unnecessary distance between Owen and himself. Then he stopped, turned back and gave his mouth a little twist.

"If you cut the line all the way through and empty all the fluid at once, the driver would know it right away." He squinted and tilted his head. "And if you make a small cut, you can't make sure that the brakes fail at a critical moment. Not only that, but before they failed, any alert and careful driver would notice a soft pedal."

All that was not what Owen had wanted to hear. "Yeah. I know. That's why you thought Virginia was reckless. She ignored a soft pedal. But there must be some explanation other than that. She was not reckless. Distracted or not, I'm positive she took good care of that car. But the brakes failed, the seatbelt didn't work properly, and the airbag didn't open. Why?"

They were by now in the office, a small but neat little room off the work bays, and Chet was handing over Virginia's keys. Owen could imagine from the exasperated look on Chet's face the reaction the police would have if he went to them with his concerns.

As he took the keys, he tried a new tack.

"Chet, come look at the car with me. I haven't opened the trunk or the glove compartment. But I guarantee you'll be impressed with the way they look. They won't look like they belong to a careless or reckless person."

Owen backed out of the office. Chet followed, his lips pressed together in irritated silence. But they relaxed and he stroked his chin when, as Owen expected, despite some disarray from the crash, the opened trunk looked as clean and well equipped as Virginia's medicine cabinet. Spare tire fixed tight to its rack, jumper cables, aerosol can to inflate a flat, wiper fluid, flares and flashlights, all in a plastic box. Even a folded shovel and chains for snow. Not a loose piece of junk to be found.

The interior of the vehicle was neat—no candy wrappers, coffee cups or other trash—and spotless, except for the bloodstains around the driver's seat. A packet of business cards was clipped to the sun visor and her cell phone and a small purse lay under the passenger seat, almost entirely hidden from view. Owen took the phone and the purse, surprised at the carelessness of the original search by the police crew.

The glove compartment, too, was a testament to Virginia's compulsiveness. Registration, insurance card, neatly folded maps, a little notebook and some index cards wrapped in a rubber band. The top card in the pack had a neatly printed message to call Barbara Steele in New York in the event of emergency. Owen also found a set of the "Judgments and Mortgages" pages from the Brokers Title document that looked identical to the pages Owen had found in Virginia's apartment. Complete with Marian McNeil's work number.

He got out of the car and straightened up. "What do you think now, Chet? Is this the car of a reckless girl?"

Chet tucked his lower lip into his mouth and said nothing for a few seconds. "Well, she was certainly neat and prepared for anything. I'll give you that. But even if she wasn't careless, that always leaves suicide as a possibility. Doesn't have to be tampering."

Owen nodded. "Sure. To be honest, until this morning, I assumed that she'd committed suicide—or at least been distracted by some personal issue while she was driving. I'd seen her apartment. It was as neat as this car and I knew she hadn't been reckless. But . . ." Owen paused and breathed hard through his nose. *Oh, what the hell.*

"But . . . ahh . . . I recently learned that another girl . . . a girl who'd been with her just before her crash . . . and later wrote her a note saying she was scared about something . . . ah . . . that girl also died in a car wreck. I also know that the girl who drove this car was being stalked."

Chet spread his feet apart and planted himself in front of Owen. "And you suspect foul play, right?"

"Well, yes." The tightness in his chest made him answer with less conviction than he felt in his gut.

Chet frowned. "Nah, I still think you watch too much TV. Coincidences do happen. What's more likely, a double murder or two car accidents? I say two accidents. Even two suicidal accidents. Believe it or not, one of my customers had three daughters who all had separate accidents on the same day." Chet seemed ready to walk away. But he stayed put, studying Owen, apparently thinking over what he'd just said. "Tell you what. I'll take another look at the car. See if I find anything."

Owen's mouth opened in a silent cheer. But seeing it, Chet added, "I can't do it today. And it'll cost you a hundred bucks, payable in advance."

"That's a deal, Chet. Where's the nearest ATM? I'll get the money now." Owen's chest expanded as he took a huge breath.

Chet directed Owen to a bank in Mt. Holly proper. It took no more than five minutes to get there. A small, typical, old South Jersey town, Mt. Holly consisted of a few blocks of low-rise commercial district blending quickly into a surrounding residential area of neat bungalows. He drove down the main street, noticed the office of Brokers Land Title and Insurance Company and parked just a few doors away in front of the bank Chet had suggested. He got his money from the ATM and then went into the coffee shop next door where he sat at the counter debating whether or not to pay a visit to Brokers Land Title.

As he sipped his coffee, he noticed a "Copies Made" sign in the window of the drugstore across the street and had an idea. He paid for the unfinished coffee, went across the street, and asked an emaciated older woman behind the counter for some white out. Using the counter as a workspace, he took the Judgments and Mortgages paperwork he'd found in Virginia's car and carefully whited out Marian McNeil's name and phone number from the margin on the second page. He asked the clerk to make him a copy and, after inspecting it, touched it up with a little more white out and asked for another copy. That one looked good enough to him.

The Brokers Title office was less than a block away. As he walked, he crumpled up the good copy of the Judgment and Mortgages and then smoothed the pages out against the window of a hardware store.

The suite of offices he entered seemed sizeable for a town like Mt. Holly. A secretary/receptionist sat close to the front door in a room with a seating area for eight or so and one other desk, not currently occupied. Maybe that was Marian's desk. To the rear of that space, to the right, he could see a conference room and, to the left, what appeared to be a private office. Door closed.

Owen was already standing in front of the receptionist when he closed the front door.

"May I help you?" She had turned from her computer. Owen recognized the voice from his phone conversation. He hoped she didn't recognize his.

"Yes. My name's Owen Delaney. I've just come from Chet Odum's body shop down the road. I was inspecting the damage to a friend's car. Unfortunately, I have become responsible for winding up her affairs. She died in an accident."

Owen held out the crumpled pages he brought with him.

"I found these in her car. Don't know what they are; but they have your company name on them. I thought you might need them for something."

The receptionist skimmed the papers.

"Oh. These are from a title report. If the report is from this office, I'm sure we have the complete version in our files. We really don't need these. But thank you for your thoughtfulness."

Owen opened his mouth in what he hoped looked like surprise. "Title report? Does that mean Virginia was buying a property? I didn't know that." Owen prayed that he didn't sound too disingenuous. "What was she buying? I may have to let somebody know that she won't be going through with it."

The woman looked at the papers in her hands. "I can't tell from just these pages. If you had the front page of the report, it would all be there. But if the report was generated by this office, Mister Scalero might know. Hold on."

She buzzed an intercom and explained the situation to Scalero. Owen couldn't hear Scalero's end of the conversation but the receptionist read one or two items from the pages in front of her and eventually asked Owen to wait until Mr. Scalero came out of the closed door at the back of the office.

Scalero, a huge man, six feet three or so, in his mid-forties, was a walking cliché with a weightlifter's build and a swarthy complexion. Though his suit jacket was off, it was obvious from his slick trousers, red suspenders and silk necktie that he had worn an expensive looking suit to work that morning. His style seemed to Owen to be out of place in simple Mt. Holly.

Scalero scowled, his dark brows almost touched each other above his nose and his lips pressed together into a mere slit below it.

"I'm sorry, Mr. Delaney. We can't help you. Our files are confidential. All I can say is that the property covered by this report is not being purchased by a single woman."

"Okay, that's enough for me." Owen wasn't going to push things further with the guy. "I was just afraid I had more details to worry about."

Scalero stared at him and didn't say a word. The receptionist, eyes wide and darting between Owen and Scalero, piped in to break the silence. "Well, I guess that's it. Thanks for coming in, Mr. Delaney."

As Owen turned to leave, Scalero went to the door, opened it, and followed him out. He stood on the sidewalk and watched as

Owen walked to his car. From his car, in his rearview mirror, Owen could see Scalero take out his cell phone and make a call.

Owen was happy to be leaving Mt. Holly. But he wished he hadn't used his real name. And he wished Scalero hadn't seen his car. Its license plate was probably readable from where Scalero stood. On the receiving end of Scalero's stare, Owen couldn't help but remember Marian McNeil's note. "I think we were spotted today. I'm scared."

Owen drove back toward Chet Odum's at a pace that could have led a funeral cortege, uncertain whether or not to press his request that Chet re-inspect Virginia's car. He pulled off the road a few hundred yards before reaching the body shop.

On the one hand, he was truly afraid that he'd introduced himself into a dangerous situation. Even though a few short hours ago the online stalker was his "prime suspect"—he almost laughed as the voice in his head used that very term—Scalero's suspicious behavior was now, for Owen, practically an admission of guilt. He could imagine Scalero's cronies already tracking down his license plate. Maybe he would be scheduled for an "accident" somewhere on the way back to Chestnut Hill.

On the other hand, he might just be getting carried away again with his own goofy fantasies. Like the times when, as a kid, he and his mom would make up wicked stories about the commuters who walked past their house late in the afternoon and, in time, he'd enjoy believing the stories were true. He remembered running in the house one afternoon when the man who had imprisoned his wife and children in his attic passed by while he was playing in the front yard.

He eventually decided to go ahead and stop at Chet's with the money. After all, if he'd stirred up a hornets' nest, dropping his request for the re-inspection was not going to improve the situation. And if Chet found out anything useful, maybe Owen could get some protection from the authorities.

When he entered Chet's office, Chet was on his cell phone. Owen showed the money, about to drop it on Chet's desk, when Chet took the phone from his ear and held it to his chest. "Wait till I finish this call, please. I have something for you."

The call was about rescheduling orchestra practice. Owen recognized a French horn case sitting behind Chet's desk. *Interesting guy.*

Chet looked up at Owen once he'd finished the call.

"I play in our community orchestra. Scheduling practices can be more of a production than the practices themselves." He fumbled for a piece of paper on his desk.

"Here. I made some calls about that other accident you mentioned. It was probably the Chevy brought to Pete Thomasian's yard in Rancocas. Pete was pretty sure the driver was a woman." He handed the paper to Owen. "Pete's address and phone number."

Owen took this little research to be a sign that Chet now thought Owen's worries might have some merit. He took the paper and handed his five twenties to Chet. "Thanks Chet. When do you think you can check out the Honda?"

Chet suggested Owen call him around noon on Wednesday, was interrupted by another phone call, and apparently recognizing the number on his caller ID, rolled his eyes. "More orchestra crap. Sorry, I have to take this."

Owen waved and left.

• • •

Rather than head directly back to Philadelphia, Owen drove to Rancocas and found Pete Thomasian's yard outside of town. Pete's office and Pete himself were more like what Owen expected from a body shop. The requisite pin-ups and NASCAR posters were taped to the walls of the sloppy and overheated office which Pete had furnished with a dinged metal desk and two tattered armchairs, all too big for the small space. Owen had even noticed two motorcycles parked outside.

Pete himself, about forty, overweight, with longish, greasy-brown hair, wore jeans and a filthy white tee shirt. He sported a tattoo of a torpedo on his flabby right bicep. After the predictable asides about Owen's "pretty boy" hair to two similar-looking forty-year-olds sprawled in the armchairs, Pete confirmed that the Chevy he'd towed from Westhampton Road had indeed been registered to a Marian McNeil.

"Do you know how the accident happened?" Owen asked, hoping that Chet had established his bona fides with Pete. Owen was rarely able on his own to establish any rapport with guys like Pete and his friends, or employees, or whatever they were.

Pete smiled and looked at the two others. "Chet Odum says our friend here—what did you say your name was?"

"Owen. Owen Delaney."

"Yeah. Owen here is doing a little detective work. He thinks our wreck and one over at Chet's are connected some way. Maybe not accidents. Whadaya think, boys?"

The hulk sitting closest to Pete took off his Eagles cap, ran his hand through his thinning hair, and squinted with mock seriousness.

"Pete, I think what we got here is the making of a new TV series. Faggot detective solves crimes by asking stupid questions." The other hulk pressed his hands to his stomach and faked restraining a laughing fit.

Owen's heart sank. Not this shit again.

"What Carl here is saying, pretty boy, is that we just tow 'em. Go to the police if you want information. Leave us be. We got work to do."

Owen, who had never sat down, murmured a "thanks anyway" and turned to leave. As he opened the door he heard Pete laugh. "And tell that Chet Odum to send over a real woman next time. Maybe we'd have more information for her."

After slamming his car door and seething in Thomasian's parking lot for a few minutes, Owen decided to take Pete's advice and go to the police. It couldn't possibly be more frightening or humiliating than the conversation he just had or his earlier meeting with Scalero.

He asked for directions at a gas station and soon pulled his Highlander into one of the two visitor spaces next to a simple, one-story brick building on Highway 234 that served as headquarters for both the Rancocas police and its road department.

At the far end of the building's small entry foyer, a beefy but pleasant-faced policewoman, maybe fifty, sat behind a half-wall topped by a thick glass partition. Her blue uniform was more than a tad too tight. She lit up when she saw Owen. It could have been her normal manner or maybe it was his hair. But in either event, his body tension eased when he noticed her smile. When she asked how she could help, Owen was moved to try out what he used to think of as his boyish charm.

He smiled and scratched his head as he introduced himself.

"I'm really not sure that I have any reason to be here, but I'm curious about an accident that killed a young woman on Westhampton Road last week."

The woman's smile faded by a hair. But her sing-song tone was still motherish. "And why, pray tell, are you curious about that accident?"

Owen decided that at least partial honesty was the best policy. "A friend of mine, who'd been working on a project with the girl killed on Westhampton Road, was also killed in an accident last week." Owen paused and read the woman's nametag, Sgt. P. Kelly. Her smile was gone. "In my opinion, Sergeant Kelly, the circumstances of my friend's accident were unusual. I was just trying to put some pieces together so they made sense to me."

"What were the unusual circumstances, Mr. Delaney?" Sergeant Kelly folded her arms across her breasts.

"Well, I thought my friend had committed suicide by purposely crashing into a tree near Mt. Holly. But when I learned that Marian McNeil was also killed in an accident, I began to wonder." Owen debated mentioning Marian's note.

Sergeant Kelly said nothing for a few seconds and then, unfolding her arms with her palms up, spread her hands out wide. "And?"

Owen had feared that gesture or something like it. But he barreled on. "And . . . and I found a note from Marian saying that she was afraid of something involving her and my friend."

"Can I see it?"

"I don't have it any more. Didn't think it was too important when I read it." Owen's voice trailed off as he spoke.

Sergeant Kelly slumped in her chair, then leaned back. "Okay. I'd have liked to see it. But, anyway, what is it you think? They both committed suicide?"

"Well yes. Or maybe they were both murdered." Owen felt ridiculous saying what he truly felt. He stood slack mouthed as Sgt. Kelly got up from her chair, saying she would be back in a minute, and walked out of her cubicle behind the glass.

She returned soon, holding a file. Sitting in her cubicle again, she opened the file and read through it for several minutes. Owen agonized as he waited, remembering conversations with Hank about his desire for a literary career which Hank had always treated as an outlandish prospect. The disconnect between his most truly felt impulses and Hank's reaction to them had always left him sweating and almost nauseas.

But Sergeant Kelly had apparently decided to go easy on him. "This is the file on the McNeil accident." She slid the file through the slot at the base of the glass and looked squarely at Owen. "Read it over. Nothing in it suggests suicide. Murder, too, seems very unlikely. If we could find the driver of the other vehicle, we could probably charge him or her with some form of manslaughter or vehicular homicide. But intentional murder? No way." As if anticipating Owen's objection, she added, "And that note you found doesn't change anything for me."

Owen read through the accident report with some difficulty because of the sloppy scribbling of the officer who had completed it. But he quickly got the gist of the story. The accident happened at night on an unlit portion of Westhampton Road, a country road about four miles from town. A teenaged couple parked on a farm lane just off the road reported that they'd noticed a beat-up van weaving across the midline of the road as it rattled past them toward the bridge where the accident occurred. They then heard Marian's car break through the guardrail and crash below the bridge. But otherwise occupied, they had not noticed much about the van when it passed them. The kids couldn't even remember whether it was light colored or dark. The report did mention that neither the deceased's seatbelt nor air bag had been working properly.

Owen slid the file back to Sergeant Kelly. He had no trouble reading the report as describing the tampering with Marian's seatbelt and airbag and the intentional running of Marian's car off the road, at precisely the spot where it could be fatal. He remembered that Virginia's stalker had written that he loved to cruise in his van; and he was about to try out the intentional accident scenario on the sergeant when a tall, crew-cut and barrel-chested officer entered Kelly's cubicle. He stood behind her and stared at Owen through the glass. Sergeant Kelly looked back at him over her shoulder.

"Oh, Chief. This is the fella. Owen . . . Delaney, was it?"

"Yes, ma'am."

The chief picked up the file and patted it with his free hand. "Son, why are you so interested in this? Who were these girls to you?"

"Actually, I didn't know either of them. I was asked to clean up some details after the first girl was killed."

Sergeant Kelly snapped her head up. "I thought you said one of them was a friend."

Owen could feel himself flush. "It was a friend who asked me to clean up those details and . . . as I said . . . I got suspicious with that note and the second accident."

"And you like doing police work, right?" The chief looked pissed.

"Not really. I just . . ."

The chief interrupted. "We all assume the van was filled with migrants who were either drunk or driving too long without rest. Lots of worker movement with the change of seasons. And nothing you've told us changes that theory."

Afraid to push his case, Owen asked if the police had any leads on the van.

The chief put the folder back on Sergeant Kelly's desk. "No. Since the girl's car hadn't actually been hit, we had little to investigate. There are hundreds of beat up vans around here. We have no make or color to narrow down the field. And since there would be no telltale evidence on the van itself, the job is pretty futile. Besides, the van could have just been passing through."

Owen could feel himself slump as he exhaled with more force than he had expected. Sergeant Kelly shook her head sympathetically and her smile now returned. "Son, I'm afraid your imagination has gotten the best of you. I'm sorry about your friend or whoever she was. But accidents do happen."

Chapter 8

Back on the road after his visit with the Rancocas police, Owen passed an old-fashioned diner and remembered he hadn't eaten since breakfast. He swung back, parked in the diner's crumbling lot and went in. The only customers were two heavy-set guys in denim overalls and green John Deere hats sitting at the counter. He took a booth in the far corner and waited for the waitress to finish serving the overalls. As she waddled to his booth with her order pad, he noticed she was uncomfortably pregnant and felt guilty for having made her walk.

After ordering, he asked if there was a newspaper around that he might read.

"Don't know. I'll look."

He followed her to save her a return trip and leaned against one of the stools as she poked around under the Formica counter. Her hair fell over her young face and she moved it back with a practiced flick.

She frowned as she looked up at him. "Charlie must have taken them home when he left. Let me check in the back." She straightened up, massaged her right side with her palm and then pushed through the swinging door to the kitchen. Owen decided she deserved a big tip.

She was back in minutes holding a paper. "Sorry, all we have is our local weekly. Boss did take the Philly papers when he left."

"That'll be fine. I'll read anything. Thank you." Owen accepted the paper and took a seat in a booth closer to the pass-through in the counter that gave the girl access to the booths. He told himself he should have sat even closer, at the counter even. But he was afraid the overalls might try to engage him in a conversation.

As he set the paper on the table, he heard two noisy motorcycles slowing down on the highway outside the diner. Through the window, the riders looked like the greasers from Pete Thomasian's office. Owen couldn't be sure because of the helmets, and their type all looked the same to him anyway. But he felt his chest tighten as he pictured them swaggering into the almost empty diner.

Then, one of the riders raised his right hand to his mouth in a pantomime of drinking and pointed up the highway. The second rider nodded and they picked up speed and continued on their way. Owen exhaled and turned to the paper in front of him.

The front-page headline jumped out at him. "Accident Kills Local Woman." Below it there was a picture of Marian McNeil's mangled Chevy, a picture he recognized from the police file. He read the story. It essentially repeated the version of the accident Sergeant Kelly had shown him, with the upsetting addition that the flimsy guardrail Marian broke through had been due for replacement the following week.

Owen gazed absently out the window for a while and then turned back toward the counter. The waitress sat on a stool near the cash register. She noticed his look and got up and went into the kitchen. He hadn't meant to bug her about his food and bit his lip. If he stayed there much longer, his tip would be bigger than his bill.

The girl swung back through the kitchen door and struggled onto her stool again. "A few more minutes, sir."

"Thank you. No problem." Owen flipped through the pages of the paper while he waited. Toward the back, on the Obituary page, the caption *McNeil*, in bold type, sat sedately above a brief obit. He slowly read the six short paragraphs, thinking again as he had after his mom's death how sad it is for survivors that the world just goes on when a loved one dies. He had wanted the world to stop everything to mourn with him. But no. People on the street noticed nothing different about him. He had fantasized about wearing black for the rest of his life to show the world his grief. But Colgrove had trumped all other aspects of his grieving. Stopped it in its tracks. Even now he found that he had barely focused on what he was reading as his anger at Colgrove had him breathing noisily.

But two items in the McNeil obit were interesting. Among the survivors were listed only a father, a brother and a partner, Fran Resnick, all of Rancocas. And memorial contributions were directed to the New Jersey Gay and Lesbian Coalition.

The possibility that Virginia and Marian had been seen in a sexually compromising situation had been one of Owen's themes since he'd first read Marian's note. Maybe their sex had been witnessed by Marian's partner who became murderously jealous. But unless Fran was a butch auto mechanic, she was unlikely to have the know-how to sabotage Virginia's Honda or the balls to run Marian off the road. So maybe a guilt fueled double suicide was possible after all.

The waitress quietly slid his food in front of him as he stared out the window, wishing he had somehow been able to refuse Rick's request in the first place. He was not up to dealing with these messy complications. But of course, then he wouldn't have met Barbara,

84

for what that's worth. At this point, to be honest, just food for more fantasy.

He picked at his spaghetti and wondered if he should call Barbara. No, it was probably too soon. And it would be awkward with what he now suspected about Virginia. Maybe he should try to find out more about Fran Resnick while he was in Rancocas.

He asked the waitress for a phone book. She dug one out from under the counter and started to walk around to him. Owen jumped out from the booth to take it from her before she had made it out of the pass-through.

"Thanks. When's the baby due?"

"'Bout two months. It's my first."

"Good luck with it." It amazed Owen how simple it could be to deal with people sometimes. Yet he had been resisting it for months.

He found a business listing for an F Resnick in Rancocas, but no residential. The business was Gold Star Realty on Chestnut Street. He wrote the address on his paper napkin and gobbled down most of his food. To leave it all on his plate would be insulting. When he finished, he went up to the cash register for his check and directions to Chestnut Street. The girl put the totaled bill in front of him and pointed with her left hand. "Go left out of the lot. Bear right at the Y. That'll be Stuart Avenue. Take Stuart about a half-mile. Chestnut is on your right." Owen noticed she was not wearing a wedding ring. His tip was more than generous.

Gold Star Realty was housed in a pale yellow bungalow with a low-railed porch across the front. A downspout was askew on the side of the building where he parked and the place badly needed a paint job. The interior had been jerry-rigged into two apparently small and awkwardly shaped offices off a tiny entrance hall. Owen stopped in the entry area near a door with *Gold Star Realty, F. Resnick* engraved on a cheap nameplate of wood-grained laminate.

He realized he had no idea what to say when he went inside. If Virginia and Marian had indeed had a romantic or sexual relationship and been *seen* by Fran, Owen would not be very well received as a friend of Virginia's family. If Fran had somehow been directly involved in either or both of the girls' deaths, that reception would be even worse, maybe dangerous. Then again, maybe Fran was completely ignorant of the relationship. Maybe, there wasn't even a relationship other than their work, and they were "seen" by Scalero or the stalker or someone else. She would then be nothing more than a grieving partner who might welcome his consolation and be sympathetic to his inquiries. He decided to hope for the best and approach the conversation as though Virginia had indeed committed suicide. He opened the door and went in.

The one-person office was small and cheap: vinyl floor and, except for a rack of coat hooks next to the door, bare walls. An oversized work station was jammed against the far wall and two hard wooden chairs, maybe taken from a dining room set, sat against the door-side wall.

A middle-aged woman in jeans and dark blue sweater was sprawled at the big desk working at a computer. She appeared to be entering data from a stack of bills in front of her. Turning toward Owen, she spoke with a New England accent.

"Yes sir? May I help you?"

"Fran Resnick?"

Owen wasn't sure what he'd expected her to look like. But what he saw was not it. Age all wrong, of course. And her parchment colored face was drawn and hard. Smoker's skin. He could even smell the nicotine on the jackets hanging on the rack next to him. Her dark hair, cut medium length but hugging her head because of its wiry texture, was graying noticeably. Rimless glasses. Other than a pale lipstick, she wore no makeup. She looked more like a mechanic than Chet Odum.

The woman nodded in the direction of a door to Owen's left that he hadn't noticed.

"He's on the phone. Shouldn't be too long. Have a seat." She turned back to her work.

Damn. There I go again. Full-blown theory based on wild assumptions. Owen felt foolish as he sat down. The undeniably male voice in the adjacent room had been faint background noise when he entered the office; but the walls were flimsy and he'd ignored the voice and other building noises while he focused on the woman he took to be Fran. Now, as he sat and tried to figure out what approach to take with *Mister* Resnick, the voice got louder by increments until Owen could understand almost every word Resnick was saying.

"God damn it, Joel. You know I can't do that. And besides, the collateral you have is more than adequate. You have the appraisals."

The woman at the computer turned to Owen and shrugged. Owen wondered what Joel wanted Resnick to do.

"Joel. Please go back to your committee and ask them to reconsider. If they keep pushing, they'll end up dealing with me in bankruptcy court. I just need a little more time. I'm expecting some new capital soon that should solve the problem."

The voice went silent for a while. Then, "Okay Joel. We'll talk in a few days." Owen could hear the phone being slammed back in its cradle.

The woman at the computer turned toward the closed door and hollered, "Fran. There's someone out here to see ya."

After a pause during which Owen's mind went blank, the door to Resnick's office opened and a tall, lean, red-faced thirty something stepped through it and glared at Owen.

"Whatever you're selling, I'm not buying."

He wore khakis, a blue buttoned-down oxford shirt, and brown walking shoes. Intelligent face. With close-cut blond hair, wide set eyes and firm jaw, he looked like the high school teacher all the kids wanted to be like. But his eyes were tight and his nostrils flared. And Owen was a little intimidated. He got up from his chair.

"Not selling anything. I'm just hoping you could help me figure something out about the death of a friend of Marian's."

Owen struggled to think of what to say next and blanked again when Resnick took two quick steps and towered in front of him, probably three inches taller.

"What friend is that? And you know, Marian herself was killed last week."

"My friend was named Virginia Steele. Marian was the last person she saw before she had an accident that looks like a suicide. I have been trying to figure out what was bothering her. I was looking for Marian when I learned that she had died too."

Resnick was still breathing hard through his nose.

"Never heard of a Virginia Steele. And I don't appreciate your snooping around. Marian's dead. I wouldn't let her speak to you if she was still alive." He turned to the woman at the desk. "Paula. I'm going to the job site. Won't be back till tomorrow morning."

He grabbed a windbreaker from a hook by the door and left, slamming doors behind him. Owen looked out the front window as

Resnick hopped into a big-wheeled pick-up parked at the curb and roared away.

"That's some vehicle he drives." Owen leaned against the window to watch it roll down the street.

"Yeah. He's a car nut. Always tinkerin' with this or that. He's got half dozen old wrecks. At least he works on my car for free. It's his only hobby."

Owen turned back from the window. "Is he always so hospitable?"

She took off her glasses and rubbed her eyes.

"No. Things have been rough for him lately. His housing project near Mt. Holly is behind schedule and over budget. The bank is hounding him and we're way behind with our bills." She waved an arm over the pile on her desk. "And then Marian was killed in that crash. Only a few days after they had a horrendous argument. I think he feels responsible somehow."

"I understand. Maybe I was out of line coming here. Tell him I apologize."

"No need. He'll forget about it by tomorrow." She put on her glasses and turned back to her work.

Owen opened the door to leave, but in a move that reminded him of the Columbo series he watched in reruns, he spun back to Paula.

"You know, I read Marian's obituary and I was wondering. Why did the family ask for contributions to go the New Jersey Gay and Lesbian Coalition. Any idea?"

"Sure. Her brother. He's very active in that group and they were very close."

89

"And Marian's life insurance. Who'd that go to? Her brother or Fran?"

Paula knit her dark brows and pulled her chin into her chest as if she had received a blow. "It's none of your damn business; and I wouldn't know that anyway. I doubt she had any insurance. She was only twenty four years old."

"Sorry. I seem to be crossing the line a lot this morning. But thanks for your help."

Sitting in his car, Owen could feel his ears redden at his foolish enthusiasm for the theory of the fatal love triangle involving Virginia, Marian and that woman Fran. So he squeezed his eyes shut and wrinkled his nose, resisting the impulse to develop a new theory, this time about the cash-strapped real estate developer who killed his fiancée for money from an insurance policy he had secretly taken out on her life.

• • •

By the time Owen coasted down the long drive of his Chestnut Hill house late that afternoon, he couldn't decide whether the two accidents were or were not just a coincidence.

After a bowl of micro-waved soup and some bread and peanut butter, Owen called Rick Jennings at work. The operator said Mr. Jennings was not available and no one knew when he'd be free. Having heard legends about all-nighters imposed on new associates as a rite of passage in big New York law firms, Owen imagined it might be the next day before he could reach Rick. So he went to his computer to set out his quandary in an email.

The email went on forever. Owen painstakingly detailed what he knew about Virginia's character and how it was inconsistent with the neglect of her car, paraphrased the alarming note from Marian McNeil, assumed Rick would be shocked that McNeil, too, had died in a recent automobile accident, and highlighted the possible significance of the excerpt from the title report for the real estate transaction Virginia and McNeill seemed to be working on (which he sent along as an attachment). Then he summarized his encounters with Scalero and Resnick and ruminated about the possible involvement of the online stalker he had discovered in Virginia's emails.

While he thought his analysis was perfectly sensible, Owen hesitated when he had the long message finished. He fretted that Rick would react as he did to that history paper Owen had slaved over in high school trying to prove that JFK had been assassinated by the mafia in an attempt to get Robert Kennedy off their backs. In his convoluted theory, because LBJ hated Bobby Kennedy, he'd never keep him on as attorney general when he succeeded to the presidency. And Bobby's campaign against organized crime would end. Both Rick and Mr. Koonz (who gave him a C) thought the theory was imaginative but ridiculous.

Owen leaned back and sighed. His shallow breaths caught in his chest and for several minutes he stared blankly at his knees. Finally, he rolled his neck and went back to the keyboard.

What do you think? Should I go to the police? Report my suspicions to Fletcher & Rhoades? Am I just imagining things?

Owen

With a smirk and a lift of his eyebrows, Owen tapped Send.

• • •

It was still light outside when Owen finished his long email. And it would be light for a while since daylight savings still had a few days to run. Owen felt like a drive down to the Wissahickon Valley Park for a walk. The park had been on his mind since the Sunday meeting with Barbara when he'd imagined going there with her for a stroll along the creek. Besides, he had not taken any exercise in months and either had to lose some weight or buy a whole new wardrobe of pants. He put on sneakers and a sweat suit. Maybe he'd even jog a little.

Owen elected to forego the upper trails climbing the slopes of the valley and confined his walk to the more level bridle path that follows the Wissahickon Creek through the entire valley bed. The canopy of turning foliage over the path was reflected in the quiet creek like an Impressionist painting and the shimmer of sun-kissed rust and gold that surrounded him almost made him cry. His lungs devoured the crisp autumn air and the powerful sensory input stimulated fond memories of childhood walks down the bridle path with his mom: to see the fishermen in the creek on opening day of fishing season, to be pulled on his sled in the winter snow, to feed the ducks in front of the old creek-side inn anytime the weather invited it. As a teen, he often rode his bike along the path with his friends; and he'd often run there during college. But he hadn't been back for years.

He began a light jog. Within a few minutes he'd worked up a sweat. He forced himself to walk and jog for about three miles down the bridle path and back to his car, finishing up tired but exhilarated. On his way home, he even stopped at the newsstand in Chestnut Hill for an *Inquirer* which he hadn't read for months.

At home he showered, put on a clean set of sweats and checked his email. Nothing back from Rick.

He made himself some cheese and crackers, took a Coke from the fridge and sat at the kitchen table to snack and read the paper. After checking every article on the front page, he skimmed the sports section, which was filled with stories about the Eagles comeback win the day before. He had completely forgotten about the game in the excitement of seeing Barbara. Then a picture on the first page of the business section caught his eye. Phil Gordon, in shirtsleeves again, standing with some architect types and a hard hat or two, out in the country somewhere.

The caption under the Phil Gordon photo indicated that planning for the development of a new state college campus on the old Morris estate in Solebury Township was nearing completion and the professionals involved in the deal had met at the site to finalize details before the official closing of its purchase. There was no accompanying story.

Owen recalled the old Morris estate from his boyhood. It must have been three hundred acres of beautiful rolling hills and woods. Fantastic stone house and outbuildings. The name of the estate went back to the days of the robber barons. Old Man Morris had been a railroad mogul with Jay Gould. Owen couldn't remember the name of the elderly couple who owned the place when he was growing up but they'd have to be in their nineties by now if they were still alive.

John Frazier lived near the old estate and had held a Memorial Day picnic at his family farm each year for a while. Everyone had to pass by the Morris estate to get to the Frazier farm and the comparison made John's place look modest. But in fact, the Frazier farm was pretty nice, too. His Coke and cheese tasted better just thinking about the place and the fun he'd had there as a kid.

After a few more minutes with the paper, during which he was actually tempted to call for a ticket to the Springsteen concert promoted in the Entertainment section, he decided to watch a movie while he waited for Rick to call or email. He loaded the DVD with one of the action movies his mail order vendor had in its wisdom decided he'd like—probably because he had actually picked some similar brainless films when he signed up in June and had never bothered to upgrade his request since then. He barely remembered to return the discs he had watched.

He found the movie ridiculous and realized he had let his love of film go the way of everything else enjoyable in his life.

When the movie ended, he checked his email again. Nothing from Rick. He called Rick's office number but got his voicemail. Same result with his cell phone.

He loaded another film, but halfway through, shook his head, cringed and went back to his computer. Still no reply. Then he went upstairs to bed, like a kid trying to rush Christmas morning.

Chapter 9

Barrett was watching TV when he got the call from Giunta. He wished they'd picked someone else to deal with him. He never liked the arrogant sucker.

"Real nice work, Al. We're all happy about it. Not a drop of suspicion about the accidents. From what we heard, the police guess the first girl was a suicide. And they're blaming the second one on some migrant workers who disappeared into the sunset." Giunta sounded like he'd won the Trifecta at the track with a system he'd worked on for months.

Barrett grunted. The police never suspected anything with his jobs and he wished Giunta would lose the childish enthusiasm and realize he was dealing with a pro. But that would be too much to expect. When things went well for Giunta, it just confirmed his own hot shit image of himself. What Barrett didn't like was that when things went bad, the wuss crumpled and hid. Barrett could not remember him ever having a screaming confrontation with anyone, let alone a real fight. For better or worse, Barrett himself was the confrontational sort. He decided to cut Giunta's celebration short.

"Whend'ya say I'd be getting paid?"

"Sometime late next week. We won't get ours till next Monday and it'll take a few days to get your cash together."

"Fine. Give me a call when it's ready" Barrett hung up and shook his head.

TUESDAY
October 25

Chapter 10

Owen woke a little earlier than usual on the morning after sending his long email to Rick Jennings. When he rushed downstairs to Hanks office, he found that Santa had left a present.

Odee,

I don't know what to say. But for the stalker and the "coincidence" of MM's death, I'd say you were just imagining things. You have a tendency in that direction, you know. Even so, it's possible that Virginia and MM met to discuss some personal matter. Who knows what they were doing when MM thought they were seen? And they could both have had accidents because they were upset about the same thing.

Owen understood Rick's theory was as plausible as any of his own. Part of him was relieved. But another part didn't want to let go of his more dramatic versions. They excited him in the way running from the man who had imprisoned his wife and kids in his attic had excited his childhood self. And it also seemed necessary to pursue his own theories just in case Scalero and or Resnick had, in fact, set their sights on him. So the rest of Rick's email quickened his pulse.

If I were you, though, I would check out the judgments and mortgages listed on the title report. Just go to the Bucks County recorder of deeds and ask someone how to look them up. The books and pages where they're recorded are recited in the title report. The judgments will tell you the owner of the property and the mortgages will give you the property in question.

Rick

Bingo. Why hadn't he thought of that?

Owen downloaded directions for the Bucks County Recorder of Deeds, located in the county courthouse in Doylestown. As he clicked and scrolled his way to the information, he realized how little law school actually prepared its students for the day-to-day practice of law. Not only that, but he'd never had an interest in real estate law and had taken only the basic Property course in first year. He understood from Rick and the woman at Brokers Title that Virginia had copied her list from a report of a title search. But he really didn't know much about what lawyers did with a title report and he had no clue what could have interested Virginia so particularly in the one she had copied.

Owen pulled up the Wikipedia site and typed in *Title Search.*

It wasn't exactly law review research, but Owen quickly understood what a title report and title insurance were all about. In order to get an independent guarantee that a Buyer was getting good title to a property, the Buyer and the Seller had to convince the title company that the Seller was the rightful owner of the property and that all of the liens and mortgages on the property that were matters of public record, as evidenced by a search of those records, had been paid or would be paid at the time of sale. When these items are settled, the title company will issue insurance to the Buyer and the Buyer's mortgage bank that the title is good.

Owen studied the list of judgments and mortgages he'd taken from Virginia's apartment. There were a total of ten items on the list: four judgments in the Bucks County Court of Common Pleas and six mortgages. Apparently, the seller of the property was having financial difficulties. The six mortgages were from three to as much as twenty-five years old. The oldest mortgage had been given to Hamilton Bank, a Philadelphia bank swallowed up years before by a bigger bank which had, in turn, become part of the food chain of bigger and bigger banks over the years. Owen couldn't remember which of the megabanks in the area was Hamilton's current successor. The other five mortgages were to companies that had "Finance" or "Investments" in their name. Owen assumed that this meant they were second or third or even further subordinated mortgage lenders of some type. It also meant that the underlying property must have some real value if so many institutions were willing to lend against it.

None of this explained Virginia's interest in the property, assuming that, in fact, she had a particular interest. Possibly, she had brought home the list accidentally and it had no meaning at all. Maybe it had just been a handy spot to jot down the phone number for Marian McNeil, to contact her outside of work. But, of course, she would not then have written down Marian's work number. And she wouldn't have kept a second copy in her glove compartment.

After digesting his research on title insurance, Owen left about ten and drove thirty five minutes northeast of Chestnut Hill to Doylestown, hopeful that he could finish at the Recorder of Deeds in time to make it to John Frazier's Union League seminar that afternoon. He had no real interest in the seminar; but at this point, Frazier was the only person other than Rick with whom he felt comfortable sharing his concerns about Virginia.

The Bucks County Courthouse, in a modern complex of county offices, sat next to a classical style building that had served as the county legal center since the nineteenth century. The town itself bespoke a similar mixture of new and old: Victorian houses on tree lined streets; a huge, new, regional high school; a 1940s movie theater renovated into an art-house triplex, all suitably reflecting the evolution of the county from elegant rural to bustling suburban.

Owen parked two blocks from the courthouse. Another crisp, bright day had him sweating slightly by the time he reached the broad courtyard around which the new complex was built. The elderly guard in the entry hall directed him to the Recorder of Deeds office.

The office itself was huge, a wide space divided roughly in half by a long counter on which were set numerous computer terminals for use by the public. Behind the counter were desks for about ten clerks who all at least looked busy stapling papers, moving to and from filing cabinets, staring at their own computer screens or talking earnestly with one another. It took forever for one of the clerks to notice Owen, standing expectantly at the counter.

The clerk who rather reluctantly asked if she could help him was big haired, big breasted and chewing gum. She predated the new courthouse by decades. Owen showed her the pages from the title report and asked how he could find the documents identified in the report. The clerk seemed to want to be helpful, but apparently the typical users of the office were professional title searchers who knew what they were doing. It was hard for her to know where to start with a newbie. But in time, he had a rough idea of how to proceed and, by two o'clock, he'd dug up plenty of information.

The subject property was owned by a Paul and Estelle Dixon. Some of the judgments were against Paul and some against Paul and Estelle. The court judgments were all relatively recent and in amounts totaling about $125,000. They had all been entered in the past year or so and were easy to find in the computerized records.

The three newest mortgages, also in computerized records and all to finance companies, totaled $790,000. They were placed on ground described only by lot and parcel numbers. No street address. The lots and parcels were in Solebury Township.

The older mortgages were another matter. They were all on microfilm and it took Owen an inordinate amount of time to find the correct reels, thread them in the machine and spool to the proper pages. He couldn't even find one, to First America Finance, of Philadelphia, dated March 17, 1994, for $950,000. Called a "Reverse Mortgage", it was not the biggest mortgage amount. That honor went to Hamilton Bank for $6,000,000. But it was a sizeable chunk of the $8,000,000 and change in mortgage debt.

Owen asked the big-breasted clerk for assistance.

She snapped her gum as she took the title report from him.

"Hon, if it's not at the book and page the title report says it should be, the title report must be wrong. The searchers who create these reports can make mistakes when they're working with these old documents. The computers help, but God knows our people sometimes make mistakes too."

Owen's wrinkled brow must have elicited some sympathy.

"What you should do is think number reversals. Let's see." She spun Owen's papers around so they could both read them. Owen pointed to the First American Finance Reverse Mortgage. She skimmed an orange fingernail along the lines he'd identified.

"Your report says Deed Book 457, page 365. Try Book 475 or 547. Or page 635. You get the idea. Just keep looking. You'll find it."

Owen checked his watch, then exhaled and rubbed a hand through his hair. John Frazier's symposium started at four and he

101

was eager to talk with him. Frazier might have a way to check out that guy Resnick. And, if the girls' deaths were connected to the title report on the Solebury Township property, Frazier might be able to tease out the connection. He'd have to put off this last piece of title research or find a better way to track down that final mortgage.

Chapter 11

Dense traffic slowed him down as he entered Center City, Philadelphia, an hour after leaving the courthouse, and he was already late by the time he pulled into a parking lot on Sansom Street. He jogged over to Broad and was a little out of breath when he approached the Union League.

A white haired gent in uniform was polishing the brass handrails that curved up the gentle stairway leading to the entrance centered in its brownstone façade. At least the exterior of the club still had the venerable look he remembered. At one point, many of Hank's partners had been members of the club, lunching there every day and holding firm parties in one of its big upstairs rooms each Christmas. But, as the old ways died, membership had fallen off dramatically. Even as a child going to Christmas parties over the years, Owen had noticed the club's gradual decay. He had heard that, to stay alive, the club was forced to admit women and minorities, even Democrats. He didn't know what to expect inside, but once through the heavy doors, the bustle and sparkle of the place amazed him. New blood had worked wonders.

An elegant concierge at the reception desk directed him to the bar association symposium on the second floor. Noticing the clock behind the desk read quarter past four, Owen bounded up the steps two at a time.

The symposium room held about fifty chairs. He found a seat in the half-full audience near the side aisle. John Frazier sat at a dais in the front of the room together with three other men and two women. One of the women, maybe forty-five, severe hairstyle, dark tailored suit, was speaking.

"John, I'm quite sure we all understand the changes you describe. However, I think they are best seen as a result of the opening up of the practice and, indeed, the opening up of our society as a whole."

Frazier gave her his full Prince John treatment. Elbow on the dais, hand gently holding his chin. Head cocked in interest. She continued. "This opening of society made for a bigger and more heterogeneous legal profession. That, in turn, made it more competitive. As the pie has not grown, particularly here in the declining Northeast, the increased numbers had to fight harder for their piece of that pie. But on the whole, I would prefer the openness and the competition to the closed world you remember from the old days."

A graying man of about fifty sitting at the end of the dais, evidently the moderator, called on a brown-suited contemporary of Frazier. He had jabbed his hand in the air to get the moderator's attention. He was obviously the other panelist representing the old guard, but he was bald and altogether without Frazier's regal bearing.

"John, you also have to remember that, at least at its higher levels which we are discussing, our profession has become very specialized. Just like the medical profession. And with this specialization, we've lost some of the relationships with clients and other lawyers that we used to have."

Frazier, still in his high concentration pose, nodded as the bald head elaborated. "Tax lawyers in your firm talk primarily to tax lawyers in other firms, labor lawyers to labor lawyers, and so on.

Even the clients now send only their specialists. There are no generalists anymore. Frankly, you have to work harder as a specialist. You are expected to know everything. As a generalist, it was possible to take your time a bit, pose issues to yourself and your clients. Get back to them after a little research. While I don't like our intense specialization and our clients' expectation of instant answers any more than you do, I see it as necessary. The world has grown so complex that specialization is an absolute necessity."

Frazier sat back in his chair as the speaker finished. He raised his hand. The moderator acknowledged him.

"All that may be true, Helen, Robert. But one problem I believe to be at the core of the change is that lawyers today think they should be earning too much money."

He smiled handsomely and the audience chuckled.

"Seriously, many of us aspire to inappropriately extravagant lifestyles, spending fortunes on homes and offices. No wonder our fees are so high. They must be, to cover overhead. Call it the curse of the baby boomers."

Owen remembered Frazier's rant in the office the previous Friday and worried that he might go off again. But the public Frazier was too controlled for such an outburst. Sonorous and calm, he reminded Owen, for a hateful moment, of Colgrove. "In a sense, that is one reason for the specialization that has developed. How can you charge $600 an hour, or more, to give general advice? You have to work on the same problems over and over again until you are like a computer for your field. But what kind of life is that?"

With this plea for a more balanced work life, Frazier seemed to Owen both more human and a little pathetic.

A hand raised in the audience. Owen had not noticed Carter Brock before. Brock stood up when the moderator called on him.

"John, with all due respect, you should keep in mind that when you started in the practice of law, most big firms in this city were run and, for that matter, typically staffed, by men of means. Old families like yours. Old money that didn't need to hustle for the better things in life. As the old money got spent or lost or spread around to grandchildren who had moved to California, the influence of the old guard waned and the profession opened up. But the new guys didn't already have everything; and they were willing to work for it. I agree with Helen. We are better off with an open and competitive profession." He sat down quickly and gave Frazier a brisk salute.

The discussion went on like that for another forty minutes. Only Frazier seemed to defend the old ways. Owen felt sorry for him, unable to change the white shoes he'd first put on as a boy. He was fighting a losing battle to preserve a style that was known only to him and a shrinking number of Philly blue bloods.

When the discussion ended, Owen waited near the front of the room for Frazier to finish the post mortems with the other panelists and a few members of the audience. Frazier spotted Owen and approached him when the little crowd dispersed.

"Owen. Owen, my boy. Thanks for coming. What did you think?"

"Well, Mr. Frazier, it looks like you're fighting a rear guard action."

"That is so, Owen. That is so. I feel like such a relic. But I cannot give up my allegiance to the clan. I just don't feel I belong anywhere else. Don't know whether to scream at the world or cry."

Hand on Owen's shoulder, Frazier guided him toward the doorway of the emptying room. "And you, how did your work with Virginia Steele's affairs turn out?"

Owen's moment of truth had arrived.

Owen had tried out various approaches to Frazier while driving from Doylestown but hadn't picked a best option. So he took a baby step.

"Not finished yet. Still have to get her apartment emptied. But I did want to speak with you about it."

Frazier stopped walking. "What can I do for you, Owen?"

His direct gaze made Owen's pulse quicken. He took a deep breath before answering.

"I don't know that there's anything to do, actually. But I'm concerned Virginia met with foul play. Possibly connected to something she was working on at the firm. Or maybe a personal matter."

Frazier leaned toward Owen and spoke softly. "Tell me more, Owen."

The old man's features wrinkled delicately as he listened to Owen's story about the car, Marian McNeil's worried note and her death a few days later. Owen described the excerpt from the title report and the coincidence that Marian had worked for the title company. He told Frazier about the meeting with Marian's fiancé and the financial troubles he was having and the big argument he'd had with Marian before she had died. He didn't mention the stalker.

Afraid to hear Frazier's reaction just yet, Owen followed up his story with a quick question. "The title report was for a large piece of land in Bucks County owned by a Paul and Estelle Dixon. Are they clients?"

Prince John's typically erect posture gave way a bit. "No Owen, but they are my neighbors. Do you remember the old Morris estate? Estelle Morris married Paul Dixon when I was in college." His eyes brightened and he smiled. "I still remember the wedding out in one of their fields. The newlyweds left the ceremony in an antique horse-drawn carriage. It was all quite beautiful." He then shook his head and sighed. "They are in their nineties now with no heirs. They own all that land but, from what I've heard, they have little cash left."

Another big exhale and he straightened his shoulders. "They're selling the property to the State College system for a new campus. We represent the State. Phil Gordon got the work through his connection with Vince Fiore."

"The politician from South Philadelphia?"

Owen had been reading about Fiore and seeing him on TV for a few years, since he'd become a power in Harrisburg. He was reputed to have his fingers in every lucrative pie in Philadelphia, both legitimate and illegitimate.

"Yes. We only get to handle the land purchase." Frazier was standing erect again, his energy returned. "Morgan and Jones gets the big job working on the development of the campus itself. I've got my toe in the deal because I have been friends with Winston Gates who represents the Dixons. He and I went to Choate together."

They resumed walking out into the hallway as Frazier continued. "But I can see nothing in the matter that could endanger Virginia Steele or Marian whatever her name was. It's a straightforward business transaction. I think your imagination has gotten the best of you, Owen."

"You're probably right, Mr. Frazier. But I wanted to get your reaction before I got carried away." Owen shuffled his feet and decided not to mention he'd hired a mechanic to inspect Virginia's car and had even talked to the police about his theory. But when he remembered his email to Rick Jennings, he decided to fess up just a little bit. "I did mention it in an email to a my friend in New York. He thinks I'm imagining things too." He concluded that, for the time being, another white lie wouldn't hurt. "Other than that, you're the only other person I've talked to about it."

"That's good. Frankly, Owen, I wouldn't want people to get the wrong impression about you. It's kind of a crazy idea."

Owen felt the impulse to laugh. Oddly, he was relieved that Frazier was so dismissive. "I'm glad you think so. It makes me feel a little better."

"Do feel better about it, Owen. Get her apartment emptied and get on with other things." He patted Owen on the shoulder. "You know, despite the way Phil Gordon sounded the other day, we'd be happy to have you interview with the firm if you decide you want to practice. Think about it." He stopped again after three steps down the hall. "In fact, maybe I should put the hard sell on you before you think about it. Have you got any dinner plans?"

Owen was flattered. "No. I haven't had dinner plans for months."

Prince John flashed his electric smile. "Well, why don't we get something to eat here in the club. They have great prime rib on Tuesdays. Okay with you? We'll charge it to the firm's recruiting budget.

Feeling a lightness in his chest, Owen was tempted to prop an arm around Frazier's shoulders. He realized he'd loosened up quite a bit in the few days since he'd last seen the old man. "Sure, why not. I guess I can take the sales pitch for a free meal."

Frazier took out his cell phone, held it up for Owen to see it and started to walk out of Owen's hearing: "Just let me make a quick phone call home before we go down to the dining room."

Though bored within a half hour by Frazier' attempts to tout the firm while still lamenting the changes in the practice of law, Owen more or less enjoyed himself. Other than the coffee and bagels with Rick and the girls on Sunday, it was the first social meal he'd had since he'd left New York and it felt good. He even shared with Frazier his sense of loss over his parents' deaths and the problems with his ongoing depression. Several times during the dinner, his heart ached when he remembered he'd not been able to have such a conversation with Colgrove the previous Christmas. Maybe he wouldn't have fallen into such a funk if he had.

As the waiter took their dessert orders, Frazier caught the eye of a tall black man entering the dining room. He wore a boxy brown suit and had distinguished gray hair. Frazier waived him to the table.

"Commissioner. Nice to see you. Have a seat for a moment, will you? This handsome young man here is Owen Delaney."

The Commissioner reached a strong hand to Owen. "Police Commissioner Ted Barnes. Nice to meet you, Owen." He sat down and nodded at Frazier. "What's up, John?"

"Probably nothing, Ted. But I wanted to give Owen a chance to meet you and describe a situation he told me about earlier. Get your opinion."

The Commissioner turned toward Owen. "Shoot, Owen."

Owen felt a tingling sweep up the back of his neck and didn't say a thing. Frazier finally prompted him. "Ted, a young paralegal in our office was killed in an auto accident a week or so ago. Owen

110

was asked by a family friend to wind up some of her affairs here in town. She was from Iowa. No family here. And he has developed some suspicions that the accident was . . . well, maybe not an accident. Is that right, Owen?"

"Yes. That's about it." He then struggled through his litany about Marian's note and her subsequent death and the title report that linked the two girls.

The Commissioner heard him out, then glanced at his watch. "And what do you think, John?"

Frazier leaned back for the waiter to place a crème-brule in front of him. "I don't know, Ted. I'm familiar with the transaction the two girls were working on and I can't see anything about it that could give rise to foul play. I just thought Owen would want another sounding board; and who could be better than the police commissioner?"

The commissioner took a business card from his wallet and wrote a something on the back. "Owen, I tend to agree with John. Probably nothing to worry about. If you've been in the police business as long as I have, you've seen plenty of coincidences more bizarre than yours. But if you really think you need help, call Detective Kopinski." He pointed to the name and number he had written down. "He's one of the best."

The commissioner pressed both hands on the table. "I see my guests are arriving. I have to go join them. Nice seeing you again, John. Nice meeting you, Owen."

Frazier and Owen half stood as the Commissioner left, then settled into their desserts.

They didn't finish until almost seven-thirty, and as Owen said good-bye and left to get his car, with two wise old heads having counseled against further worry, his mind was free of thoughts about Virginia Steele for the first time since he read Marian McNeil's desperate note.

He strolled in the dusk to his car wondering, as he walked among the suited classes moving toward home after late hours at their offices, what it would be like to have a life among the living.

Although the rush hour had already passed, Owen decided to take the scenic drive home along the Schuylkill River, a slower route than the empty expressway would be at that time. With dusk just settling, bikers and joggers still dotted the paths between the drive and the river; and the water, like the Wissahickon Creek the day before, was so quiet that the reflections of the bridges and the trees on the riverbank showed barely a ripple.

Chapter 12

It was dark when Owen arrived home from his Union League dinner, a little before nine. He parked behind the house, went in the back door, grabbed a Coke, and turned on the TV in the family room. No good sports to be watched so he settled into a cable movie, a romantic comedy set in contemporary London. Dozing off toward the end of it, he dreamed of Scalero staring at him, face tight, using an elbow to nudge Resnick standing next to him with his arms crossed. Owen woke with heart palpitations and sat up rigid on the sofa. Then he eased his weight back and, with a faint tightness in his stomach, began thinking about the Virginia affair again.

Rick Jennings, John Frazier and Commissioner Barnes were undoubtedly correct. Owen's imagination and shaky emotional state had gotten the better of him. Other than the stalker, whom Virginia had essentially ignored, and the proximity of the two deaths, there was really nothing unusual in anything he had *discovered*. As Frazier had said, the sale of the Dixon estate was straightforward business. The knot forming in his stomach loosened and he took a sip of his warm Coke. As the credits for the movie rolled, his mind idled until it settled on his inability to locate that mortgage to First American Finance. He recalled that it was a reverse mortgage. He knew from aging movie personalities in late-night TV commercials that a reverse mortgage was typically taken out by older property owners looking for funds to live out their lives. It required no payments during their lifetimes but accrued interest while they were alive and was ultimately paid by their estate after death. Made sense, given what Frazier had said about the Dixons.

He hadn't asked the clerk whether, maybe, those mortgages were recorded in a separate system. But Owen saw little point in driving back to Doylestown and trying to find it. From what he could tell there was nothing unusual about the other five mortgages. Why should there be with that one? And would he be able to tell if there was?

But on an unexplainable impulse, he rose from the sofa and went to Hank's office, sat at the computer and Googled "First American Finance"

Nothing.

Odd. But maybe irrelevant.

He next Googled the Pennsylvania Secretary of State, which he vaguely remembered as the office where firms doing business in the state had to register. Sure enough, there was a link to search for any business entity registered in Pennsylvania. He clicked, chose entities with names beginning with "F," and scrolled down until he came to First American Finance. Checking further, he found that First American Finance was an active corporation with offices at the South Philadelphia address he remembered from the title report. Incorporated five months ago.

Five months ago! He flushed with goose-bumps. How did this brand new company loan money to the Dixons in 1994?

Owen called Rick Jennings, waking him from what he claimed was his first early night's sleep in two weeks. Owen rushed through an explanation about the missing mortgage. Rick understood, but said he was too groggy to respond intelligently and begged off.

"Let me call you back in the morning, Odee. Maybe someone in my firm will have an explanation for all this. Or at least some idea of what to do next."

Owen wished he had the nerve to tell Rick to wake up. He himself was in full alarm mode, sure he had discovered something important. His foot tapped wildly under the desk and his breath was rapid and shallow. But still a little gun-shy, all he said was "Okay, Rick. Thanks," and hung up.

He sat at the desk for a few moments, unsure whether he could sleep. He envisioned a long night of tossing and turning ahead. Or maybe a Sports Center marathon.

He finally rose to go upstairs. As he entered the front hall, intending to take the front stairs for a change, he caught his breath when he noticed the door to the vestibule was wide open. He exhaled when he saw that the outside door of the vestibule was closed. But it was very strange. He never went in or out of that front door. Always came and went through the kitchen in the back.

He closed the door and walked back into the office. Hank's old desk faced him from across the room. As usual, he had walked around the right side of the desk to get to and from the desk chair. He now noticed papers strewn on the floor to the left. He knew he hadn't done that and he shivered. Was it possible he'd surprised an intruder when he came home, scared him out the front door as he came in the back? He couldn't be sure, but he thought maybe some items on the desktop had also been rearranged. Or was he imagining the whole thing? Nothing seemed to be missing; and remembering the reception he had gotten at the Rancocas police station the day before, he didn't feel up to calling the cops to report that he thought, maybe, someone had been in his house but not taken anything.

He inspected the first floor carefully for other signs of an intruder but found none. So he secured the latches on all of the first floor windows, made sure the front and back door were locked, and went upstairs to bed, wishing Hank had installed an alarm system.

WEDNESDAY
October 26

Chapter 13

Owen didn't sleep well after discovering those signs of a possible break-in. So he got out of bed before daybreak and pulled on a pair of sweats for another jog in the Wissahickon.

He was on the dimly lit bridle path before seven and back at his car by eight after a calming walk, trot and a little canter alongside the early morning horsemen who rode out of the stable at the west end of the valley.

He toweled himself off and changed to a dry but almost comically oversized sweatshirt that had been in his back seat since May. It reached down to his thighs and he assumed he looked ridiculous. But he took a deep contented breath and stretched his arms out wide. Sunlight was by then streaking through the trees and it promised to be a beautiful day. He felt great. He also felt like a coffee and bagel from Dellasandro's, even though it was a bit of a drive from the Wissahickon to Germantown, particularly at that hour on a weekday morning.

As he drove in the rush-hour fits and starts along Germantown Avenue, he couldn't help but compare the drive to the one he'd taken Sunday morning. The streets were empty on Sunday, and for the first time in months, his thick fog of depression had thinned in anticipation of meeting Barbara. Today, on the other hand, the avenue was clogged and the bus ahead of him stopped at just about every corner. And despite his endorphin high, even thoughts of Barbara couldn't calm the slight quiver in his stomach about that First American business.

118

When he pulled up in front of Dellasandro's, a collection of panhandlers were hanging around on the sidewalk. He sighed. Three of them. There had been none on Sunday. They paid close attention as Owen opened his car door. Twisting out of the car, he realized he had left his wallet at home. He bent back in, managed to scrounge a few dollars in change from the console, and hoped it would be enough.

The handful of change just barely paid for his coffee and two bagels after an awkward little chat with old Mrs. Dellasandro, who still remembered him. She hadn't been in the shop on Sunday when he was in a better mood for a conversation. He left regretting he hadn't been a little friendlier, telling himself he could have spared her a few more minutes, particularly since he knew he'd have to run the gauntlet of panhandlers who pestered everyone for change as they left the store.

There were now four of them. The three who'd been there when he arrived shuffled off when he said he'd spent his last dime inside. But the new guy was more persistent, blocking Owen's path to his car.

"C'mon buddy. Don't give me that shit." He looked like one of those Iraqi war vets who had never settled back into civilian life. Bundled up for winter even on a mild fall morning. Hands pressed into the deep pockets of a heavy, army-surplus jacket worn over a hooded sweatshirt. Unshaven. Big, wraparound sunglasses.

Given where Owen had been emotionally the past months, he had sympathy for all disturbed people. But he really didn't have any money.

"Sorry pal. It's true. Didn't bring my wallet with me. You can have a bagel if you want."

119

The panhandler didn't move. He just glared at Owen.

"Fuck you, asshole."

His voice was low and raspy. As he spoke, he pulled his right hand from his pocket, flashed a three-inch knife blade, and lunged at Owen's heart.

Owen's last thought as he dodged to his right was that this guy seemed a little old to be an Iraqi vet.

The knife punctured Owen's left side but slid off into the folds of the big sweatshirt. As the mugger tried to pull the knife back out for what Owen feared would be a second try, it snagged in the armpit of the sweatshirt. Owen threw a right fist that connected with the mugger's jaw. And, to the surprise of both of them, one of the three other panhandlers cracked the mugger's right arm with a length of pipe that, Owen later learned from the police, the guy always carried in the long pocket of his cargo pants for self-defense.

The mugger dropped the knife, sprinted to the corner and turned up the side street. The panhandler who had helped Owen followed him around the near corner, but came walking back within twenty seconds, shrugging his shoulders and extending his palms at his waist.

Owen sat on the curb, looking vacantly at the hole in his sweatshirt. The area around it soon darkened with oozing blood. Dizzy, he leaned against his car, not in great pain and amazingly relaxed, drowsy enough that he thought he just might fall asleep.

Alerted by one of the panhandlers, Mrs. Dellasandro came out of the store and called the police. She stayed with Owen for the endless wait. He was very grateful for her company but didn't say a word and may have drifted into sleep off and on as she quizzed the three panhandlers gawking at the scene. None of them had ever seen Owen's attacker before that morning.

When the police finally arrived, they had with them an emergency medical team who examined Owen and assured him that he'd be okay. He had apparently evaded the most serious possible consequences with his quick move away from the knife. But he would need stitches. The medical techs dressed the wound and set him on a gurney for transport up to Chestnut Hill Hospital and further evaluation.

Owen resisted going in an ambulance. "What about my car? Can't I drive to the hospital myself?"

The medic at the head of the gurney, a young black man about Owen's age, carried himself with a confidence that, even in his semi-conscious state, Owen recognized and envied. "No way. You'll have to ask someone to pick it up for you."

Owen realized he had no one to ask. He had no friends but Rick, who was hours away. Same for Barbara, although he snickered at himself for even thinking they had such a relationship yet. With the sharpness of his mugger's blade, it hit him that, other than those two stretches, he had no idea whom he'd name as an emergency contact if he had to. Parents gone. No other family to speak of. The downside of being an only child.

Like dried flowers in one of his mom's fragile scrapbooks, a collage of memories faintly pressed themselves into his consciousness: his mom helping with school projects, Hank finding their seats at a Phillies game, family weekends at the Jersey shore. He began to cry softly and was reminded of that day in Kentucky that Colgrove had made him feel so alone and unwanted.

The young black medic noticed. "Don't worry, bro. You'll be okay. The hardest part will be waiting for your turn in the emergency room."

Owen didn't bother to explain as they slid him into the ambulance and drove, siren blaring, up Germantown Avenue to the hospital in Chestnut Hill. Owen envied the siren's full-throated wail, a cry he felt but just couldn't let out.

• • •

Two policemen interviewed Owen in the emergency room as he waited on his gurney in one of the curtained alcoves that lined the bright aisle running the length of the treatment area. No, he didn't know or recognize his assailant. No, he really couldn't give a good description of the man other than what he wore. He could hardly see his face.

When the medical team pulled back the curtain to start their examination, the cops gathered up their clipboards and walkie-talkies. The older of the two, with a bulge around his middle exaggerated by the Kevlar vest under his uniform, stared at Owen, his lips on the verge of a sneer.

"One last thing, Mr. Delaney. Most muggings are random acts. But is there any chance someone had a grievance against you?" Owen noticed the old cop's eyes move toward his hair. "We're supposed to log in anything we think might be a hate crime. Have you ever been mugged before? Could the attack have been personal? Did the guy say anything?"

Though exhausted, Owen flushed. His whole body tensed. "No. I don't think so." He raised his voice. "This is not about me or the way I look." But, as the nurse swished the curtains closed behind the departing cops, he fought away those heart-stopping images of Scalero and Resnick staring coldly at him.

Chapter 14

In Germantown after his knife attack failed, Barrett walked the last block to his pick-up, not only because he was out of breath after sprinting away from that crazy with the pipe, but because he didn't want to call too much attention to himself. A white guy racing down the sidewalk in that part of Germantown would be like a black guy doing the same on, say, the posh street in Chestnut Hill where the blond kid lived. And he needed to calm himself down. He was still grinding his teeth when he yanked open the pick-up door.

Despite the brisk weather, heat flushed through his body as he imagined screaming at Giunta, face to face, holding him in place with a death grip on his fancy silk tie. The twenty-five they had agreed on for the girls had sounded fine. Maybe more than fine, given his typical rates. But then the extras started. First the break in. No biggie, even though he hadn't done much of that stuff since the old days with Richie Caputo. And he wished they'd given him more time to pull it off: he'd had to scoot out the front door when the kid pulled up to the back. But whatever. At least reading the kid's emails gave him some idea what Giunta and Nicky were up to. But when they added the deranged panhandler plan, he told them the plan sucked, that he'd have to follow the kid all day to find a situation that made any sense and that knives were not his thing. He doubted that he had seriously hurt the kid, let alone kill him. And who the fuck would've guessed one of those bums would step in? He was gonna tell Giunta he needed more money.

He sat for a while in the pick-up, breathing deeply. It had been his first screw-up since he started in the business. And it was their fault. This third job wouldn't'a been necessary if they hadn't screwed up somewhere along the line. He wondered if The Rake had ever messed up. He doubted it. The way people talked about his old man, he must've batted a thousand till he got sick. Hell, they lived in the same house, more or less, for fifteen years before he ever knew what the guy did. And, even then, it was only because Mike Walsh called him the son of an assassin during that screaming fight on the bus to Newman High.

But for Mike Walsh, he probably never would've wondered about the chunks of cash The Rake would plop on the kitchen table every now and then. Although maybe he should've figured it all out by his mom's reaction. When she first saw them, she'd put her hands to her face and moan. Just let the money sit there. The Rake would say something like "Dot, you and Carmela need some new clothes" or "Al's tuition is due next month." And, in a few hours, the money'd be gone and Dot would prepare a big meal that evening. And The Rake would stop bitchin' at him for a day or two. Like they were a real family.

The house was not the same with everyone gone. The Rake and Dot both smoked themselves to early graves, and little Carmela married and moved to Maryland. He would've liked to keep up the family tradition with cash on the table, but there was no one to see it. So the best he could do on paydays was send Carmela a money order, "for the kids", and go say hello to Rich Caputo at his deli.

Barrett doubted Richie actually knew what he meant to him. Truthfully, other than Dot and Carmela, Richie was the only person who had ever showed him even a drop of loyalty. Till this day, he was amazed Richie hadn't plea-bargained. Who would've blamed him for a little snitch on his partner. But he told the cops he worked alone, even though all he'd done is keep the car ready and then fence the stuff later. It was the fencing that got him caught. He shouldn't've used the same pawnshops over and over. But whatever, Barrett smiled at the idea that Richie had finally bought that deli. And his jaw relaxed when he imagined himself popping in there to say hello again when he got paid.

Chapter 15

It was past noon by the time Owen had been examined, stitched up, gotten his health insurance information from his insurance agent (his wallet was still at home), and been given a prescription for pain medication. The head nurse, after a long interrogation about possible family or friends who could pick him up, finally called a cab.

The cabbie took him home where Owen asked him to wait while he went in to get his wallet. Though the nurse had advised him not to drive for a week, when he came back out of the house, Owen told the cabbie to take him down Germantown Avenue so he could get his car.

When they arrived at Dellasando's, the scene of the crime now looked so innocent Owen had to shake his head. A couple of panhandlers were still there, but they weren't part of the morning's crowd. Customers were swinging in and out of the shop door and pedestrians flowed along the sidewalk as though nothing had ever happened. He did notice a few darkened bloodstains where he had sat down after being attacked. But he became fatigued and heavy limbed when he recognized that the stabbing, so dramatic an event for him, had almost no perceptible impact on the world around him.

His head bumped the headrest as he leaned back for the slow, one-handed drive back home. When he needed two hands, the effort pulled on his wound and it hurt. But at least he didn't have to worry about the car being parked in that neighborhood. And he would have it at home if he really needed it.

Creeping into the parking space behind his house at about one-thirty, his stomach churned at the thought of going inside again. Suppose Scalero and Resnick *had* been behind the mugging. That would confirm they knew who he was and where he lived. And, by now, they might know the mugging had failed and would've had time to plan something else. He sat in the car for ten minutes.

Finally he forced himself out of the car, crept up the back steps, unlocked the kitchen door—at least it was still locked—and froze in the middle of the kitchen to listen. No sounds other than the heater in the basement. He took off his shoes and tiptoed around the first floor, but found nothing.

After checking the upstairs, he sat on his bed, took Commissioner Barnes's card from his wallet and called Kopinski's number. It was answered on the first ring.

"Kopinski here." He sounded like Clint Eastwood.

"Detective Kopinski?"

"I just gave you my name. Who's this?"

Owen swallowed. "My name is Owen Delaney. Your name was given to me by Commissioner Barnes. I spoke to him last night about suspicions I have that two girls have recently been murdered. He told me to call you if I developed any more evidence." Owen knew he had made a wrong choice of words. "Developed more evidence" would make him sound like a kook.

"What department are you with, Delaney?"

"Oh, I'm not a cop. I met the Commissioner at dinner at the Union League. I . . . ."

Kopinski interrupted. "Let me get this straight. You told the commissioner that you think two girls were murdered and he mentioned my name and said to call me when you get more evidence?"

"Yeah. That's about it."

"And what's your new evidence?"

"Uhm, I was mugged today and I think it was connected to the murders." God, he sounded like an idiot, even to himself.

"Well, I'll tell you what to do, Delaney. Go down to City Hall, ask for an assistant DA, and tell them your story. If they think there's something there, they'll contact us. Either that or I might bump into the commissioner at the Union League myself and he can tell me all about it personally." Kopinski hung up. Owen hadn't had a chance.

Owen stretched out on the bed. His sleepless night and the trauma of the day had taken their toll. And Kopinski's quick verbal beating had fully drained him. He decided to take a nap and was dead to the world in minutes.

The cell phone on his dresser chimed about two-thirty. He fought his way awake to answer it but the call had gone into voicemail by the time he got to the phone. He flopped back on his bed and closed his eyes, still exhausted. When he remembered that Rick had promised to call after he had some made inquiries about the First American puzzle, he got up, yawned, and checked his message.

As usual, Rick's voice rang with energy. "Odee, give me a call as soon as you get this. I have some information for you about that First American Finance."

Owen couldn't tell from Rick's tone whether the information would explain away or confirm his anxieties. He quickly called up his contact list, scrolled to "Rick-Office" and pressed "Send," realizing that he no longer remembered Rick's actual numbers.

Unbelievably, he got through on the first try. "Answering your phone today, Rick? What's up? No work to do?"

Rick sounded almost embarrassed. He voice was a little weak and Owen could imagine him massaging the back of his neck. "Actually, I finished a big project yesterday and I slacked off a little today so I could follow up on some ideas one of our corporate guys gave me about that First American Finance. Here's what he told me."

Rick paused for breath or maybe just dramatic effect.

"There are a couple of ways to explain the inconsistency you described to me last night, that a corporation organized this year is the mortgagee on a mortgage more than fifteen years old. The first is that, for some reason, First American Finance decided to reincorporate with a new set of articles, by-laws, and so on, rather than just amend the old ones. It apparently is done. The old corporation transfers its assets and liabilities to a new one and then goes out of business. Same thing could happen with a merger of a new corporation with an older one. Keep the name but change the ownership and governance in some way."

Owen could follow everything Rick said so far. It sounded like, once again, his worries were going to be assuaged. He began to pay more attention to the pain in his side than Rick's explanation.

"But," Rick's emphasis refocused Owen, "in either of these two instances there would be a paper trail in the office of the Secretary of State in Harrisburg. Not one you could access on the Internet; but one that local searchers in Harrisburg could quickly follow. I got permission from Bob Slevin—he's my guy in the corporate department here, about five years ahead of us in law school—to call up our Harrisburg search outfit to see what they could find."

"And?" Owen sat up straight.

As Rick continued, Owen realized that his friend enjoyed this.

"They found nothing. Nada. No 'out of business' affidavit. No merger document. No history of any prior corporation with that name. None incorporated in Pennsylvania until this year. And no out-of-state corporation with that name ever registered to do business in the state."

Owen said nothing as the implications of the search sunk in.

"And here's the kicker." Rick was speaking more slowly now. "Although I didn't ask them to, the search firm went to the incorporation documents for First American Finance. As you know, they were filed in May of this year. You may or may not know that big firms like ours and Fletcher & Rhoades often use an outside service to prepare and file new incorporation papers."

Owen didn't know that, of course. *How could he? He wasn't a lawyer and never would be.*

Rick went on. "Someone who works for the service will sign the public filing as the original incorporator; and then, in private documents not filed with the state, turn over control to the real directors and shareholders of the new company. So, at least until some other type of filing is required from the new company, there is no public record of its true ownership. Nothing underhanded about this. It's done all the time."

Owen interrupted. "So what's the 'kicker,' Rick?"

"Just wait, Owen." When Rick called him Owen, he knew Rick could not be rushed. And, true to form, Rick took a while to continue.

"But sometimes, a firm will do the filing themselves and have someone at the firm sign on as the incorporator. Or an individual who is part of the new company will do the filing and name himself as the incorporator until the company gets more fully organized. Something like that was done with First American Finance this May. And the original incorporator was none other than . . . ta da . . . Virginia Steele."

Owen stared out his bedroom window. Barbara would be upset to think her sister had taken a wrong path when she left her on her own in Philly. He spoke only after a full twenty seconds had passed in silence.

"Wow. And what do you make of all that, Rick?"

"I just don't know." Rick said, and then took his own twenty seconds of silence. "At the very least, that 1994 mortgage is probably bogus. No wonder you couldn't find it. That will undoubtedly come out when the buyer and seller get together at settlement. But I can't believe Virginia was involved in anything shady. I don't think we should tell Barbara about it. But I'll talk to Bob Slevin. Maybe he has some ideas. Let's touch base later in the day."

Owen swallowed hard before saying "Okay. Talk to you later." He didn't want to hang up and almost called Rick back—he'd even forgotten to tell Rick about his mugging, for God's sake—but he just slumped on the edge of his bed, alone and completely exhausted.

But staring at his carpet, thinking about all he'd learned, he could feel his breath quickening. He could see the rough shape of the puzzle, but not the details. Someone had obviously planted a bogus mortgage in the title report for the Morris estate. But who? Marian and Resnick, with Scalero's help? How was Virginia involved? And more important, why would anyone do such a thing? Did they really think they'd collect at settlement? Wouldn't the sellers know it was bogus? It reminded him of those computer hackers who spread Internet viruses. They wreaked havoc. But how do they gain from it?

Owen sat up straighter and blinked wildly at the powerful sunlight splashing through his window. He felt compelled to action but didn't know what to do. He thought of calling that arrogant Kopinski again, but tensed up when he remembered the snarky tone of his voice. Maybe he should go down to the DA's office, like Kopinski said. That was probably the sensible thing to do. It just didn't feel right. What the hell was he going to tell them that would move them to action? But with nothing better to offer himself, Owen struggled up from his bed and went to the bathroom to wash and shave with the intent of making himself a little more presentable.

But toweling off the last spots of shaving cream, he grinned at himself in the mirror. He'd had a better idea. He wasn't sure what he'd do there; but he felt like Rick the high-school fullback breaking through his line. Why not just keep going?

So he dressed as quickly as he could with his wound making movement difficult, limped downstairs, got the address for First American Finance and headed for South Philly.

Chapter 16

Barrett called Giunta when he got back to his house on Fourth Street. The conversation was predictable. When he told Giunta that he doubted the kid was anywhere near dead, Giunta said, "Shit, Al, how could you fuck that up?" like the wuss would've done better himself. And when Barrett reported what he'd read in the kid's email to his friend Rick, Giunta's voice went shrill. Barrett could imagine his face turn ashen and his lips tremble just like in the old days when he'd threatened to piss on Giunta's new pants or rub dog shit on his white loafers. He felt an adrenaline rush knowing Giunta was scared. But he also wanted to get paid. So he let his face go hang-dog while Giunta hyperventilated through a confused ramble about the mess they were in. Finally Giunta told him to go up to Chestnut Hill, hang around the kid's house, see if he ever got home in one piece, and wait for a call.

When Barrett got to Delaney's house, the kid's Highlander was parked near the back, halfway down the long driveway that ran on another hundred feet to an old stone garage. He parked across the street and waited. About three o'clock Delaney popped around the rear corner of the house and got into the Highlander. Barrett pulled away as the kid was making a three-point turn in a wide section of the driveway. He doubted the kid would recognize him, but no sense taking chances.

Barrett noticed in his rear view mirror that the Highlander was behind him and he pulled over so he could get behind it and maybe figure out where Delaney was going. He followed the kid through

Mt. Airy and on to Wissahickon Avenue, which probably meant he was headed downtown. So, on impulse, he backtracked to Delaney's house, pulled into the driveway, parked in the back and used his picks to open that flimsy lock on the back door again. Funny, through his ten years in the service, no one had touched that set of picks just sitting on the dresser in his room. With The Rake already gone, maybe no one in the house even knew what they were. But he had been good with them, before they caught Richie and he started to worry about his own future. Joining the service was probably his best option at the time, although if that recruiter hadn't sold him on the glamour of Special Forces, he'd have tried to get a job on the docks. Shit, the Rake had been, theoretically at least, a union organizer down there.

Tiptoeing around Delaney's house, Barrett was more impressed than he had been from the outside. You could get lost in the place. Though, upstairs, the kid's room looked like a teenager's. Clothes scattered all over, bed unmade. Kid could've used some military training. The thought occurred to him he ought to take something as a present for Richie. Sort of a sentimental thing. He poked around the kid's chest-high bureau, noticed the prescription for *Zohydro*, and rolled his eyes realizing that his supposedly fatal street violence had caused so little damage it could be treated with a little medication.

As he was examining a leather-bound diploma from a law school in New York, and thinking he might take it and replace the diploma with some kind of Deli Owner Certificate for Richie, his phone rang. It was Giunta. When he told Giunta where he was, the little prick went ballistic and told him to get out of the house. He said they were working on a new plan to neutralize—that was actually the word he used, "neutralize"—the kid, and he should get somewhere safe and just fuckin' wait for a call. They might need him.

Barrett poked his tongue into his cheek and inhaled sharply as Giunta ranted. When Giunta finished, he could see in the mirror above the bureau that his face was red. Had Giunta been there, he might have punched him. But like he was defusing another IED out in the field, he forced himself to stay calm and said "Sure, but if you do call, it's gonna cost you another fifteen. And I ain't gonna be using any knife this time. All that last stupidity cost him was a prescription for some shit called Zohydro."

Barrett was about to hang up without saying another word when he remembered his appointment. "And Don't call till after dinner. I got a meeting at the Social Club with some new clients who need a good ka-boom." Giunta was probably too dense to realize he was also saying he was a free agent in these matters; that he, not Giunta or Nicky or whoever they were working with, called the shots. And not only that, but these new guys completely understood his expertise was explosives, not bullshit knives or guns.

Chapter 17

First American Finance was on Snyder Avenue in South Philadelphia. Driving slowly, avoiding the expressway and the River Drives in case he had trouble with his wound, Owen took almost an hour and a half to make the forty-five- minute trip from Chestnut Hill. When he finally arrived at the address he'd copied from the title report, it was already four-thirty and he couldn't find any evidence that First American Finance actually existed. The physical address was the home of South Philadelphia Community Savings Bank, a storefront bank. To its right was a windowless one story stucco building with "Downtown Social Club—Members Only" lettered on its solid wood door. To its left was another store front office, this one for a law firm called Giunta and Giunta.

Owen pulled past Giunta and Giunta until he found a parking spot. He struggled to parallel-park, wincing from the pain in his side, then walked back to the bank office and went in. The place was empty but for one teller behind a counter and an unnaturally red-headed woman at a desk in the front.

He approached the front desk.

"Good afternoon. I'm looking for a company called First American Finance. I thought it was located at this address." He glanced down at the paper on which he had written his note.

The red-headed woman looked up and shrugged. "Might be. The Giuntas have lots of businesses. Sometimes they use this address, sometimes next door. I can never keep track of them all."

"You mean the law firm next door?

"That's it."

Owen gave his thank you and left.

The offices next door were a little more plush than the bank, but still unpretentious. Owen sat in a waiting area after introducing himself to the pretty young receptionist who manned the phones and also had a computer at her workstation. When she learned he had no appointment, she spoke on the phone to one of the Mr. Giuntas and, taking just a little longer peek than necessary at his hair, told him to wait. They would both be out of a meeting shortly and could see him then.

Owen had half-finished an article in Philly Digest about the impact of the Phillies success on the city's economy when the door to a conference room off the waiting area opened and three men stepped out. One, about fifty, he recognized from TV and the newspapers. There had even been a picture of him in the magazine sitting on his lap. Vince Fiore, the South Philly politico.

Fiore was not as tall as Owen would have thought, but he was hefty, with a full head of wavy, dirty blond hair above a pudgy youthful face. He had the obvious vitality of a student council president and his dark suit was noticeably well tailored.

He shook hands with the two other men. They were both older and thinner and had dark-haired comb-overs doing a poor job of disguising their balding heads. Neither wore a suit-jacket. Both wore Clark Kent glasses and suspenders. They were clearly brothers and had the studious hardworking look of old-world Italian gentlemen. They watched from the conference room door as Fiore left. He nodded at Owen and smiled, then tapped his finger on the receptionist's desk as he bounced past her.

"Bye, Patricia. You look great today."

Patricia thanked Fiore then asked Owen which Mr. Giunta he wanted to see.

"Don't know. I had some questions about First American Finance. It's a new company that gives the bank next door as its registered address."

The Giuntas tilted their heads and raised their eyebrows to each other. The one with slightly more hair, who seemed maybe a tad older, stepped toward Owen with his hand extended.

"I'm Tom Giunta. This is my brother Frank. Why don't you come in and sit down." He gestured toward the conference room. "What did you say your name was?"

Owen swallowed hard. "Jennings. Rick Jennings." It was the first name that came to mind.

They sat around a modern conference table. The Giuntas looked at each other and then at Owen without speaking. After an awkward silence, Tom Giunta said "Well?" and took a quick peek at his watch.

Owen took the cue. "I'm doing research for a law school project on new incorporations in Pennsylvania. I selected First American Finance as one of my case studies. Came down here to its registered address to find out how things were going. They told me next door at the bank to see you."

"What law school do you attend, Rick?" Frank squinted. He spoke like a parish priest hearing confession.

Owen named his law school in New York. "But I live in Philly."

"Where exactly do you live, Rick?" Frank was gently turning Owen's investigation into one of his own.

"Not too far from here. In Society Hill." Owen knew he'd never pass for a South Philadelphian. Society Hill was more believable.

At that point, Tom Giunta held up a hand.

"Rick. We should cut this short. Our firm has been serving as the registered office for out-of-state corporations and small domestic start-ups for a few years now. We handle state paperwork, file annual reports, receive service of process if necessary. That sort of thing. It's a decent sideline business. But unless you have an official reason for asking, we are not going to share any information about our clients with you. I'm sorry."

Owen could think of a dozen reasons why this sounded like a lie. Why not ask him what kind of information he was after? Why not just give him the name of the true principals of First American Finance so he could pursue his research with them directly? But his limbs were shaky as he contemplated confronting the Giuntas' quiet strength. He realized he'd been naïve and stupid to pop in on them in the first place. There was something shady going on. That was certain. And the sooner he got out of there and got help, the better.

"Okay. Sorry to trouble you. There are plenty of other new companies to study."

The Giuntas rose, extended their hands for a gentlemanly shake and walked him to the reception area, apologizing that they couldn't be of more help. Owen thought, as the receptionist said goodbye and took another quick peek at his hair, that if the Giuntas or Vince Fiore had any reason to compare notes with Scalero or Resnick, his hair would be a dead giveaway. Hopefully, without emphasis on the *dead.*

Outside, the late afternoon sun smacked him in his face. He shaded his eyes and turned left to avoid the glare, staggered a few steps toward the bank and the social club, and saw three toughs bumping down the sidewalk in his direction. When they reached the door to the club, one turned and buzzed an intercom while the other two stood, more or less facing the street, surveying the avenue. Owen froze. One of the surveyors wore a hooded sweatshirt and wraparound sunglasses. He no longer wore the heavy jacket, but Owen was almost positive he was the guy who'd attacked him that morning.

Owen turned his face away and remained motionless for the milliseconds it took to make an instinctive flight or fight calculus. In his condition, he couldn't defend himself against another attack. Or run, for that matter. Afraid to look back, he cocked his wrist, just a guy checking his watch, and took elongated strides to his car.

Opening the car door, he could see from the reflection in the storefront windows that the threesome had not followed him. But his heart was racing. He drove slowly down Snyder Avenue until he found a space large enough to pull into without painful parallel parking. Like it or not, he had to call Kopinski again.

Kopinski's number rang a half dozen times before it was answered by a female voice.

"Kopinski's desk."

"May I speak to Detective Kopinski, please?"

"He's gone for the day. Anyone else help you?"

"No thanks. I'll try again tomorrow." Owen sagged in his seat and stared at three little girls playing hopscotch on the sidewalk. He didn't want to wait until tomorrow. He assumed the DA's office would be closed by the time he drove to Center City.

He decided to call John Frazier. Frazier had pooh-poohed his concerns but at least he'd been civilized about it. He might even make a personal call to Police Commissioner Barnes once he heard the latest details. His clout was Owen's best bet.

Frazier hadn't left for the day and the Fletcher & Rhoades switchboard operator put Owen though. Frazier answered quickly.

"Yes, Owen. What can I do for you?" How many times had Frazier asked Owen that same question, no doubt understood from years of use to establish the proper relationship between Prince John and his listener.

Owen didn't hesitate. "Mr. Frazier? You remember at the Union League when I said I thought Virginia Steele had been a victim of foul play?"

"Yes, Owen. I still think that is a ridiculous idea." Frazier sounded testy, stressing each syllable in *ridiculous*.

Owen was in the open field now and not about to be taken down by a little exasperation at Frazier's end.

"I'd hoped so too, sir. But I'm more convinced than ever that she was either involved in something illegal or uncovered something illegal. I'm pretty sure it had to do with that Morris estate sale. Can't go into all the details on the phone. But let me say this. Somehow, my suspicions have become known and I think I'm in danger. My house was broken into and I was mugged today."

"That does sound serious, Owen. Have you called that detective the commissioner referred you to?"

"He wasn't in. So I called you."

"Well, we should get together and talk about this. From what I know about this transaction I can't believe there's anything illegal about it. But who knows when Vince Fiore is involved?"

Owen shivered at the thought that he'd just left the lion's den. He was about to describe the scene at the office of the First American shell when Frazier continued.

"I have a meeting of the Museum board tonight and appointments all day tomorrow. I won't be free until tomorrow evening. I know you're upset but I'm sure this will hold until then. I should be home by eight. I'd like to meet there. Do you remember where I live?"

"Sure." But Owen hoped he could get Kopinski or the DA on the case so he wouldn't have to make the painful drive all the way to Solebury Township.

"Can you be there about eight-thirty? We can go over this carefully together then."

"Okay. I'll see you tomorrow night at eight thirty." Owen clicked off his phone then dropped his head and closed his eyes. Despite Frazier's support, Owen took the delay as further evidence that no one was taking his concerns seriously. Could he really be that wrong? How would he convince Kopinski?

• • •

Owen arrived home from South Philly an hour and a half later with his side burning in pain. He searched through the mess on his dresser top for the Zohydro prescription he'd been given at the hospital earlier in the day. He couldn't find it though he knew he had put it there. Where the hell was it? Had he had another visitor? No. There it was, on the floor.

In the car again a few minutes later, he made a slow, painful drive to the pharmacy on Germantown Avenue where he had to wait twenty minutes for the pharmacist to fill the prescription. Then back home again. It took another hour before, sprawled on his bed, fully dressed, he began to feel better.

At nine he called Rick Jennings and filled him in on the trip to South Philly and the details of his mugging, which he'd forgotten to report in the shock of learning that Virginia Steele had been the incorporator of First American Finance.

The pitch of Rick's voice rose when Owen claimed to have seen the mugger on Snyder Avenue. "Can't be, Odee. And even if it was, it can't mean what you seem to think it means. Are you saying that the mugging was planned, that someone was following you?"

"Well, yes, that's what I think, Rick." If he was going to be doubted, Owen figured he might as well lay everything out. "And I even think there was someone in my house when I was out yesterday afternoon. Things were disturbed in the office and the front door was open."

Rick apparently chalked up that last tidbit to Owen's penchant for fantasy. "But who could it be Odee? Who even knows you're suspicious about Virginia's death?" He sighed heavily.

"Other than John Frazier, the only ones who could have a clue would be that Scalero at the title company and Marian McNeil's boyfriend." Owen paused to massage his neck. "I doubt that Scalero believed the story I gave him about returning the title documents to his office. And that guy Resnick was off the wall when I tried to talk to him."

"But how would either of them track you down?"

Owen answered in a rush. "I gave my real name to Scalero. And, if he got my license plate as I left his office, he could easily have found out where I live. I don't know how Resnick could find out. I never got a chance to introduce myself. But he could have gotten my plate number as well."

"That's true, Odee."

144

Owen's back and neck muscles relaxed for a split second at Rick's concession. Until Rick cleared his throat and continued. "But it all still seems farfetched to me. Are you sure the guy you saw in South Philly was the mugger?"

"Pretty sure. Can't be positive. It was so quick and the sun was in my eyes. But he had the same sweatshirt and glasses. And I did see a little of his face up close this morning. I think it was him."

Rick sighed. "Not enough for a court of law, Odee. And frankly, not enough for me."

Owen wanted to cry. He remembered being in tears in the family room when he was about seven, insisting to Hank that there had to be a Santa Claus.

Rick interrupted his flashback. "But the mugging is beside the point, in a way. Whether you saw the mugger again or not, we know there is definitely something fishy about that title report. The question is what do we do about it?"

Owen was glad Rick had said "we". The whole enterprise was numbing his mind.

"Well, tomorrow I'm going to call a police detective whose name I got from the police commissioner himself when Frazier introduced us at the Union League. I spoke to him already but he didn't think much of my story. But if he puts me off again, I might call the DA. I also have a meeting with John Frazier tomorrow night at eight-thirty to go over everything. Maybe he'll have some ideas."

"Is he involved in the Morris estate sale?"

"Only marginally. He's an old friend of a lawyer named Winston Gates who represents the sellers." Owen surprised himself remembering the name of the Dixon's lawyer. Frazier had mentioned it only in passing.

"Apparently, Frazier was brought in to deal directly with Gates, old guard to old guard. Frazier also knows the Dixons, the old couple who own the Morris estate. He says there's nothing unusual about the deal. But he's a little suspicious of Vince Fiore's involvement. Fiore brought the work to Fletcher and Rhoades." Owen paused for breath. "And I haven't even told him about the bogus mortgage yet. I'm sure that'll get his attention."

Rick didn't respond immediately and Owen could imagine him tapping his forehead like he did during law school exams. Finally, he said "I'll be interested to hear what Frazier says when he learns about that mortgage. Call me after you meet with him. Eight thirty?"

"Yeah. At his farm in Buck's County. You ever go there with us to one of his Memorial Day parties?

"Down the road from the Morris Estate, wasn't it?"

"Right. Great little farm. I guess it'll be too dark to see much of it tomorrow night. But I loved that place." Owen's breathing slowed a bit as he pictured Frazier's rolling fields in hazy dusk.

"Don't forget. Call me tomorrow night. Good luck, Odee."

Owen exhaled and rocked in his seat. At least Rick agreed that the bogus mortgage had to have some significance. Now he just had to convince someone else, whoever that might turn out to be.

THURSDAY
October 27

Chapter 18

The next morning, first thing, Owen called Kopinski.

"Kopinski here."

"Detective Kopinski, this is Owen Delaney again."

"Who?"

"Owen Delaney. Commissioner Barnes gave me your number. I called you yesterday about the two girls I think were murdered." Owen winced. Why had he thrown in the 'I think'?

"Oh yeah. Oh yeah. The friend of the commissioner. You were mugged yesterday and you think that proves you're on to something."

"Right. And I saw the mugger yesterday afternoon in South Philly. Next door to the office of some people I think are involved in the murders. And Vince Fiore was there."

"Is that so."

"Yes, it is." Owen could feel his face turning red. "Don't you even want to hear the story?"

"Not really. I told you yesterday to give your story to the DA's office. Or better still, have the commissioner give me a call."

Kopinski hung up.

Owen decided on the spot that he wasn't going to expose himself to the same treatment from the DA. Let Frazier handle all these guys. Once he knew all the details, he and Owen might just get the commissioner to give Kopinski a nasty call. Sweet.

Owen was sitting at Hank's desk. A full day lay ahead before his meeting with Frazier. He might as well make it productive. So he called a local mover to arrange transport of Virginia's furniture to the Salvation Army in Roxborough. The movers were free that very morning but otherwise not available until the following week. He agreed to meet them at the apartment complex at ten-thirty.

They were already at the complex when Owen arrived and he led them to Virginia's apartment. Unable to lift anything himself because of his wound, he gave them instructions and then checked Virginia's mailbox again (it was empty) before going to the office to return Virginia's keys.

The office was chilly. Neither the manager nor Rose was around. At Rose's desk was a young man in a wheelchair, with a tremendous upper body but shriveled legs that barely reached the footrests of his wheelchair. He had draped a leather-sleeved varsity jacket over his shoulders, but otherwise wore only a navy blue tee shirt and jeans rolled up to the length of his little boy's legs. Except for strong, gleaming teeth, his features were dark and irregular. But the overall effect was pleasing.

He smiled and deftly swung his chair from behind the desk and closer to Owen.

"How can I help you, sir?" At such close range, Owen could read an emblem in the design of a basketball sewn on the left placard of the man's jacket: "Philly Wheelchair League—Champs." The name "Roman" was stitched in script under the basketball.

"I'm emptying Virginia Steele's apartment this morning. We should be finished in less than an hour. I thought I'd give you back her keys now."

"That'll be fine." As Roman reached out to accept the keys from Owen, his jacket slipped off his right shoulder, exposing a powerful hairy forearm. Above his wrist on the inside of his forearm was a tattoo the size of a computer mouse: a cartoon Popeye shooting a basketball.

Owen felt like the hairs on the back of his neck were standing on end. *Popeye@xxxx.com.*

But he kept his cool. He'd been shocked repeatedly over the past few days and had gotten better at controlling himself.

"Where's Rose?" he asked, perching his butt on the corner of Roman's desk, like he had all day to chat. "Doesn't she work here anymore?"

"Oh, she still works here. But I fill in every once in a while. Think she's taking care of her grandkids today." Roman had already swung back behind the desk and was tying a white tag on the keys.

"Must be hard for you getting here on short notice. Or do you live in the complex?" Owen found it hard to imagine that Roman could have been somehow involved in Virginia's death; but that on-line stalking was another matter.

"No. I live in East Falls. But Rose always gives me plenty of notice. And I do drive. That van out there's specially equipped for me." He pointed out the office window to a brown van with doublewide side doors and a few inches of what must have been a hydraulic lift protruding along their bottom edge.

Maybe Owen felt more confident than he would have had Roman not been in a wheelchair. And maybe Owen's impression that stalker types were basically timid gave him some added chutzpah. But for whatever reason, he felt a vein twitching in his neck and he turned fully toward Roman. Owen's nostrils were flared and he was breathing noisily.

"Roman—I see that's your name." He pointed to the jacket. "When I was cleaning out Virginia Steele's apartment, I reviewed her emails." He paused and gave a hard stare at Roman who bulged his eyes and dropped his lower lip a quarter inch. "I saw that you've sent her a lot of them. What's that all about?"

Roman's powerful chest heaved as he leaned back in his chair, and his wide eyes darted around the room. Had he been ambulatory, he might've run out the door. But he said nothing.

Owen's jaw tightened. "Well?"

Roman buried his head in his hands. His jacket fell to the floor and his muscular shoulders shook in tiny convulsions. He finally spoke.

"Yeah. I email all the pretty girls who live here. I read their files then I pretend I'm watching out for them and know all about their lives. It's harmless. One or two of the girls even answer my emails." Roman slid his face up through his hands. His eyes were moist and his dark features contorted.

"Virginia never answered. But I think she knew who I was. She had a funny look on her face one day when she came in to pay rent and saw my tattoo."

Owen sat down in one of the chairs across the desk from Roman and thought for a moment. Roman couldn't possibly have done any tampering to Virginia's car. And whoever ran Marian off the road had to be a skilled driver. No way Roman could've done that. Besides, what motive could he have had to do such things? As he thought more about it, he realized that Virginia probably knew Roman was her stalker and had just let it go.

But Owen was reluctant to let it go. Though Roman's disability and his obvious remorse made Owen feel like a bully just thinking about picking on him, he simmered over the deaths of Virginia and Marian and over the insults he'd taken the past few days from

151

Thomasian and Resnick and Kopinski. He imagined the fear Roman's emails had stirred in the girls at the complex who weren't as observant as Virginia and he felt alive being in a position to correct at least one little wrong.

"Roman. You know this is really a police matter. I should report you. But I've got a better idea. Do you have a list of the girls you've been harassing?"

"I haven't been harassing them. I let them think I watched but I never actually spied on them. Like I told ya, it's harmless. But yes, I have a list."

"Let me see it."

Roman reached into a pouch attached to his wheelchair and pulled out a small spiral notebook. He threw it on the desk.

Owen flipped through the pages. The first ten or so were full, each page with a name, email address and other information, including emergency contacts, clearly copied from rental applications. After that, the book was blank.

Owen rose from his chair, notebook in hand, and walked to the door. He turned to face Roman, who sighed in apparent relief that Owen had merely confiscated the notebook. But Owen had more to say.

"Roman, I'm going to email the girls on this list and tell them who's been sending those emails." Roman stiffened as Owen continued. "If they already knew who you were, so be it. But I'll encourage them to spread the word so if you keep doing this, everyone'll know who's behind it."

Owen's side hurt as he stupidly reached for the doorknob with his left hand. Roman pressed his balled fists down hard on his scrawny thighs and his eyes narrowed. The little room was warm with his impotent rage. Owen remembered his own fierce reaction to Colgrove's cold-bloodedness and softened his tone.

"I sincerely hope you don't lose your little job over this, Roman."

As Owen went out the door, Roman spit at him so violently that Owen thought he saw the wheels of his chair lift off the floor.

Within a half-hour of leaving Roman, Owen was leading the movers to the Roxborough Salvation Army. By one o'clock he was back home at Hank's desk, working on a checklist.

After sending a series of emails to the girls in Roman's book, he called Virginia's auto insurance carrier and reported the accident. Didn't give many details. Just that Virginia had died and the car had been totaled.

Dealing with Virginia's auto insurance reminded him that he hadn't alerted Barbara about Virginia's life insurance. He pulled out the card Barbara had given him. Rather than email her, he decided to call her cell phone.

"Hello?" Her voiced sounded strained and hesitant. Strange number on her caller ID? Or maybe just uncomfortable getting a personal call at work.

"Barbara? This is Owen Delaney."

Her voice lightened. "Oh Owen! So nice to hear from you. I've been meaning to send you a note to thank you for a wonderful afternoon. I really enjoyed talking to you."

Owen did a little dance in his seat.

"I enjoyed it too. Hope we can do it again. Maybe I could get up to New York sometime soon." If she only knew how such a trip would've been unthinkable a week ago.

"That would be nice. Are you calling to make a date?"

153

"I guess we could. But I actually called because I just realized I never mentioned there's a life insurance policy in the things I gave you on Sunday. Virginia named you as beneficiary. I didn't want you to miss it. I think it was for ten thousand dollars."

Barbara didn't say a thing and Owen could hear her breathing. Or was she crying? Finally, she spoke in a quiet voice. "I'm not sure how I feel about that. In a way, it makes things worse. First, I let her down. Then I benefit from her death. It doesn't seem right."

"Oh Barbara. You're being too hard on yourself. I'm sure Virginia would hate that." He wanted to tell her she had absolutely nothing to do with Virginia's death; but that would have to wait until John Frazier sorted things out with the police.

They chatted for ten more minutes and ended with a plan to go to dinner in the city over the weekend. Owen had not been so excited in over a year, and he scuffed his chair up closer to the desk and grabbed that checklist.

Next was Virginia's money. Owen realized he hadn't found any banking information in her files, surprising for a girl who still posted her appointments by hand on a calendar. She must have tracked everything online and paid her bills electronically. He could have checked her computer; but he'd already given that to Barbara. And he wasn't going to call her back and ask her to look stuff up for him.

So he called Fletcher & Rhoades and asked for Carter Brock.

"Hi Owen. Nice to talk again. What's up?" Owen tensed at Brock's pleasant tone, remembering his promise to get Barbara's contact information to him. Under the circumstances, however, Owen chose to ignore his guilt as well as the original request.

"I'm still trying to clean up Virginia Steele details and realized I don't know where she banks. I thought I could get the information from you, since you direct deposit to her account."

Brock took his time responding. Owen wondered if he was debating whether or not to be helpful, since Owen hadn't gotten him that requested information. But Brock didn't mention Virginia's sister.

"I don't see any problems giving that information to you. But you know, her bank will need formal authorization of some sort to release her money."

Owen grabbed a pen and held it above a yellow writing pad he pulled from a desk drawer. "I assumed that. But at this point I don't even know which bank."

"I understand, Owen. Hold on and I'll try and find out."

Owen waited, drumming his fingers on the desk, energized about scratching one more item off his list. He told himself that he ought to thank Rick for asking him to do all this. The forced activity had woken him up.

Brock came back on the phone. "I found it. She banked at South Philadelphia Community Savings Bank. We put the money in her checking account. Don't know if she had any other accounts there."

God. The Giunta brothers' bank. Too many coincidences, thought Owen. "Isn't that an odd bank to use. So out of the way. She lived on City Avenue."

"Not really." Brock's tone was matter-of-fact. "Quite a few of our staff bank there as a favor to Phil Gordon. He has an interest in the bank. It's run by his brothers."

"I thought the Giunta brothers owned that bank." Owen instantly wished he could take those words back, shaky at the thought his inside knowledge my set off alarms in Brock.

"It is. Tom and Frank Giunta. They're Phil's brothers. John Frazier convinced Phil to change his name when he joined the firm."

Chapter 19

Owen felt a shiver as he mumbled a thanks and something about not forgetting that Brock wanted to reach Virginia's sister. He then hung up in a daze and slid down in his chair, thumping his head against the top of the backrest, and noticed some peeling paint in a corner of the ceiling. He felt weak, and struggled to process his new information.

At least Brock's candor made it unlikely he was involved in the First American mess. Owen's breathing came easier with that realization. But he got goose bumps when he recalled Gordon bumping into him outside of Fletcher & Rhoades with those questions about Virginia. He must have been trying to figure out what Owen knew. Well, maybe Owen knew now what Gordon was afraid he knew then: that he and his brothers had set up the fictitious First American Finance as a vehicle for the Morris Estate scam; did it privately to keep it off the firm's books and used Virginia Steele as the incorporator; probably had her drive to Harrisburg to do the filing in person.

And if First American and its mortgage were bogus, that meant that Scalero or someone at Brokers Title had to be in on it too.

As the state's attorney, Gordon wouldn't allow the state to buy the Morris place unless the title was clear. The Dixons couldn't sell their property and get out of their financial jam unless they paid the bogus First American debt. That payment would get split by the three Giunta brothers and Scalero, maybe even Vince Fiore.

But why would the Dixons actually pay that money? As a reverse mortgage it would, by now, on paper at least, amount to more than two million dollars in debt. Owen shook his head and tightened his brows at the thought that anyone would pay a two million dollar debt they didn't owe. Maybe, at ninety plus, they were confused about their finances, maybe even afraid to raise doubts about the existence of the First American obligation. But they must have advisors, a lawyer or an accountant who would know better. What about that Winston Gates? Or was he too part of the scam?

Owen considered the scheme quite elegant, except for the probability that the Dixons would never pay. And except for the fact that Virginia happened to read the title report with her typical care and noticed the date on the First American mortgage. She probably at first thought it was a mistake and called Marian McNeil. In time, they realized a scam was underway. They met in person to strategize and were seen, who knows by whom. They were disposed of and the Giuntas and Scalero continued on their way.

Owen sat very still, taking long, slack mouthed breaths. While the scam might never have worked anyway, it certainly would not go ahead now. Owen could stop it all. Lay it all out to John Frazier. Frazier would know what to do, if only to alert Winston Gates. And Frazier would definitely want to know that his recruit, Mr. Giunta-Gordon, had been a very bad hire.

Owen wanted to be in on that phone call to Police Commissioner Barnes.

It was not even two, almost seven hours before his meeting at Frazier's farm. His heart was now beating wildly and the pain in his side seemed to have increased with his agitation. What should he do while he waited?

He called Rick Jennings. Not available. He persisted, raising his voice to the operator. "It's *very* important."

"The best I can do is put you through to his voicemail." She spoke as though she hadn't heard Owen's words or the urgency in his voice. "Would you like that?"

"No thanks." Owen's side twitched with pain as he slammed down the phone.

He went to his computer and sent Rick a long email, setting out the new details he had discovered about Phil Gordon and his brothers and First American Finance. As he did, he mouth went dry when it occurred to him that he might have been too hasty in his conclusions. Perhaps it was all the doing of Phil's brothers, in cahoots with Vince Fiore. Maybe they'd asked Phil's help in setting up a new corporation for one of their clients and he and Virginia had unwittingly participated in the scheme. Or was it possible that Virginia and Marian McNeil had planned it themselves, to help Resnick out of a financial jam? Somehow used South Philadelphia Community Savings as their bank and official address?

Suddenly Owen felt exhausted. He wanted to cry, or maybe just take another nap and shut down his flood of worry: worry that Gordon might have pried Owen's crazy ideas about the Morris Estate from Frazier; worry that Gordon somehow knew Owen would be meeting with Frazier that evening and that he'd want to prevent that; worry that the break-in and his mugging were not just coincidences.

He decided to get out of the house and not come back till he'd talked with John Frazier.

Owen was in worse shape as he pumped gas at the Sunoco on Germantown Avenue in Chestnut Hill. He was by now almost nauseous with worry. But the worry now was coated with a profound sadness at the realization that his months of isolation had left him with no friends to call on for aid or comfort.

A van gassing up on the opposite side of the pump island obscured his view of the avenue. And his eyes were misty with self-pity. So he wasn't sure. But he thought he saw his old friend, the Iraqi vet—his mugger—driving a red pickup past the gas station in the direction of his house. He turned his face away from the street, shut down the pump, and hopped into his Highlander.

Holding his breath, Owen drove in the direction the pickup had headed and spotted it turn onto his street. He turned as well, but pulled over to the curb, afraid the guy would somehow know his car. The pickup slowed as it approached his house, then pulled in his driveway.

Drivers often did this, thinking the long wide drive was a small lane off the street. They'd turn back quickly when they realized their mistake. But this was no mistake. The pickup didn't come back out. Owen pulled away from the curb and headed down the street, coasting past his house. He could see the pickup in his parking space near the back door. But after circling the block for a second look, the pickup was gone.

Had someone been left behind to go inside? Should he check? Silly idea. Should he call 911? No, he was tired of trying the police. Better let John Frazier request an escort for him when he came home.

Chapter 20

Barrett had gotten a couple of calls from Giunta since his meeting at the Social Club the previous evening. Apparently, Giunta's partner thought he could deal with Delaney himself. But Giunta told him to consider himself "on call". Damn, how he hated that guy's self-importance. Why couldn't he deal with Nicky instead? At least he was a regular guy. A bumbler, maybe, but not an asshole like Phil Giunta. If he'd been paid for the girls already, he'd have told Giunta to shove the whole Delaney thing. Get someone else if his partner couldn't handle it. But twenty-five Gs was a big payday and he knew he'd have to stay on the string. Phil had said their own payday was just a week or so away.

This "on call" business made him itchy and he went for a walk around his neighborhood. The area around St. Andrea's hadn't changed much since he was a kid and there were still plenty of people who said hello or nodded as he passed by. When he edged around a group of paunchy old guys in a sunny semi-circle of beach chairs on the sidewalk, his thoughts turned again to The Rake. He felt like he understood him better now that he had taken up the old man's profession, so to speak. And, sucking in his cheeks as he thought about it, he realized they'd both developed their deadly skills in the so-called service of their country: The Rake in Vietnam where POWs could be a logistical nightmare and were often disposed of behind the lines, and he, a generation later, in the Middle East defusing IEDs. But he wondered whether he might have turned out different if The Rake had not been such a mean bastard

161

to him most of the time. He probably wouldn't have been so hell bent on proving himself as a bad ass. And he might have accepted his success with those IEDs without becoming so cocky about it that the whole unit hated him.

Barrett instinctively put his hand to his throat. Thinking about that last fight and his discharge always made him poke around there to see if he could still feel any pain. There was none, and there hadn't been any since that flare up about a year ago. But from what the VA docs had said, his voice was never gonna be normal again. Probably served him right, picking a fight with a black belt.

When he turned back on to Fourth Street, he noticed a legal spot in front of his house and decided to move his truck away from the hydrant up the block where he'd parked it the day before. Never once got a ticket on his block, but there was always a first time. So he hopped into the pick-up and circled the block. But by the time he arrived back in front of his house the damn space was taken. He groaned theatrically, then laughed out loud. It never paid to do the right thing.

Rather than pull up at the hydrant again, he just kept cruising down Fourth Street, daydreaming with an empty feeling in his stomach, thinking he should tell Giunta to fuck off if he called, but knowing he wouldn't actually do that. His neck and jaw went stiff as he recalled Phil screaming at him over the phone while he was poking around Delaney's bedroom. The he remembered that leather bound diploma and again thought it would be a nice gift for Richie. Not the thing itself—hell, he could buy a nicer one in Center City— but the idea that he would've stolen it for him was kinda cool.

He turned on McKean towards Broad Street and then headed north towards Chestnut Hill.

He had never been up to Chestnut Hill before that break in on Wednesday night. But this would now be his third trip in two days. He liked the area. Big houses, lots of trees, fancy shops on its cobblestoned main street. And, by now, he could pick open Delaney's back door in his sleep.

Delaney's driveway was empty. He turned in and rolled to a stop by the back door. Grabbing his picks, he was inside and upstairs in the bedroom within minutes. The diploma was still on the bureau. He snatched it and bounced downstairs, locked the door behind him, jumped into his truck, made a reckless three point turn in the driveway and pulled out to the street. The whole thing took no more time than a drive around the block.

Chapter 21

Blowing hard short breaths to calm himself, Owen circled his block three times checking that his driveway was still empty. It was, but he shivered at the thought he could have been at home.

He still had no idea what to do until his evening meeting with Frazier, but driving aimlessly for a while, he finally decided to head up into the Bucks County countryside. That way he could check his recollection about the location of John Frazier's farm while it was still light. He hadn't been there in years.

He stopped for a Big Mac and Coke at the McDonalds in Flourtown and then headed on the back routes to Doylestown. Driving slowly to avoid straining his throbbing side, it took almost an hour to reach Doylestown. Seemed like so long ago that he had been there at the courthouse checking on the Dixon liens and mortgages. Yet it was just two days. He had changed in the last few days. Maybe *recovered* was a better description. While his side was killing him and he was clammy with fear for his life, he realized he actually preferred the way he felt now to the way he'd felt then.

He pushed back his shoulders and found himself making some resolutions. Get back in shape. That Big Mac in Flourtown was his last for a while. Call the Inquirer for delivery service. Get closer to Barbara. See if she might be the one. The image of a bear coming out of hibernation came to mind. And, despite the knot in his stomach, he was no longer tempted to sit down and skid to a stop.

Avoiding main roads, it took Owen another hour to find the Frazier farm which, with normal driving, was about a half hour northeast of Doylestown. He remembered it could be reached from the road that ran along the Delaware River. River Road, they called it. He took several false turns up narrow, winding roads leading away from River Road before he found the right one. By that time, steering had become very painful and he had to take another pain pill. The only one he'd brought with him. Should have taken it a while ago. And should have brought the whole bottle.

Coming up from the river, he recognized the Frazier farm first. Same two stone pillars at the entrance to the drive. On his right, with the Morris estate in the distance. They had always reached the Frazier's' from the other direction, approaching it from Route 611, a busy highway he avoided with his side so sore.

The old farm looked just as he remembered it. Lush bluegrass meadows and split rail fences hugging the rolling hills. White run-in sheds for the long-gone animals dotting the fields. Red wooden barn, still in good repair, sitting peacefully just off the winding driveway. The stone house on the hill up at the end of the drive looked a little smaller than he remembered, but it was still stately, lording it over the expanse of green, white, and red. The flat, neatly mowed area behind the barn, where the Memorial Day picnics were held, could host a picnic tomorrow.

Ah, those picnics. He smiled and almost laughed out loud as he remembered the men-versus-kids tugs of war, with the kids allowed to win each year until they became real threats and the fathers actually had to try. They ended one year when the rope broke and everyone went flying backwards onto their rear ends. As a little kid, he had loved to play hide-and-seek in the huge barn. As a teenager, softball games were big. Hot dogs, hamburgers, ice cream. One year there was even a brass band playing Sousa.

165

He drove past Frazier's and came quickly to the immense Morris estate. Many times the size of Frazier's, the years had not been kind to it. The Dixons' financial troubles could be read in the missing fence boards along the long road frontage, the uncut fields now sprinkled with tall weeds, and fallen trees that hadn't been removed. Like an aging beauty queen who still had her figure but little else, the estate's hair had thinned, skin had parched, and posture sagged. It looked like it was managed by ninety-year olds.

Owen continued carefully down the road. Each of the small farms beyond the Morris estate was more picturesque than the last. He enjoyed the drive. At an intersection a few miles from the Frazier's, he stopped at a pub for a beer and a break. It was now five-thirty. Three hours to go.

Owen called Rick from the pub but was told that he'd left for the day. He asked for Barbara Steele but was told that she'd left as well. As Owen started to call Rick's cell phone, the bartender across the room pointed to a sign on the wall behind him. "Sir. No cell phones please."

Owen turned off his phone and slid it back in his pocket. He'd call Rick later.

He had been reading the local paper and nursing a beer at his window table for about an hour when he noticed a red pickup pull into the intersection from the direction of Route 611, and then head down the road toward the Frazier farm. He couldn't see the driver clearly but whoever it was didn't look like the Iraqi vet and took no notice of Owen's Highlander which was in full view from the road. He told himself to relax. There were millions of red pickups.

Owen asked for some pretzels and another beer and continued staring out the window toward the intersection. It crossed his mind that if, by chance, John Frazier had finished his appointments early and headed home, he might spot him on the road and speed up the timetable for their meeting. He didn't know what kind of car Frazier drove so he had to strain in the fading light for a glimpse of each driver who passed by. Most were women. But when the male drivers all began to look like Phil Gordon or Scalero or even Carter Brock, he concluded his imagination had trumped his vigilance. He knew, as Rick had said, he had "a tendency in that direction, you know." He even began to doubt his whole take on the Virginia affair. After all, if there was a valid explanation for the apparently bogus First American mortgage, he could have been chasing phantoms all along.

Owen remembered reading about a curious aspect of the JFK assassination. Though the day of the assassination was warm and dry, with an overnight rain shower having long passed, photos showed a man dressed in a heavy black suit holding an open umbrella over his head, standing in the street-side crowd at precisely the spot along the motorcade route where the shooting began. Once you saw him in a news photo, he stood out like a bright beacon in the open sea. He surely had to have been an accomplice to the shooting.

However, when investigators tracked him down, he turned out to be protesting the pre-World War II appeasement policy of the dark-suited, umbrella-toting Neville Chamberlain, who was abetted in that policy by JFK's father when he was ambassador to Great Britain. Apparently, the man with the umbrella had lost family in the war, which he believed could have been prevented with different policies.

Maybe the obvious signs of foul play associated with Virginia's death that screamed "look at me" like the man with the umbrella were no more incriminating than that man's gesture had been. Certainly it could have been a personal matter that brought Virginia and Marian together. He knew little about Virginia, and any number of far out scenarios were possible. Rick had pointed that out. And even Barbara's story about Virginia's mysterious fight with her girlfriend in Des Moines made him wonder how far out she might actually be.

The two deaths could have been coincidental accidents, just as they appeared. He really wasn't positive that the mugger at Dellasandro's was the same guy he saw on Snyder Avenue. And the red pickup parking at his house could have made the same mistake as that couple years ago who thought his big house was a nursing home where their uncle was staying.

If the First American mortgage could be explained, there'd certainly be an explanation about the registered address at the Giuntas' bank. And he still couldn't figure out how the schemers, if there was a scheme, could be sure that the Dixons would pay the First American mortgage at settlement if they didn't actually owe the money. Maybe he'd gone overboard with all this. Maybe he should be very tentative in his explanation to John Frazier.

By six he was hungry and ordered a Caesar salad with chicken, giving a crisp nod to the barkeep as he ordered from the "Lite Fare" menu. He stopped scanning the intersection and watched the news on the bar TV from six thirty to seven. The last hour of waiting was tedious. As darkness outside blanked his window, he worked puzzles on the paper placemats at his table, thumbed through the local paper again and washed up in the men's room.

He left by eight and drove slowly back towards the Frazier farm. In the dark it was hard to tell one farm from another. But finally he recognized the broken fence line of the Morris estate and knew that the Frazier place would be coming up soon. When he located the drive, he turned in and could see lights in the house at the top of the hill. There were no lights on the winding driveway and his headlights cut an eerie swath through the night as he maneuvered its turns.

He parked in the circular drive in front of the house and crunched across the gravel to steps leading up to a wide patio that stretched across the entire width of the building. There was no doorbell, but a big brass knocker hung on the heavy front door. John Frazier responded to its metallic clunk within seconds.

"Welcome, Owen. Thanks so much for coming. Any trouble finding it?" He was still dressed in his dark business suit.

"No, Mr. Frazier. I more or less remembered it from those picnics you used to have here." Not to mention that he'd been sitting a few miles away for hours, hiding from real or imagined bad guys intent on doing him harm.

"Good." Frazier closed the door behind Owen. "So, let's go to my den and try to sort out this Virginia thing once and for all."

Frazier led him through a foyer to the living room and then into an elegantly furnished den. Owen remembered the den from a weekend meeting with Frazier his father had dragged him to when he was about twelve. He had sat doing homework in the adjacent dining room, behind two closed sliding doors, while the men talked.

Frazier motioned for Owen to sit at a leather wing chair facing his desk. Owen sat and sighed in relief, looking around the room and noticing the intricate paneling of the two nearby sliding doors, while Frazier moved to his desk and, carefully pulling up his pants legs so as not to stretch out their knees, dropped into his high-backed desk chair.

"You want something to drink, Owen? A soft drink? Something stronger? My wife's away so I can't offer you much in the way of food unless we want to see what there is in the fridge for a sandwich."

"No. I'm fine, Mr. Frazier. Stopped to eat on the way here." Owen tapped his foot, strained with all the waiting.

"My wife is on her way to visit her sister in D.C. Driving herself. I always worry about her driving. And she doesn't carry a cell phone. Makes the worrying worse. I've been meaning to buy her a phone and insist she learn how to use it. But there are so many choices now."

Owen could feel his Lite Fare churning in his stomach as Frazier rambled on.

"What kind of cell phone do you use, Owen?"

Owen took his phone from his pocket and passed it over to Frazier.

"I got this a little over a year ago. It's simple and it gets great reception. There are newer models, but I haven't bothered to change. Didn't want to have to learn how to use one of those smart phones. But I guess I really should pretty soon." He realized he'd never called Rick or turned his phone back on after being cautioned by the bartender at the pub.

Frazier pulled out an index card from a desk drawer. "Let me write down the make and model. Might be a good choice for my wife. She's put off by all those apps she hears about."

Owen exhaled through his nose and hoped he was not showing too much exasperation.

As Frazier wrote on the card, he said "So tell me again, Owen, why do you think there is something afoul with the Morris estate sale?"

Owen answered in his best law-student fashion, summarizing the parts of the story he'd already told at the Union League, but adding the fact that one of the mortgages on the title report appeared to be bogus.

Frazier had seemed unfocused while Owen repeated the basic facts, but the detail about the mortgage woke him up.

"What do you mean, 'bogus'?" Frazier leaned forward on his desk.

"Very simply, the mortgage can't be found in the Bucks County courthouse, and it was dated 1994, when the supposed lender was not incorporated until five months ago." Owen sat back in his wing chair after delivering this last bit of news as though he expected applause.

"But Owen, have you considered the possibility that the newly incorporated lender is merely a successor to an older, preexisting entity?"

Owen couldn't tell whether Frazier was puzzled or angry.

"Yes, John." Warming up to this Perry Mason stuff, Owen surprised himself with his informality. "But there *was* no previously existing entity. No history of First American Finance until five months ago, when it was incorporated by Virginia Steele. And the address of the new corporation is the bank in South Philly owned by Phil Gordon and his brothers."

With that, the doors behind Owen slid open.

"Okay. We've heard enough." It was Phil Gordon. Standing next to him was Scalero, with a pistol in his hand pointed at Owen's head.

Chapter 22

For a few seconds, Owen thought he was going to pee. He stopped breathing, scrunched down and could focus on nothing but Scalero's pistol. When he finally exhaled, he glanced at Frazier and realized he was not alarmed.

Frazier finally spoke. "I think you're right, Phil. Unfortunately."

Frazier swiveled his head in a tiny gesture of disappointment and puckered his lower lip. "I had hoped we could send poor Owen back home with all his Virginia Steele worries behind him. But he's done too much homework. If what he knows ever got out and old Winnie Gates got wind of it, our jig would be up."

Owen almost laughed at Frazier's quaint, old-fashioned expression. The turn of speech made Frazier seem somewhat harmless and Owen crossed his arms and leaned forward. "Then I guess you'll have to kill me too."

Owen could see from Frazier's scowl that his brazenness had pissed the old man off. But he was quite sure they wouldn't try to dispose of him right there in Frazier's den.

"Yes, Owen. This deal is getting messy. First time we've had any trouble. But we have had it in spades." Frazier pressed his palms together and tapped his fingers, a gesture than must have conveyed deep thought to thousands of clients over the years.

Frazier's posing quickened Owen's pulse. He squinted at Frazier and said "First time? You mean there have been other times?"

Frazier picked up a yellow pencil and drummed its eraser end on his desk. He answered after a long pause.

"Many. Ever since I met these two." He nodded his princely head in their direction. They both smiled like praised children.

Owen massaged his chest as he blinked at Frazier. "But why, John? Why you?"

Frazier closed his eyes and shook his head. Owen hoped he was asking himself the same question. Why would a man who had everything take up with two lowlifes like Gordon and Scalero? Owen didn't expect an answer. He doubted Frazier could even give one. If Owen had to guess, he'd have said Frazier was a thrill seeker, bored in his old age, and enjoying the risks he was taking with these guys.

So Frazier surprised him when, opening his eyes, he lowered his voice as he had during their conversation in his office the previous Friday and said "Money, dear boy. Money. It costs a lot to keep up one's position in society. Do you have any idea how much I have to give each year to stay on the Museum board? Or the Symphony? If I made money at the firm the way some of my esteemed younger colleagues do, I would be fine. But you know, today everything is based on productivity. And we old fogies aren't very productive. We have no *specialties.*" He spit the word out like it had been stuck between his teeth.

Frazier's face was turning pink as he looked over to Gordon. "Do you know Carter Brock is looking into sending legal work to India where young people like Owen will draft contracts and do research for a tenth of what even *he* would expect to be paid here? Where would that leave us? All we have left to do is those damn real estate contracts."

Scalero waved his gun. "I've heard all this shit before, you two. My question is what do we do with this kid now? And, if something happens to him, what do you think the guy in New York will do? Jennings, or whatever his name is."

Owen realized that someone had indeed been in his house checking his emails. Rick was right back in law school. 123456 is not much of a password. Whoever had checked his emails had probably done so while he was having his clubby dinner with John Frazier. He remembered Frazier moving out of earshot to make a call before going down to dinner. And that charade with the commissioner. It was a gamble on Frazier's part; but he was betting his pal the commish would take his cues and politely dismiss Owen's story.

Owen's chest heaved and his breath quickened as his disappointment in Frazier turned to the kind of anger he had experienced during his face-to-face with Colgrove. Another betrayal.

Gordon stepped toward Scalero, lifting his gaze to yell at the much taller man. "Damn it, Nick. If your buddy from the Social Club had done his fuckin' job we wouldn't be in this mess. So just hold on."

Owen's heart sank. His mugging was, in fact, an attempted murder.

"Calm down, gentlemen." Frazier spoke as though resolving a budget issue at a board meeting. "I have put some thought to our dilemma. It turns out that Mr. Delaney is experiencing a bout of depression, and as we know from your, ah, associate at the Social Club, he has also been given a prescription for pain medication which, I have discovered, is lethal when taken in quantity."

Owen caught Frazier's drift before he spelled it out.

"Unfortunately, poor depressed Owen is going to take his own life with an overdose tonight; but only after sending a farewell email to his friend in New York." Frazier looked toward the ceiling and again pressed his palms together and tapped his fingers.

"The email will say that everything about the Morris estate transaction is explainable. That this Virginia Steele matter has been a wild goose chase and has only confirmed his sense of life's futility and his failure to make something of his own. You get the idea." He tilted his head and smiled.

Owen was sure Rick wouldn't believe that email. At this point he knew enough to be suspicious if he got it. Maybe even suspicious of Frazier, since he knew about Owen's meeting at the farm. But that didn't mean that Owen wouldn't be dead when the email arrived.

Frazier began giving orders, speaking with a chilling calm and formality. "Nick, you escort Owen in his car back to Chestnut Hill. Phil, you follow to compose the suicide email. Also, Nick, you should tell your friend at the Social Club to meet you at Mr. Delaney's house so you can access his email if he proves uncooperative. He might also be able to help getting Owen to take his medicine."

Frazier smiled to himself again and Owen ran his fingers through his hair. How could Frazier be so heartless toward Hank Delaney's boy. Like a Disney hologram Owen had as a kid that showed Mickey Mouse from one direction and Donald Duck from the other, John the Handsome Prince of High Station had magically turned into a cruel old man without a conscience. His voice was flat as he went on.

"Tell your boy not to park at the house but to walk the last block or so. You too, Phil. Don't want the neighbors to be aroused by a strange car in the driveway."

Owen told himself it was good to understand their plan, even if he was its victim.

As Scalero yanked Owen from his seat and pressed his pistol into Owen's burning side, Frazier added, "And one last thing. If anything out of the ordinary happens and the police get involved, tell them you're taking Mr. Delaney to Doylestown hospital for psychiatric commitment at my suggestion. They may tell you it can't be done without Owen's consent; but have them call me if they do. I believe Owen is a danger to himself and others."

Given the craziness of what he'd tell the cops, Owen worried he wouldn't win that battle over consent if it occurred.

"Call me when things are done." Frazier stood at his desk as though ending a friendly client meeting. "Our closing is scheduled for Monday morning. Let's just say that we won't be describing this 'Condition Satisfied Prior to Closing' in our closing memorandum."

He smiled at his little joke, walked around the desk and put a hand on Owen's shoulder. "Sorry about all this, Owen." He frowned with deliberate insincerity. "But we are too far down our road to turn back now."

Owen felt like Roman must have earlier in the day. He wanted to spit.

Chapter 23

Barrett's cell phone rang while he was watching TV. Guinta explained they had Delaney at his partner's farm up in Bucks County and needed Barrett's help when they brought the kid back to Chestnut Hill. When he described the new plan, Barrett slapped his palm to his forehead. What the fuck were they doin'. Forced overdose, faked emails. No way. Phil's voice was wavering and Barrett could imagine a sheen of sweat on his face. Phil was scared shitless. Barrett wanted out, or at least that extra fifteen Gs.

"I told ya this afternoon, Phil, if you needed me for anything else it was gonna cost ya."

"Jesus Christ, Al. This has already got to be your biggest payday. Why so greedy?"

"Inflation, Phil. Inflation. That and I don't like the way this thing is goin'. Poor management at the top."

"You don't know what you're talking about, Al. Everything's under control."

"In that case, a little extra's not gonna be a big deal. My price is forty."

Giunta was silent for a few seconds before sighing like an exasperated parent. "Okay, Phil. If my partner don't agree, I'll pay the extra from my share."

Barrett almost wished Phil had refused and given him an excuse to quit. He was out of his comfort zone. On the other hand, socking away an extra fifteen would bring him that much closer to retirement.

178

"Good. It'll take me about forty-five minutes to get to Delaney's house. What time'll you be there?

"Give us an hour. And park down the block. Don't want neighbors remembering strange vehicles in the driveway tomorrow when they learn the kid's dead."

Barrett agreed and thought it wasn't bad thinking on Phil's part. Or maybe it was someone else's idea.

Chapter 24

Outside of Frazier's house, the evening had gotten warmer and, under any other circumstances, Owen would've taken off his red fleece jacket. Had his wound not been so tender, he would have taken it off when he first sat down with Frazier. But he'd worn it throughout the entire session in the house and was now sweating from the temperature as well as fear.

A full moon had risen above the barn and Owen remembered his family staying so late at one of Frazier's picnics that they too had left in the moonlight. But leaving this time was not as pleasant. Shaking and faintly nauseous, he took mincing steps as Scalero pushed him toward his own car. When they reached it, Scalero shoved Owen into the passenger seat and, with Gordon standing guard, walked around to get in the driver's side. Once inside, Scalero held the pistol in his left hand, awkwardly pointing it at Owen as he held the steering wheel with his right. He didn't look too experienced in such things. Gordon then walked to the back of the house and brought his own car around to the front. He followed as Scalero rolled down the drive.

Owen considered unlocking his door and jumping out as they passed the big barn halfway down the drive. He remembered some great hiding places in there from those picnic games of hide-and-seek. But this wasn't a kid's game. Too easy to wait him out while he hid. Besides, they might forget about the suicide plan and just shoot him. A gunshot or two in farm country wouldn't be that unusual. And they could dispose of his body and his car. Frazier would claim he knew nothing. Again, though Rick Jennings would be suspicious, Owen Delaney would be dead. Better to wait and pick a better spot to jump. No way that he wanted to reach his house and that bottle of pills.

As they pulled onto the main road, Owen decided to engage Scalero. Maybe distract him a bit.

"One thing that puzzles me about your scheme is how a mortgage as old as the one you guys will claim to be holding can be believable with no paper trail of bills or annual reports to the Dixons. Why wouldn't Gates be suspicious?"

Scalero checked the rearview mirror, making sure Gordon was behind them. "That was never my job. All I do is make sure I get their stuff in the title report. Those two are fuckin' geniuses with the documents."

Owen needed more conversation from Scalero if he was going to get him to let down his guard. "What do you mean?"
Scalero glanced at Owen, and even in the moonlight, Owen could see Scalero's thick eyebrows arch with a 'how much do I tell this guy' look.

"Oh, what the fuck." Owen guessed Scalero took some professional pride in their scheme, had probably wished he could talk about it to somebody and told himself that Owen, who would be dead soon, was a safe audience. "When they did up the mortgage papers, they also did a batch of annual reports that supposedly went to an old bookkeeper who worked for the Dixons before he retired." Scalero was jerking his head from Owen to the road like a pigeon poking around Rittenhouse Square. "He naturally claims he never got them. But Phil's got the fuckin' lender's copies. Phil says it's his

181

word against a forgetful old crock who should have sent in a change of address when he retired."

Owen thought it would take more than that to convince him to pay up two million dollars that he didn't owe. But Scalero wasn't finished.

"John took Gates aside and told him not to embarrass old man Dixon and his bookkeeper. These old guys will do anything John tells them to do. Fuckin' A. He must have been something when he was younger."

"And who arranged for the automobile accidents?" Owen pictured the Iraqi vet unplugging the air bag in Virginia's Honda.

Scalero jutted his chin in Owen's direction. "You mean they weren't accidents?" Then he smiled. "The boys from the Social Club are fuckin' geniuses in their own way too, you know."

Scalero's must have assumed Owen knew about the Social Club because both Gordon and Frazier had mentioned it. Or more probably, the Giuntas had reported Owen's visit to their office.

"And what did the other Giunta brothers have to do for their share? And Vince Fiore?"

Scalero wrinkled his nose and squinted at Owen through the corner of his eye. "What? Are you fuckin' crazy? Vince might have been interested in our operation if he knew about it. But Tom and Frank would have had Phil fuckin' arrested if they knew what we were doin'. They're as straight as they come."

They had been sliding through intersections as Scalero drove along the country roads outside of Doylestown and had never slowed down enough for Owen to consider jumping. But as they approached the town, traffic increased and their pace slowed. Owen began looking for a chance to escape, but their slower speed also meant that Gordon was following almost immediately behind.

Entering Doylestown proper, Owen hoped for a red light. They hit one at the corner just past the old movie theater on Church Street. Only one car idled between them and the light. He'd had to make it quick before the light changed.

"Wow! Look at that guy." He pointed vaguely to Scalero's left. Scalero turned and Owen nearly screamed as he twisted out of Scalero's reach, popped the lock and opened the door. Almost falling out of the car, he raced toward the corner and turned right, up Main Street. His stitches felt like they would tear open and his entire left side seared with pain. He knew Scalero wouldn't shoot in such a built up area. But both Scalero and Gordon were out of their cars chasing him. Horns blared as the light changed green. Scalero and Gordon stopped and turned back. Geniuses they were not.

Owen limped around the small block back to Church Street where he could spy on them. Their two cars were parked along the curb near the Main Street corner, and they were on the sidewalk gesticulating wildly at each other. Owen crossed the street and slithered into a doorway just before the movie theater. He cursed himself for surrendering his cell phone to Frazier, pissed at falling for Frazier's elegant trick.

It looked from their gestures that Gordon planned to follow the route that Owen had taken up Main Street and Scalero would backtrack down Church, past the movie theater, but on their side of the street. Owen had to get out of that doorway.

When Scalero poked his head into the café directly across from the theater, Owen scurried into the theater lobby. The three shows had long since started and there was no one in line outside at the ticket window. But inside, the ticket taker was still on duty and asked for Owen's ticket.

No way Owen was going back outside to buy one, so he gave the ticket taker a twenty-dollar bill and told him to buy him a ticket and keep the change. When the confused kid went out to the ticket window in his uniform, Owen worried he might look suspicious if Scalero noticed him. His shoulders tightened when he heard the kid's loud conversation with the girl in the ticket booth describing what had just happened.

He decided not to wait to find out if Scalero could make out what the guy was saying from across the street, and went into the first movie on the left. He sat at the very back, where it would be easier to keep an eye on anyone coming in. His wound pounded with pain, although, from what he could see and feel in the dark, the stitches had held. His shirt was not bloody.

He sat with his pulse thumping in his ears for about a half-hour, during which no one entered the theater. He could hear the theater next door emptying. So he left his seat and mixed with the crowd in the lobby, moving close to the front door where he could look outside. Scalero and Gordon were inside the big-windowed café across the street, sipping coffee at a table near the door and staring over at the chatting crowd leaving the theater. They had probably guessed he was in the theater and had decided to wait for him. He went back to his seat.

The movie seemed to be coming to an end. What should he do when it ended? He could have the theater manager call the police, but the hairs on the back of his neck prickled when he imagined a scene with Gordon explaining to the cops that the disturbed young man needed hospitalization. No, there had to be a better way. His luck with the police the last few days had not been good anyway. He thought of borrowing a cell phone and calling Rick. But Rick's numbers were in his auto-dial, and he had no clue what they were without his own phone handy. He had the little card Barbara had given him with her numbers on it. But the idea of explaining his situation to her was too much for him. *She* might even think he was crazy.

He noticed a man's sport coat and an old Phillies cap draped over an empty seat in front of him. They suggested a feeble plan.

Owen struggled out of his own red jacket and placed it alongside the coat and cap. When the movie ended he'd leave his jacket behind, take the other coat and hat and try to lose himself in the crowd. He hoped his "disguise" would at least buy him enough time to get to the Main Street corner. With any luck, Scalero and Gordon would assume he was still in the theater with the third show.

The first phase of the plan worked just fine. Owen left as the credits trickled on to the screen, and whoever owned the other jacket did not notice the switch during the few minutes it took Owen to get into the lobby with the first wave of the crowd. As they left the theater for Church Street, he put on the Phillies cap, turned up the collar of his new, smallish sport coat and slinked along with the crowd moving toward Main Street.

He could see his car at the corner across the street and remembered that he had a spare key in a magnetic box under the left front fender. If he could get to that spot unseen, he'd be shielded from Scalero and Gordon by the car itself, maybe long enough to grab the key and get away.

The crowd thinned at the corner, some turning left, some crossing Main, and some crossing Church toward his car. He hid behind a big guy in the group crossing Church and managed to get to the corner without a burst of bodies running from the café. He squatted behind the front fender and felt for the magnetic box. The awkward position made the pain in his side scream fiercely. He rarely needed to use that spare key; but each time he did, he had a hard time finding it. The underside of the fender was crusted with road dirt.

He found it after an agonizing minute during which he feared the box had fallen off or maybe not been replaced after he last used it. He slid the box open and picked out the key. Then he crawled toward the front door, reached up to unlock it, and opened it as little as needed to squeeze inside. He lay on the front seat breathing heavily, and put the key in the ignition. He turned the key when the light turned green. The motor hummed. He sat upright and drove off with the traffic. In his rearview mirror he could see Scalero and Gordon race out of the café.

Weaving his car down Church Street, Owen could see Gordon's car pull away from the curb. He had about a one-block head start, which was good while in town. But he had to lose them entirely. He scrambled up and down side streets until he came to the Route 611 bypass, a short expressway that ran around Doylestown to avoid slowing the heavier Route 611 traffic.

He couldn't see them in his rearview, but assumed they were only one turn behind. So he took the expressway hoping he could speed up enough to get some distance on them before they too got on the bypass.

Breaking the speed limit he widened the gap, but as the expressway ended and became old 611 again he could see a pair of headlights swerving into the oncoming lane in a risky attempt to pass traffic behind him. He made some reckless passes himself and maintained his lead. But his throat tightened.

As the road curved to the right and he thought he couldn't be seen, he turned on to a side road, switched his lights off, and drove in the dark. The further away he got from 611, the darker it got. Tall trees and dense shrubbery lining the country road blocked most of the moonlight, and he either had to slow down or put his lights on. He slowed down and finally stopped altogether to twist around and study the road behind him. The twisting was painful and he could only hold the position for a few seconds. He saw nothing. But he had no idea whether they were still speeding down 611 or somewhere on his safe little country road with their own lights off.

He breathed a little easier after crawling more than a mile without seeing anything behind him. So he turned on his low beams and picked up speed with a growing conviction that he was in the clear. But he still had no idea where to go or what to do. He decided to head for New York and stay with Rick, or maybe Barbara.

In another half-mile, he turned onto a farm lane and coasted to a stop behind some evergreens he thought would hide the car from traffic on the country road. Satisfied with the hiding place, he labored through an agonizing three-point turn in the narrow lane so he could face the road he'd just left. He turned off the engine, squirmed out of his too-small sport coat, and waited.

As his adrenaline rush subsided, the throbbing in his side increased. He was hours overdue for his medication. Obviously, he'd have to get to New York without that bottle of pills. He tried slow rhythmic breathing to ease the pain and almost closed his eyes as his tension ebbed. But he maintained a tired watch, fearing that Gordon and Scalero might backtrack and notice the turn he'd taken. If they did, even in his dark nest, a glint of moonlight reflecting off his vehicle could be fatal.

Within minutes a pair of headlights moving at normal speed wound down the country road from the direction of 611. It was probably someone else. He couldn't see well enough to tell. The car passed the lane and continued on its way.

Some minutes later, a car came along the country road from the other direction, driving much slower. Had they been in that first car? Turned back in disappointment? Or just for a second look? Owen's hands went clammy when he noticed the evergreens didn't provide cover from that side.

Owen pinched the ignition key as the car lights slowed near the entrance to the farm lane. They passed it by, but then stopped and backed up. Owen trembled as they turned in the lane.

He started up his car and tried to back further up the lane without lights. But in seconds, the lights from Gordon's car caught him head on. He stretched to look out the rear window as he accelerated. He could barely see, and the stretching felt like someone had stuck a fork in his wound. The dark lane made a curve he didn't notice and he backed into a drainage ditch. His wheels spun as he tried to pull forward. No chance. He got out and started running into the adjacent field.

His burning side made running almost impossible. The field had recently been plowed for fall planting and was lined with furrows. He tripped repeatedly. After one spill he looked up to see two flashlights coming after him. They gained ground as he staggered forward.

It was over in a minute. Scalero grabbed him by his shirt collar and then twisted his left arm behind his back. Owen again imagined his stitches popping as his side screamed in pain.

Scalero whispered in his ear. "You little faggot. If it was up to me, I'd shoot you right now."

Owen almost wished he would do just that.

Gordon had been thirty yards behind Scalero. But by the time he reached them, he had his cell phone out and had Frazier on the phone.

"We got him, John. What now?"

Owen and Scalero panted heavily. But otherwise, an eerie silence held as Gordon listened for instructions from Frazier.

When he finished. Gordon slipped his phone back in his pocket. "John says bring him back to his farm. One car this time."

The threesome stumbled back across the field to Gordon's car. Owen's pulse quickened when he saw it was a two-door sedan.

"My car's got more room." Owen's throat was so tight he could barely get the words out.

Neither Gordon nor Scalero even bothered to look over at the Highlander with its door hanging open. Owen realized he'd left the key in the ignition and was about to say something when Scalero began muscling him into the back seat of the two-door. Owen yelped as his side scraped the doorjamb when Scalero pushed him through the narrow space behind the front passenger seat.

"Shut the fuck up, kid." Scalero poked the barrel of his pistol between Owen's shoulder blades as he squirmed into place. Scalero then started to squeeze himself into the back as well.

Even before Scalero put his first leg into the small space, Owen felt woozy. The last time he'd sat in a back seat without doors was that panicked ride in high school. Since then he'd just explain that he was morbidly claustrophobic. Most people understood. Lot of luck with that approach this time.

Owen knew they wouldn't let him sit up front again. His best shot was to keep Scalero out of the back. They should realize he wasn't going to escape if Scalero sat in front. What was he going to do? Strangle Scalero from behind and grab the gun? No way. He decided to chance making a suggestion.

"No need to sit back here. These windows don't even open."

Scalero stared at him. At first, Owen thought that he was considering the idea of sitting up front. But no. Probably just suspicious.

"Fuckin' kid always has to put his two cents in." And with a groan, he thrust his bulk through the narrow opening. Owen half expected to hear a pop.

"Jesus, Phil. You need a bigger fuckin' car." Scalero spread out across most of the back seat, shoving Owen to the far corner.

Owen closed his eyes and conjured up images of a wide beach, empty except for a few seagulls pecking away, waves rhythmically lapping the sand. He rolled his head to loosen the cramped muscles in his neck.

Gordon got in, started the car and began to back out of the farm lane. It was a difficult stop-and-go process, during which Owen concluded that both Gordon and Scalero had learned Fuckspeak at an early age and remained quite fluent with it. Their shouts and the overpowering sweetness of Gordon's cologne drove the peaceful image of Owen's beach far from his mind. Owen hugged his stomach.

Chapter 25

Barrett was waiting in the parking lot of the train station not far from Delaney's house when the next call came through. Thank God, it was Nicky. He'd had his fill of Giunta for the day. But, as usual, Nicky was a little confused. They wanted him to leave Chestnut Hill and meet them at Frazier's. It was the first time he'd heard that name, but he assumed Frazier was the "partner" Phil was always referring to. But Nicky was weak on the directions and had to check with Giunta. Eventually Nicky handed his phone to Phil. Barrett's stomach turned.

"Al, you got something to write on?"

Barrett picked a pencil from his sun visor and reached into his glove compartment for a little spiral notebook.

"Okay. Shoot."

Giunta dictated the directions with a fake calm that had Barrett breathing through his nose. As he got him to the road leading to Frazier's farm, he said "You have to be careful on that road. It's very dark and you can hardly tell one farm from the next. But you'll pass a big place on your left, with a long, broken down fence. Maybe two entrances after that farm is a drive with two pillars. That's Frazier's. Should take you about an hour."

Chapter 26

Though his eyes were closed and his head rested in the far corner of the backseat through all the chatter between Scalero and Gordon and the guy on the phone, Owen couldn't relax. The image of the beach would not return and his breathing was short and shallow. He wanted to scream but imagined Scalero making things worse by holding a hand over his mouth if he did. He didn't get himself under even a semblance of control until they were on the quiet country road leading to the Frazier farm.

He noticed the pub at which he had spent most of the afternoon. It was almost midnight but there were still a few cars parked out front. He felt a surge of adrenaline, imagining himself free and running to the pub for help. But the elation passed in seconds and he sagged back into his corner. Getting free this time wouldn't be so easy.

Gordon finally pulled into Frazier's long drive and Owen could see the yellow glow of the house lights up the hill. Other than that, the entire countryside was dark. As they approached the gravel circle in front of the house, the light above the front door came on. The door opened and Frazier took a step or two out onto his patio and stood with his arms folded across his chest. He'd replaced his suit coat with a long dark robe, but otherwise was dressed as he had been earlier that evening. Tie and all. With the light at his back and his open robe billowing from the modest wind, Frazier cut an imposing figure.

Gordon got out, telling Scalero to stay put. He pulled himself up to his full little boy-scout height, and threw his shoulders back as he walked stiffly toward Frazier, who was still standing above them in his godlike pose. Owen thought he could hear Gordon sigh, like he was steeling himself for an expected tongue-lashing. He seemed much diminished from the cocky younger lawyer who'd shown Frazier so little deference the previous Friday at Fletcher & Rhoades.

Owen strained to listen. Gordon had left the driver's door open, making it possible to understand a little of what Frazier and Gordon were saying. The concentration took his mind off being cooped up with Scalero in the back seat.

Frazier didn't yell or even raise his voice. Gordon's posture relaxed. Frazier apparently felt that salvaging their original plan was a greater priority than taking out his anger on Gordon. Owen wished Frazier *had* raised his voice so he could hear better. But from the pieces he could make out—"not in my house" and "rope . . . in the barn" and " your friend"—Owen understood that he was still on Frazier's menu for the evening. He heard Gordon say, "He'll be here in about an hour" as he turned and walked back to the car with a bouncier step.

Gordon got in the car without saying anything, turned it around and headed back down the drive. He stopped at the barn, got out, walked around to the passenger side and opened that door.

"Okay. Everybody out."

Scalero took as long to pry himself out of the back seat as he had to get in; but once *he* was out, Owen slid across the seat and scrambled out, ignoring a stabbing pain as he banged his side against the front headrest. The cool night air was intoxicating. Thank god almighty, free at last.

194

Scalero still had the pistol pointed loosely at Owen. But he was looking at Gordon.

"Now what, Phil?"

"Wait here. I gotta get something from the barn."

Gordon walked to a door at the near corner of the long side of the barn. As Owen remembered, that door went into a small tack room where bridles and saddles had been stored years ago. The rest of the first floor of the barn consisted mostly of animal stalls, sometimes used for horses and sometimes for black-angus cattle, depending on Frazier's whim at the time. The stalls, each of which had a big window to the outside but no outside door, lined the front wall of the barn. The space between the stalls and the long back wall was open and used for showering and tacking up horses. The back wall had a few windows for ventilation about six feet off the ground. At each end of the barn was a heavy sliding door, the near one leading to a lane that extended about thirty feet to the main drive where Gordon had parked; the other to the fields beyond the barn. There was also a stairway next to the tack room that ran upstairs to a hay loft which had plenty of kid-sized hiding spaces in its nooks and crannies.

Owen considered running then and there. But his throbbing side reminded him of his futile escape run earlier that evening and he stayed put. Besides, Scalero had seemed just tired enough of the evening's enterprise to shoot him if he pissed him off any more.

As they waited for Gordon to return, Owen couldn't help but notice the beautiful night. The warm air had become crisp and the moon was so bright in the open area around the barn that Owen wondered if he might be able to read by its light.

By the time Gordon returned, Owen had almost forgotten his predicament and he thought of his mother, who could always focus on the beautiful rather than the problematic. But Gordon's return snapped him back to the here and now. He was carrying a bulky coil of heavy rope. It looked like what remained of the rope used for those tugs of war at Frazier's picnics. When Gordon was close enough for Owen to smell that damn cologne, he gave Scalero his orders.

"John says tie him up with this and keep him in one of the stalls till our help gets here." He dropped the heavy rope at Scalero's feet. "I'm going back to John's house to make plans. You hang around here to make sure the fuckin' kid stays put."

Gordon got into his car and spewed gravel as he accelerated back up to the house.

Scalero looked unsure of what he was supposed to do. He was certainly big and mean looking, and had apparently engaged in a longstanding run of white-collar crime. And he said 'fuck' a lot. But he seemed at a loss when it came to the nuts and bolts of actual blue-collar crime. For that matter, so did Gordon and Frazier. Obviously, those were the things they left up to the Social Club. That thought both scared him and gave him hope. He had about an hour before his fate would be turned over to someone he imagined as a professional killer. But until then, he only had to deal with the big, but maybe bumbling, Scalero.

Chapter 27

Barrett had no trouble following the directions to Doylestown, but after that it got more difficult. The roads were not well-lit and street signs were few and far between. He wished he had one of those new GPS things, but his truck was almost an antique. No extravagant purchases until his nest egg was secure.

He wondered if The Rake had ever thought about retirement before he kicked the bucket. Probably not. He was only about fifty at the time and Carmela was still in school. And from what the old guys at the Social Club told him, The Rake only had to do a few jobs a year, brought in when a job was too messy for a plain old push broom. But what would he have done if he'd lived longer? Till he was too old to practice his trade. He couldn't have anything socked away or Dot wouldn't have had to depend so much on The Rake's old clients for food money and those gift certificates to Wanamaker's.

Barrett sighed at the memories. Funny how life works. If The Rake hadn't died with his perfect record, he might not have been so quick to assume he himself was the criminal type, and he certainly wouldn't have exaggerated the meager success of his petty nighttime break ins in the neighborhood. And if Richie hadn't been so impressed, he would have waited for a job at the docks to come up rather than beg to go along with his friend the big-time burglar. And if he hadn't needed to show off for Richie, he'd've stayed in the neighborhood instead of trying those fancy places in Society Hill. And if their Society Hill spree hadn't gotten all that attention,

Richie'd never been caught and he himself wouldn't have gone in the service. And, but for the service, he wouldn't have all his marketable skills, skills which were gonna earn him the retirement The Rake never got.

He pulled into a gas station on 611 for help with directions. The Indian guy behind the counter was no help but a customer buying cigarettes knew the area and got him back on track. He had missed the turnoff for Solebury.

Backtracking and turning onto a country road with a Solebury directional sign hidden by a low hanging branch, he soon found that cruising along the country roads in the patchy moonlight slowed his heart rate. It had been racing with the difficulty following Giunta's directions and the excitement of his retirement fantasies. But the closer to the farm he got, the more overheated he felt at the prospect of dealing with Giunta face to face. That little cocksucker better not try to tell him his job. He rolled down his window and stretched his neck into the cool night air.

Chapter 28

Scalero pointed with the pistol. "Get in the barn, faggot" Owen was a little slow on the uptake and Scalero poked his painful side with the barrel of the pistol. "I said get in the fuckin' barn"

Owen moved to the still open tack room door. Gordon had left a light on in the room and, when they entered, Scalero told him to lie down in the middle of the room where the small overhead bulb cast a yellow circle of weak light on the floor.

"I need to see what I'm fuckin' doin'."

Owen struggled to get down, then lay on his back. The floor was cold.

Scalero stared at him for a few seconds, and chewed on his lip. "Turn over."

Once Owen was on his stomach, Scalero knelt on his back and yanked his left arm up and behind him. Owen groaned. The pain was almost unbearable and he felt faint. He could see that Scalero had put the pistol down beside his left ear, but he didn't care. He might have been able to reach around with his right arm but all he wanted was for the pain to stop.

Scalero tied an end of the heavy rope around Owen's left wrist. Then he leaned across Owen's back to grab the right one. The feel of the rope did indeed remind Owen of those old tugs of war. And as Scalero yanked his right wrist up onto his back, Owen instinctively wrapped the loose rope two times around his left wrist. Scalero didn't notice. Owen remembered using that quick twist to get a better grip during those tugs of war. He hoped this time it would help him loosen the rope when the opportunity presented itself. If it presented itself.

Once both of Owen's hands were wrapped behind him, it took Scalero about five minutes to swaddle his entire body with the long rope. He used his considerable strength to pull it tight as he went and, by the time he'd finished, Owen felt like a mummy. He was panting wildly. To make things worse, his cheek itched from the rough concrete floor and his nose tickled with sweat dripping from his brow. Sitting in the back seat of a two-door car was an afternoon on his fantasy beach compared to this.

Scalero then pulled Owen to an upright position and left him standing in the dim light as he opened the door leading to the rest of the barn. He came back to Owen, picked up his pistol from the floor and pointed it toward the open door.

"Hop"

Owen hopped out the door.

"Go left."

Owen hopped until he reached the sliding door to the first stall.

"Stop." Scalero unlatched the bolt on the door and slid it open. "Get in."

Owen hopped into the stall. Square, maybe twelve by twelve, the empty space was dominated by an oversized window on the outside wall at just the height for a horse to stick its head out into the fresh air. The swinging door to the window was latched outside in its open position and moonlight lit the space almost as much as the weak incandescent light in the tack room did there.

Scalero slid the door closed. "Don't fuckin' move. I'll be back in a minute. I need to get something for your fuckin' mouth."

200

Owen could hear his heartbeat thrash in his ears as he imagined Scalero shoving a rag into his mouth. Sweat beaded on his face and his eyes bulged. He sobbed in anticipation of his ordeal.

When Scalero returned, all he had with him was a roll of duct tape. "This stuff ought to shut you up."

Owen exhaled, relieved that Scalero hadn't found a dirty old rag. But why couldn't he just leave his mouth alone.

"Why bother. No one would hear me if I screamed at the top of my lungs."

"*I* would. And I intend to sit on that bench outside and enjoy the evening." With that, Scalero tore off several strips of duct tape and pressed them hard across Owen's mouth. One of them partially blocked his nostrils; but he couldn't speak to ask Scalero to move it. He made a few growling sounds and shook his head violently. But Scalero just said "Shut the fuck up. Slide down to the floor and stay there."

Owen did as he was told. Leaning against a wall of the stall for support, he managed to inch his way down to the floor by taking small hops away from the wall. As he did, he could feel some of the coils move slightly. When his butt hit the floor with a final hop, enough of the coils had slipped so that he was able to achieve a more or less sitting position. He groaned from the exertion.

Scalero pointed the pistol at Owen's head. "I don't want to hear none a your fuckin' noises. Just sit there and be quiet like a good boy." He backed out of the stall, slid the door closed and latched it from the outside.

Owen could hear Scalero's footsteps trail away from the stall and through the tack room. Soon, he could detect the acrid smell of a burning cigar drifting through the open stall window. Scalero was indeed trying to enjoy the evening.

Owen knew he had to work quickly. And quietly. If he didn't get himself free before their help from the Social Club arrived, he'd be "fuckin' fucked," as Scalero would say.

He had noticed that the coils of rope wrapping his chest had loosened a bit in his slide down the stall wall before Scalero left. Not a big change in overall tension, but it gave him an idea. Pushing himself back up the wall was almost impossible because he had so little leverage with his legs still tightly bound. And the pain around his wound intensified from the strain. But with repeated mini ups and downs, like he was scratching an itch on his back, some of the overlapping coils surrounding his upper body slipped off the coil they had overlapped and reduced the overall tension another hair. By pressing his bound arms closer together, Owen effectively reduced the circumference of his body and the coils loosened a little more. It took several attempts at this last move before he could withstand the pain enough to try and undo the short length of rope he'd twisted around his wrist while Scalero was tying him up.

But he couldn't bend his left wrist enough to fish his fingers into the loop that extra twist created. Had he been able to open his mouth, he would've screamed. He calculated the time until the guy from the Social Club was expected and gave himself about thirty-five or forty minutes. He repeated his finger work without success until the obvious occurred to him and, almost faint from pain, he pressed his arms even closer together and used his right hand to strip the added twist of rope off his left wrist. He cursed himself for the stupidity that had cost him nearly five minutes.

Even with the coils now loose enough for some feeling to return to his arms and hands, he still had a lot to do. He worked the back scratching maneuver again. But this time he tried to move the coils up his back. Little by little, one or two moved towards his shoulders and neck. The effort was excruciating and maintaining a feel for each individual coil required intense concentration. Time was melting away.

Finally, a coil slid up around his neck. Then another. When he got a third one up there, the effect was miraculous. The coils were now loose enough for him to bend and twist his head against the direction of the coiling, undoing it one coil at a time. Soon, loose rope was piling up on the floor. Except for his overkill with the winding and tightening, Scalero had not really done a good job. There hadn't been any knots keeping the coils in place. And, when all that remained were the knots around his wrists, he undid them without too much trouble. Then, with his hands free, he inched the duct tape off his mouth. It stung as it peeled away.

By his reckoning, he had about fifteen minutes to escape the farm.

The stall door had been latched shut from the outside. But its top half was made of jail-like bars so the horse in the stall could be seen from the aisle and have better ventilation as well. So, reaching through the bars and down to undo the latch was no problem. Except for the noise. The click as he slid the latch open was like a gunshot. He expected Scalero to barge into the barn in seconds. He closed his eyes. All his effort to free himself had been in vain.

But nothing happened. He waited a minute longer. Still nothing. Then, pushing on the bars, he slid the door open a few inches. There was a scraping sound but it was not very loud. If Scalero hadn't heard the latch, he probably wouldn't have heard the scraping either. Owen waited. Nothing from Scalero. He slid the door open a bit further and waited again. Finally, sure it was safe, he gave the door one more slow slide and squeezed through it.

Once outside the stall, he guessed his best option was to go out the big sliding door at the far end of the barn, away from where Scalero was sitting. He could still smell cigar smoke. Scalero had either lit another one or he smoked very big cigars. Owen pictured him with his legs stretched out, leaning against the backrest of the bench, puffing casually as he gazed at the moonlit sky. But Owen couldn't take any chances with noise. He bent down and took off his shoes and tiptoed down the aisle to the big door, carrying his shoes in his right hand. Halfway there, he remembered how heavy those big doors were. He could never open one himself when he was a kid and he was sure that shoving it open would be a noisy process even now.

What he needed was something like a crowbar to inch the door open slowly and quietly. He looked in the stalls as he crept along. No crowbars or even pipes. But in the last stall, he saw an old pitchfork. The stall door was open. He put his shoes down, went in and lifted the pitchfork, very carefully, like a giant pick up stick. He could actually feel his pulse thump in his neck as he concentrated.

On his way out of the stall, looking ahead for an opening along the big door into which he could wedge the pitchfork, he tripped over his shoes, losing his balance and nearly dropping the pitchfork. He righted himself after a few stumbling steps. No noise to speak of. But again he cursed his own stupidity. Despite his desperate predicament, he couldn't help smiling. Rick was always telling him to pay more attention to where he was walking.

Thinking of Rick reminded him of Barbara. Had it not been for seeing her picture on Virginia's desk, he'd probably never have pushed himself along the path that might now be leading him to an early death. That unhappy thought forced his attention back to the big door.

He carefully undid the big hook holding the heavy door shut and saw that he could fit the prongs of the pitchfork between the door and the immense jamb to which the hook attached. He stuck the prongs in the crack and, using it as a lever, pushed the handle firmly but steadily. The door moved a couple of inches. Barely a sound. He pushed again. A slight screech. But a few more inches and he could squirm through. He took a deep breath and leaned on the handle with a little more force. The door didn't move. He leaned harder. Still nothing. The old tracks on which the door slid must be warped. If he pushed hard enough to get the door past the bend, even a comatose Scalero would have to hear the noise.

He tried to squeeze through the opening he'd already made. It was maybe and inch and a half too narrow and he feared getting stuck if he tried to force himself through. That horrible image nearly made him vomit.

By his calculations, the guy from the Social Club should be arriving any minute.

Owen had to do something. He didn't see a ladder or anything that could boost him high enough to climb out the ventilation windows along the back wall. If he forced the big door open and alarmed Scalero with its screech, he'd have to make a run for it. But he'd learned earlier that evening that he couldn't outrun Scalero.

He decided to hide, and tiptoed back toward the tack room, forgetting his shoes as he recalled the many secret places upstairs in

205

the crazy-shaped hayloft. When he got closer to the stairs, he could smell Scalero's cigar smoke drifting through the open window of the stall where he'd been dumped. Had Scalero not even bothered to walk to the window and check on him? Guess not. Thank God it was such a beautiful night.

The old steps creaked as he climbed. Owen hoped the noise just sounded like the settling of the old barn timbers in the now cooling evening. He nevertheless stopped at each step and waited, taking almost two minutes to get up to the loft. He knew exactly where he wanted to hide, assuming the old loft hadn't changed since he was twelve.

At the gable end facing the drive was a large swinging door that opened into thin air fifteen feet or so above the ground. It was the portal for hay deliveries and, every Memorial Day before hide-and-seek began, the mothers would ask a father to go up to the loft to make sure that door was closed and securely locked. The door was now open, and peeking out, he could see Scalero puffing away peacefully on the bench below.

On each long, eave-side of the barn, built into its sloping roof, was a dormered, triple-wide window with what amounted to a window seat below. From the outside, these dormers gave the barn some architectural character. Inside, the windows gave the loft some fresh air and light. Even now, moonlight streaked through them across the warped wood floor. There were also several tool closets built out from the walls and big wooden tack storage trunks sitting around on the floor. In the old days there'd also been hay bales piled all over. The closets, trunks and hay bales all made for good hiding during their games years ago. But, even better, Owen had discovered that the two planks that made up the seat under the window facing the main house were loose, just sitting on a ledge that ran around the perimeter of the wide seat.

When he was twelve, after removing the planks, he was able to fit in the cavity underneath and pull the planks back over himself. Being able to pop up and out anytime he wanted made what would otherwise be a panic inducing imprisonment into a cozy hide-out. No one ever found him there and he'd sometimes stay put until long after the game was over, coming out of his secret place only when he was sure no one would see where he'd been. He never showed it to anyone.

But six inches taller and many pounds heavier, was he now too big to fit?

He lifted the planks and set them on the floor in easy reach from the window seat cavity. Then he climbed in and experimented with assorted positions, bending his knees, twisting his torso. The twisting pinched his wound and the pain, which he'd hardly noticed since he freed himself from the rope, shot through his left side. Unable to contain his groans, he prayed he was too far away for Scalero to hear.

He finally curled into a position which he hoped would permit the planks to sit above him without looking odd. As he had done years before, he sat up, grabbed the first board, set the far end on its ledge and rested the near end on his right shoulder. Next, the second board: far end on the ledge and the near end on his left shoulder. Then he slowly sank into the twisted and painful position he had worked on earlier, using his right hand to guide the planks into place.

When he heard the planks thud lightly on the ledge nearest his head, he shriveled in relief. Then he closed his eyes and tried to concentrate on the dots and slashes of light that were jumping about on the inside of his eyelids. His breath slowed and became more regular. He had never tried Zen meditation, but he needed something like it now. And, before too long, he was oblivious to his pain and fear.

He couldn't say how long he'd been in his trancelike state when he was aroused by the sound of tires crunching up the gravel drive.

Help from the Social Club had arrived.

Chapter 29

Barrett had crept along the road on which, if he understood the directions correctly, he'd find Frazier's farm. When he noticed a long, post and board fence on his left with half the rails missing, he figured he was close. Sure enough, a little ways further he saw a lane flanked by two pillars. He turned in, put his headlights on low, and moved slowly up the gravel lane. He could see lights on in a house way up the hilly drive, and a faint light showing through a cracked open door to an outbuilding halfway up the lane. The moon was bright but the many trees along the lane made it hard to see.

When he approached the slit of light from the outbuilding, he could see that the building was a large barn sitting in an open area well lit by the moonlight. And he saw Nicky Scalero lounging at a bench just outside. He coasted to a stop and got out. Nicky waved the cigar he was smoking, but didn't get up. Typical Nicky.

Barrett looked around before taking a seat next to Nicky.

"Nice place. Who's this guy Frazier?"

"Works with Phil. Actually, he hired Phil about six years ago when we finagled some money from a client of his." Nicky flicked the ash from his smoke and leaned back. "Yeah, I doctored up a title report with a four or five thousand dollar mechanic's lien. Frazier said it was a mistake but Phil insisted it be paid or his buyer wouldn't go through with the deal. Frazier's client was some big corporation and the money meant nothing. So they paid it. Me and Phil split the money. It wasn't the first time. We were doing it a lot."

"Beautiful." Barrett laughed. "I didn't really understand what that guy Delaney was saying in that email to his friend. But I get it now." He stood up and raised his voice. "And rather than report Phil, this Frazier guy hired him so he could play along at home? Jesus."

"Right. But he promised us bigger fish. He works with one of them big Center City firms. Lots of dumb, rich clients."

Scalero took another long drag, then said "By the way, Phil's now Phil Gordon. No more Giunta. Frazier said it sounded too ethnic. But I think Phil likes his new name."

Barrett spit on the dirt in front of the bench. "I don't doubt it. First Francine, now him. He always thought he was hot shit."

"Yeah. He still soaks himself with that fuckin' cologne."

"And what about this Frazier guy? What's he like?"

"He's old, but he's got unbelievable pull with the other old fogey lawyers we deal with in these title deals. He musta been something when he was younger. They all think he's God. They can't believe he'd do them dirty; and when they hesitate, Phil does up fake papers for him to show them. He hasn't failed even once."

"And those two girls? Phil never told me the full story."

"Yeah, well, they were just doing their jobs. One worked with me and the other with Phil. But they got in the way. Same as this kid Delaney. Don't know how the fuck he figured things out. But we can't stop now."

They both turned to the sound of a vehicle coasting down the gravel drive. Nicky ground out his cigar on the arm of the bench.

Chapter 30

From his cozy hideout under the loft window Owen heard the guy from the Social Club pull up the drive and stop where Scalero was sitting on his bench. He heard a door slam and then some muffled conversation. Casual, like two friends meeting on a street corner. Even some laughter. He then heard another vehicle, coming from the direction of Frazier's house. Gordon's car, no doubt. That vehicle also stopped near Scalero's bench. Two doors opened and closed. But the conversation that followed no longer sounded so casual.

Frazier's deep voice was doing most of the talking. Owen assumed he was resetting the plan for Owen's suicide. After a few minutes, he heard the tack room door open downstairs. Voices became clearer as the group exited the tack room and walked toward the stalls.

Scalero's voice raised above the others. "Jesus, the fuckin' door's open."

Owen could hear hurried movement. He imagined the four of them staring at the pile of thick rope and scraps of duct tape on the stall floor. He could hear Gordon.

"Fuckin' Christ, Nick. Didn't you check on him?"

"I tied him up like a goddamn mummy, Phil." Owen imagined a sagging Scalero, shuffling his feet and staring blankly into the stall.

Owen used the commotion downstairs to shift his weight and rub his side. He knew he had to get ready for the real crisis as they began looking for him. A raspy voice that had to be the new guy on the scene interrupted. "Look down there."

Owen guessed he'd pointed to the big door at the far end of the barn. He could hear footsteps herding in that direction. Then the raspy voice spoke again: "I wonder why he took his shoes off?"

"He was probably just being considerate. He didn't want to wake Nick up." Frazier's sarcastic snarl was unmistakable. Owen choked back a nervous laugh.

Owen then heard a prolonged screech as someone pushed the big door open wider. It must have been Scalero. He spoke next, a little out of breath. "He can't be moving very fast with no shoes. Should we go after him?"

Owen's twisted body relaxed and he almost snuggled in his safe little window seat. With the big barn door now wide open, it might not occur to any of them that he couldn't have fit through the narrow opening he'd made himself. If they left him alone in the barn while they searched outside, maybe he could get out of there.

But no. The professional from the Social Club had a different idea. "I think we should search the barn first. That little prick might still be in here."

Owen would have bet dollars to donuts that the raspy voice he was hearing belonged to his mugger, the Iraqi vet. It sounded like what he remembered of the voice at Dellasandro's. He shivered as it occurred to him that his secret hideaway might soon turn into a secret coffin. The raspy voice swore when he found that the light bulbs he tried to switch on all needed to be replaced. "Shit. You guys start looking. I'm gonna get a flashlight from the truck."

Owen knew they'd soon be upstairs. Except for little kids who thought squatting in the corner of an empty stall made for a delicious hiding place, no one ever hid downstairs. It was too wide open. The search down there would be over quickly.

And it was. Though no one spoke, he could hear the search party sliding open stall doors as it moved back toward the tack room and the steps leading up to the loft. By the time they got there, he could hear the Social Club guy come back into the barn through the tack room.

"Nothing down here." Gordon's voice, a little higher pitched than usual. "Let's check the loft."

As the group thumped their way up the stairs, Owen tried to re-enter the trance he'd been in earlier. It was impossible. He couldn't even keep his eyes closed. They focused on the thin slit of moonlight running between the two wide planks over his head. Footsteps echoed in the empty loft and the voices of the search party were perfectly distinct.

The raspy voice was obviously in charge.

"Nicky, open those trunks. Phil, try those closets."

Owen imagined the beam of the mugger's flashlight cutting through the dark corners of the loft. There were more footsteps as Gordon and Scalero followed orders. Then, squeaking and clicking sounds as the closets and trunks were opened and closed. Again, no one spoke.

Owen had just started wondering what Frazier was doing when he heard shuffling feet moving toward his window seat. In his mind's eye, Owen saw a pair of expensive slippers on the old man's feet, color coordinated to go with the robe he was wearing. Owen felt like his heart had stopped beating as he waited for Frazier to yank up the window seat planks and say something cute like, "Owen, my boy. Can I help you out of there?"

But it was worse than that. Frazier sat down on the window seat with a heavy sigh. The planks bent a little under his weight and the slit of moonlight running between them was interrupted with an ass-sized eclipse. And, suddenly, without the ability to free himself, Owen felt like he'd been buried alive.

Owen couldn't tell if Frazier knew he was there. And it almost didn't matter. He was about to scream.

A fleeting image of a composed Barbara, sitting in his family room with her hands folded in her lap, bought him a few calming seconds. Then, as his panic began to swell again, Frazier spoke.

"I think we're wasting time, gentlemen. He's not here. But we have to find him immediately."

Footsteps tramped across the old loft floor and stopped near the window seat. Frazier shifted his weight and Owen feared the slight bouncing of the planks would give someone an idea. But no, and Frazier had assumed command.

"I think you three should take your vehicles and start tracking him down. Without shoes, he'll want to get to a road as soon as possible. And there are only so many roads he could get to. You should hurry."

The mugger from the Social Club was not so sure.

"You're probably right, old man. But take Nick's gun. I've got one in the truck. He might still be around."

Frazier rose from the window seat. Owen imagined him accepting the gun but holding it awkwardly away from his body, like it had germs. But that comforting image was blown away by the raspy voice mugger's almost gleeful suggestion. "You just might have to defend yourself from an unknown intruder." Scalero and Gordon snickered as they all moved off towards the stairs.

Owen didn't move a muscle. He held his breath until he heard them all clump down the steps. When the tack room doors open and closed, he wiggled to get a more comfortable position but did not push away the planks. Even as he heard two vehicles start up and caravan down the winding drive, he stayed in place. Waiting for the game of hide and seek to be long over.

In a few minutes he heard what he thought was the door to the main house opening and closing. Frazier returning to his lair. Probably set that gun on the long table in the entry foyer. When he guessed Frazier was sitting at the desk in his den and the three others were prowling slowly up and down the nearby country lanes, he finally removed the planks and sat up. His arms and legs ached. His side still throbbed. He climbed out of the window seat, set the boards down alongside just in case he had to hurry back in, stood up straight and stretched his right arm above his head. Though his left arm was cramped, he knew better than to stretch out his left side.

"Now what?" he asked himself.

Owen decided he just might make it as far as the pub without being seen if he forced himself to stay off the road. Crossing the rough loft floor toward the stairs, tiny slivers of the cracking old floorboards pricked his stocking feet. The woods would be even worse. But he was afraid of taking his shoes. It would alarm the troops if they noticed.

Owen was halfway down the stairwell when he heard vehicles on the drive again.

The vehicles on the drive were crawling at a deliberate pace, like they were still on the prowl. He hurried back up the stairs and had already stepped back into the window seat when through the window he saw two sets of headlights approach Frazier's house. The lead vehicle was a police cruiser.

Chapter 31

Barrett got lost several times during the search for Delaney on the back roads around Frazier's farm. Despite the full moon, the huge trees bordering most of the roads made visibility difficult. He saw nothing and he was fifteen minutes early for the rendezvous at the pub up the road where they had agreed to meet at twelve thirty.

When Phil and Nicky arrived, he got out of his truck and stiff-legged to their car with his arms crossed. Nicky rolled down his window to talk, but Barrett felt like putting the screws to Giunta and he crossed around to the driver's side.

"What now, boss man?"

Giunta had a knuckle whitening grip on his steering wheel, staring straight ahead and wetting his lips with snake-like flicks of his tongue. He turned slowly toward Barrett and scraped his lower lip with his teeth. Barrett remembered that little tic from way back in grade school. Back then it was usually followed by tears.

Barrett snorted. "Mr. Gordon, if you don't have a better idea, I suggest we go back to old man Frazier's. Maybe he stumbled on the kid. Or maybe me and him can figure out what to do next while you shit in your pants."

Scalero stifled a laugh and Giunta snapped his head at him and opened his mouth, but said nothing. Then he started the car and screeched out of the lot in the direction of Frazier's. Barrett followed at a less agitated pace.

He caught up to Giunta at the big farm with the broken fence and the two vehicles slowed down as they approached the pillars at

Frazier's drive. Barrett could see a swirling red light at the top of the hill by Frazier's house and assumed it was the police. Frazier must have found and hopefully "neutralized" Delaney, then called the police about the prowler he'd had to shoot. Hope he has a license to own a handgun, or that gun might pose a problem.

Barrett cursed Giunta as it looked like he was going to pull up the drive. Asshole. Leave the old man to settle up with the cops. Let him explain why some rich kid was snooping around his farm all night. There was nothing Phil or Nicky or he himself could do to better the situation. From what Nicky said, the old guy was perfectly capable of lying his way out of trouble.

As Giunta's vehicle slowed to turning speed, Barrett nudged it with the front bumper of his pick-up. Giunta came to a full stop and opened his door to look back.

Barrett leaned out his window. "Get the fuck outa here, Phil. Nothing we can do now."

Giunta closed his door and continued along the road. Barrett exhaled and followed behind. About a mile and a half later, they both turned off into a small roadside park. This time, Giunta got out and approached him with a bounce in his step. Nicky lumbered behind.

"I'm guessing John got him, Al. Good thing I left him the gun. What a relief."

Barrett smirked at Nicky. He guessed they were both thinking the same thing. Giunta only had two gears, scared shitless or heel rockin' cocky. Barrett let his face go blank when Giunta smiled and said "And it looks like my plan saved me fifteen big ones."

Barrett sighed. "Yeah, well, let's all go home and get some sleep." He figured he settle up with Giunta when the time was right.

Chapter 32

From the barn Owen could see the two vehicles slow to a stop in front of the patio. A swirling red light atop the cruiser was turned on, casting a pulsing red glow across the stern grey of the house. The cruiser's siren blasted twice. No one got out of either vehicle.

Though he was afraid of being mistaken for an intruder, Owen ran downstairs and out the tack room door. He started up the drive with his hands in the air. Hope trumped the sharp pain in his side. Better to be in police custody with a chance to explain than shot as a suspect in a burglary. Frazier had probably hatched another scheme to cast Owen as a dangerous nutcase.

He was halfway between the barn and the house when the front door of the house opened. Frazier stepped out onto the patio still wearing his robe over his work outfit. The twirling red light was shut off but a spotlight was directed at the doorway. Frazier's left hand went up to shield his eyes. Owen was not certain, but it looked like Scalero's pistol was hanging in Frazier's right hand.

"Please, officer, turn off that infernal light." It was more a command than a request. The spotlight was re-directed to the ground in front of the cruiser. Frazier moved forward onto the slate patio steps, trying to catch the eye of the officer in the cruiser.

"Has someone called you about the intruder in the neighborhood?"

The officer in the cruiser opened his door and crouched out behind it with his hand ready at his sidearm. He didn't say anything.

Owen was still behind the two cars, but he continued forward, hands remaining in the air. He was afraid of alarming the policeman and also afraid that part of Frazier's plan might be to shoot him on sight and defend himself later. But Frazier's hesitated at the top of the steps. His suggestion that someone else had called the police gave Owen the impression that Frazier was puzzled by the appearance of the cops, as though he hadn't called for them himself. So he stopped moving and, hands still high, just watched.

Frazier broke the silence. "I am so glad you're here, officer. I have been terrified. There has been someone snooping around the house and barn all night."

All the officer said in response was "If that's a gun in your hand, sir, please put it down. You'll have no use for it now."

Frazier knelt and put the pistol on the step by his feet. As he did, the driver's side door of the second vehicle opened. A young man got out. From the back he looked just like Rick Jennings. He walked toward the house until he was standing next to the police officer.

"That someone would not have been Owen Delaney by any chance, would it, Mr. Frazier?"

Damn. That *was* Rick.

Frazier went stiff. Like a spooked animal. Owen could almost hear his mind at work. *What do they know? Did Owen call the police himself? How much has he told the cops? If Phil and the boys find Owen, they'll know enough not to drive up here with police around and they'll take care of Owen one way or another tonight. We can all make up some story about his odd behavior.*

Owen decided to stop Frazier's wheels from spinning before he gained enough composure to take charge. He approached Rick and the police officer and called out.

"Rick. It's Owen. I'm all right. Back here."

Rick and the officer snapped a quick look back at Owen then refocused on Frazier. Owen moved into the wide arc of light in front of the police cruiser and stared at the old man up on the patio steps. Frazier's mouth was open. Again, Owen imagined the frantic thoughts banging around in his head. *No way out. Unless I can make the kid out to be completely crazy. A long shot. But I'll have to try. Damn. Damn. Damn.*

The passenger side door of the second car opened and Owen could hear light footsteps approach in the gravel.

"Owen, I was so worried about you!" It was Barbara.

She opened her arms for a hug and Owen responded clumsily, ignoring the pain. He was speechless.

Rick interrupted. "Officer, what do we do next?" They all lifted their gazes toward Frazier, still backlit by the lights inside his foyer and lit faintly in front by the reflected light from the cruiser's spotlight. Frazier seemed unreal with his robe flapping in the breeze like a Halloween ghoul. But even so, Owen could see Frazier's face jerk back when he saw Barbara. He sat down on the step and stared at her.

"Virginia Steele?" His voice was weak. He rested his left elbow on his knee and dropped his forehead into the palm of his left hand. Owen guessed he was thinking about all he was going to lose. And his freedom was the least of it. He had stolen and even sanctioned murder to preserve his social position. Yet he'd now be remembered as a fool. And his wife, his poor wife.

Frazier leaned a little to his right. Before anyone noticed, he had Scalero's pistol in his hand and lifted it to his head.

The shot was deafening. Barbara hid her face in Owen's chest as the sound echoed in the still night.

The policeman drew his own pistol and sidestepped towards Frazier's crumpled body. It didn't move. When he reached the step where Frazier had fallen, he knelt down and felt for a pulse at his bloody neck. After holding that pose for longer than seemed necessary, he turned toward his audience frozen in the arc of light from the cruiser.

"He's dead. I'll have to get help." He pulled out a handkerchief and cleaned his hand as he walked back to the cruiser and got in, leaving the door open.

As the officer tried to reach his dispatcher on the squawking police radio in the cruiser, Owen approached the open car door.

"Officer, you should know there are three other guys out looking for me right now. I'm sure they've been involved in two murders. I was supposed to be the third."

The policeman squinted at Owen. He leaned back and seemed about to ask Owen to explain himself when his dispatcher finally responded. He raised his palm to quiet Owen and put his handset to his mouth.

"I've got an elderly white male here, dead from a self-inflicted gunshot to the head." He checked a clipboard on the seat next to him and read Frazier's address. "Please get the coroner here as soon as possible. No need for a medic."

After the dispatcher confirmed the request and the address, the officer tucked the radio handset back in its cradle, grabbed his clipboard and bent himself out of the car. He wasn't much older than Owen and Owen guessed he hadn't had many calls in his short career like the one he'd just experienced. He stood facing Owen with his mouth partially open.

Rick moved between them. "Owen, the police have no idea what's going on. They came only as a favor to the county sheriff who was called by a guy at Fletcher & Rhoades named Carter Brock."

Now Owen's mouth fell open.

Barbara joined the group, standing next to Owen and taking his hand. Owen didn't know what to make of the gesture but he liked it.

Rick continued. "I've been trying to reach you since five-thirty. But you didn't answer your cell." Owen's attention was broken by the crazy thought that he might have to frisk Frazier's dead body to get his phone back. He almost missed Rick's explanation. "When I got your email I talked to Bob Slevin about Gordon's possible involvement with that bogus mortgage. Slevin remembered a similar mortgage scam in New York some years ago. So he called this guy Brock who'd been at Sterling Moss years ago and—" Rick stopped when the young cop wrinkled his face and massaged his forehead. "I'll explain it all later, Odee."

The cop shifted his weight and pointed his clipboard at Owen. "But what was that about two murders? Who was murdered?

223

When?" He tried to cross his arms but dropped the clipboard. He left it on the ground but with a pinched expression said to Owen "What's all that got to do with him?" He nodded at Frazier's slumped body.

Owen let out a long breath and, in a tone that was perhaps a few degrees too sharp, spit out the details of the Morris estate scam. He stalled as he got to the end of the story, his stomach quivering with Barbara standing right next to him. But he had no choice.

"The scam was discovered by two woman working on the matter." He squeezed Barbara's hand. "They were both killed in faked auto accidents."

Barbara let go of Owen's hand and stifled a gasp, pressing her hands over her mouth. Obviously, Rick hadn't filled her in on all of their suspicions.

The cop exhaled noisily. He got back on his radio and called his barracks. Owen could hear both ends of the conversation and was relieved when he heard the chief wanted to hear his story directly, that the cop should bring him in once the coroner was finished.

They all took seats in their vehicles to wait for the coroner. Rick climbed in the back seat of his two door. Owen asked Barbara to sit behind the wheel. The policeman turned off the cruiser's spotlight, leaving Frazier in partial shadow, and they all settled in to wait in their private silences for the thirty minutes it took for the coroner to arrive.

Owen, Barb and Rick said very little while they waited. At one point, Rick remembered he'd promised to call Brock with an update and he did that, waking him with the call. Owen could hear Brock's groans all the way in the front seat. Brock asked if they would all come to his office about eleven that morning and they agreed.

ter. But he had a proprietary interest. He remembered he hadn't

called back Chet Odum to get the results of his inspection. He'd do

that tomorrow or, given that it was almost two am, later today.

When the coroner's men left, the policeman went up the front

steps to close the door. Owen staggered out and followed, hoping his

cell phone was still in Frazier's den and not on his body. They found

it on Frazier's desk and, when he opened it, Owen saw that there

were seven calls from Rick since he had shut it down earlier in the

In a belated show of authority, the policeman insisted that

Owen drive with him to the station. He was kind enough, however,

to stop at the barn to let Owen get his shoes.

FRIDAY
October 28

Chapter 33

None of Owen's group had more than four hours sleep that night.

First, the police interrogation took more than an hour. It was not as satisfying as Owen had hoped. To start with, he had to admit that the "murders" of Virginia and Marian were assumptions. No evidence. No police charges. Not even their jurisdiction. The detective had said, in a placating tone that had Owen crossing his arms and flattening his lips, that he'd put that matter aside for a bit. He had, however, accepted at face value Owen's claim of being kidnapped and tied up and agreed to send investigators to the Frazier farm to check out the physical evidence of his story. They also agreed to send out a radio bulletin alerting their force to be on the lookout for Gordon's car. Owen had not seen the vehicle driven by the guy from the Social Club, though he guessed it would be a red pick-up. Because it was just a guess, the detective chose not to add the truck to the alert. Then he grimaced when Owen told him that he'd never heard anyone call the Social Club guy by name.

All in all, Owen's session with the Solebury police was not much more productive than his chat with Sgt. Kelly and her chief in Rancocas, or the Philly cops in the hospital after his mugging, or his phone conversations with Detective Kopinski.

Next, they had to make the drive to Doylestown for Owen's car. During the drive Rick explained the behind the scene events that led him and Barbara to Frazier's farm. Apparently, when Brock learned of a possible scam involving Gordon, he did some research on the Morris estate file and concluded Frazier was involved as well. He called back Bob Slevin at Rick's firm in New York. Slevin patched Rick onto the call and they all worried about Owen's meeting at Frazier's farm that evening. So Brock called the county sheriff and Rick drove down from New York. When she saw him bustling out of the office, Barbara demanded to come too. They called the Solebury police on the way down and found that they hadn't treated the sheriff's call as an emergency. The chief didn't want to bother old man Frazier who was a big contributor to the township's First Responder Benevolent Fund. Rick and Barb stopped at the station to argue. But it wasn't till the sheriff called back with a report that Owens car had been found on a farm outside Doylestown with it door open and key still in the ignition that the chief decided to send a cruiser to Frazier's farm. Hearing the full story, Owen had chills thinking about what might have been.

Owen's car had been treated like an illegally parked vehicle and towed to a private lot near Doylestown. Once Owen, Rick and Barbara got to the lot, it had taken a half hour for someone to come and open the gate and another fifteen minutes to get cash from an ATM to pay the towing fee.

And finally, Owen had realized that he was afraid to go home, sure Scalero and Gordon and their buddy from the Social Club had concluded they needed to get rid of him before he could make any more trouble for them. They could have been in his driveway waiting for him.

So they all had stayed the night with Rick's parents who had plenty of room with all those grown kids flown the nest. Rick had called his mom before they left Doylestown, and she had things ready for them when they arrived. Rick went straight to bed in his old room.

But Owen couldn't sleep. And, once Barbara had heard more details about Virginia's sleuthing and Owen's take on her "accidental" death, she knew she wouldn't be able to sleep either. So they had sat alone at the Jennings' kitchen table, talking and munching cheese and grapes. Barbara talked mostly about Virginia. She was sure she could've have helped deal with Virginia's suspicions about the bogus mortgage had she only shared them with her. Then she cried, sobbing that she shouldn't have let Virginia drift off on her own. Owen moved his chair next to hers and reached up to put his left arm around her shoulder. Barbara noticed him wince.

"Oh, Owen. I'm so sorry for what I've put you through." Her green eyes were wet with Virginia tears. "This must have been the worst time of your life."

"Not really." Owen would have picked his mother's death and the episode with Colgrove. He'd been tempted to talk with Barbara about these things during her Sunday visit and was tempted again.

"But I'd rate it a close second."

Barbara wiped her eyes with a napkin and turned toward Owen. "What's first?"

Owen stumbled through a description of his close relationship with his mom and the distant one with Hank. Tears welled up as he described the deathbed scene in which he mom had told him about Colgrove, and he choked up as he told how Colgrove had dashed his brief dream of finding a real dad.

By the time he'd finished, he too was crying and Barbara had an arm around *his* shoulder. But when the tears stopped, he wondered what the big deal about Colgrove had been. Sure, it was incredible. And Barbara was obviously moved by the story. But it shouldn't really change his life. Much less tie it in knots as it had done. Suppose his mom had never told him about Colgrove? He took deep breaths as he felt the knots coming undone. When he and Barbara got up from the table, she stroked his hair.

"Has anyone ever told you that you have the most beautiful hair?"

They walked up the stairs arm in arm.

Owen had once seen a movie in which a late adolescent boy became infatuated with a beautiful young woman staying in a beach house near his family's vacation cottage. She lived alone, her new husband off in the Second World War. The boy visited the young woman often, volunteering to do chores or go to the store for things she might need. She understood his infatuation but maintained a big-sisterly relationship until, one grey afternoon, he appeared at her screen door shortly after she had received the worst of news in a telegram from the war department. In tears, she greeted the lovesick boy, took his hand and led him in silence to her bedroom. Owen had found the young woman's motivation inscrutable. But, as he and Barbara climbed the stairs, it all made perfect sense. For both of them.

In the morning, to preserve appearances, Barbara mussed up the sheets in the room she was supposed to have slept in.

Chapter 34

Rick drove them all into Center City at about ten that morning. On the way, Owen called Chet Odum for a report on Virginia's car.

"Well, I didn't find anything when I looked at first." The connection with Chet was poor.

"Say again, Chet. Can't hear you that well." Owen put his phone on speaker. Rick turned down the radio and Barbara leaned forward from the back seat.

"I found nothing. But at orchestra practice Tuesday night I mentioned your obsession to the guys in the horn section. Hope you don't mind." Chet paused and Owen grimaced. He didn't like Chet discussing the matter with others. But he had to concentrate as Chet continued.

"And when I mentioned that there had been no skid marks at the accident scene, our flutist told me to check out the Boston Brakes technique. He's a Princess Di nut. Convinced Diana was murdered using that technique."

"What technique was that, again?" Owen felt a bubble of excitement.

"It's called Boston Brakes." Chet was enunciating more clearly. "It's a technique used by the CIA and military intelligence. Involves detonating brakes or disabling steering with a remote controlled explosive that can be planted in vulnerable areas of a vehicle. They can be detonated at the critical moment by a someone trailing the target."

"And?" Owen held his breath.

"It looks to me like that Honda had both the power steering fluid and the brake fluid drained at points way up their lines where I hadn't looked before. And there were indications near those breaks that a small explosion had occurred to cause them."

Rick turned wide-eyed toward Owen. Barbara put her hand to her mouth. Owen was speechless. He barely managed a "Great job, Chet. Maybe now the police will take an interest in this. I'll be back to you."

Owen was thrilled to have evidence to support his suspicions. If Pete Thomasian hadn't been such a bastard, he'd call him and ask him to check out Marian McNeil's car for similar evidence. On the other hand, he could imagine someone placing such a deadly device in the guts of his Highlander while they all met with Brock during the next few hours.

• • •

While the three of them waited for Brock in the top floor reception area at Fletcher & Rhoades, Owen couldn't help but overhear conversations about Frazier's suicide among the passing lawyers and staff. The consensus seemed to be that *one never knew*. He was *a man who had everything*. One older woman from bookkeeping told the receptionist about the old days, before direct deposit, when they had to beg Mr. Frazier to cash his paychecks which he'd leave for weeks in the top drawer of that huge desk.

At a few minutes after eleven, a red-eyed Brock entered the reception area in shirtsleeves and led them to a conference room down the hall. The floor of the conference was strewn with open files and its big table was a mess of documents and correspondence. They all sat around one end of the table.

232

"I've been here since early this morning. Couldn't get back to sleep after you called." Brock was looking at Rick.

"So I decided to come in and review some more of the matters John and Phil had worked on together. There are a lot of them and what I found was very interesting."

Brock put the heels of his hands to his forehead and gave himself a quick massage, then panned his gaze across the three of them and sighed.

"What I am about to tell you is very sensitive from the firm's perspective. But I think it is important that you know what seems to have been going on. You already know much of it. But I think you should understand that the firm as an organization had no part in it. Just Frazier and Gordon." He stared at each of them in turn, nodding his head. Each of them gave a tentative nod in response. Then he continued.

"The firm has a big problem on its hands. We want to keep all this as low key as possible. Of course, we'll mourn John Frazier and praise him for the good he's done over the years. Not that you will want to come, but the firm will conduct a memorial tribute to John at the Union League on Tuesday." Brock sighed again before going on.

"But we also have to explain at least some of the facts to the parties involved in the Morris estate sale. That's going to be tough. We don't think we can just say the title report was wrong. The debate over that bogus mortgage has already become a big issue in the deal. We'll have to hope everyone recognizes the scam was nothing more than the work of two rogue lawyers."

Brock leaned back with his hands laced behind his head and didn't move for a few seconds. Then he leaned forward again and continued. "We'll try to keep the story about Frazier and Gordon from getting out." He turned to Owen. "But it's possible that your presence at Frazier's last night will get out to the news media. You've already given a statement to the police. So, if we're going to exert any control over this story, we'll need your cooperation. I'm sure your father would have wanted you to help us in any way you can."

Owen looked at Barbara. She raised her eyebrows ever so slightly.

"What we need is for the three of you to refer any press inquiries to me. Believe me, it will not only help us out but it'll also save you endless hassle."

Owen could certainly buy that last point.

Brock neatened some of the piles of paper in front of him. "In exchange, all that I can offer is full disclosure of what's been going on and, importantly, the commitment of the firm to redress any losses our two rogues have caused over the years. Losses, I should point out, which will probably not be covered by the firm's insurance. Does all that seem fair to you?"

Owen looked at Rick and then Barbara. They seemed to be deferring to his judgment.

"That'll be fine, Mr. Brock."

"Okay. Where do I start?" Brock folded his arms across his chest and looked down at his watch. "I guess I should start with John Frazier's story. You know he was born into a wealthy family and had a distinguished career in the Philadelphia non-profit world. He's been on the board of the Museum and the Orchestra for ages. And a big contributor to many city charities. But what you have no way of knowing is that for maybe ten, twelve years he's been considered deadwood here at the firm." Owen recalled Frazier's modest office with his old, oversized desk and sad view of the north Philadelphia wasteland. Brock went on.

"From the beginning, his role at the firm had been to bring in business. Because of his family connections, he did this very well. Even as a young lawyer. But he stopped bringing in business when his father's friends began to die off and their businesses changed hands and moved to the Sunbelt. When his rainmaking stopped, he was lost."

Owen's thoughts drifted to the scenes of industrial decay he'd observed from the train on his last trip to the firm. But Brock didn't pause long enough for Owen to think much more about them.

"John had no significant legal skills and the new generation of clients was quick to recognize this. His blue blood credentials cut no favor with them." Brock exhaled and looked directly at Owen.

"But John was still a partner and a prominent member of the community. He had once been considered as a candidate for mayor, for Christ's sake. There was no question that the firm would keep him on. He wasn't the only unproductive senior partner in the organization by a long shot." Brock rubbed his palms on the table-top.

"But his share of firm profits was cut every year to allow for greater compensation to the young Turks. And, finally, the firm put him in the real estate department doing routine deals for corporate clients and wealthy individuals. It was very simple work. No complicated development issues or construction contracts. But the powers in the firm were worried that he didn't have the proper discipline even for that. So, when he asked that the firm take on a junior lawyer to assist him, everyone relaxed a little. Particularly since Phil, the guy he wanted, was a friend of Vince Fiore." Brock stroked his frizzy hair.

"That's when things got interesting. I've reviewed several dozen files the two of them worked on and more than half seem to involve something like the scam they were trying to pull off in the Morris estate sale. The correspondence for those deals is filed with sellers questioning items on their title reports. Over the last few years, not counting the Morris deal, these questionable items totaled almost three million dollars. And all the questionable title reports were prepared by Brokers Title in Mt. Holly." Brock paused, apparently to let everything sink in.

"When our firm represented the seller, the seller was typically a big corporation getting rid of a relatively small plant or warehouse. Or maybe the client was old and nearly senile, selling off their home. Frazier would write urging them to pay the disputed lien or mortgage rather than kill the deal entirely.

"If we represented the buyer, the *seller* would be the large corporation or non-profit or elderly individual. Often as not, these sellers would be represented by an elderly lawyer who was an old friend of Frazier's. When they raised concerns about the fake lien or mortgage, John would do the persuading and Gordon would furnish them with documentation purporting to validate the claim on the title report. But like the copy of the Reverse Mortgage and the First American correspondence in the Morris estate file, the evidence was just made up. In the Morris Estate file, one of the two had left a stack of blank First American letterhead and a printing invoice from a shop on Walnut Street." Brock slid the printing bill and the blank letterhead across the table.

"They apparently got very good at these deceptions. And John got very good at convincing people that they shouldn't screw up a transaction over their own bad record keeping. The way I see it, they'd look at a susceptible transaction—one with a client or counterparty that was too rich, too old or too disorganized—and assess how much they could steal without blowing the underlying deal. The Morris estate—even though it was simple—was still a sixty million dollar transaction. They saw a big payoff. More than two and a half million dollars."

Owen knew from Frazier's comments during his kidnapping in Frazier's den that there had been other scams. But Rick slapped his hands to his head.

"God almighty! How long was this going on?"

"From what I can tell, just about as long as Phil has been with the firm, about six years." Brock hesitated and gave his temples another quick massage. Then he rested his elbows on the table, folded his hands as in prayer and rested his chin on his thumbs.

"In fact, it pains me to say that I believe, to offset his declining distributions from the firm, John recruited Phil with a plan to skim money from our clients and counterparties. Just as Phil had done to John's client a few weeks before John raised the idea of bringing him into the firm." Brock shook his head in apparent disbelief at what he had just said.

"At least that's how I read an old file of John's in which Phil represented the buyer of a vacant warehouse up in the northeast section of the city. In that file, John was writing to Phil about a $5,000 mechanic's lien that showed up on a report from Brokers Title. Our big, confused corporate client couldn't verify it from their records."

The four of them sat in silence until Owen spoke up. "I had wondered about Gordon. He seemed such an odd fit in the firm."

"That's true, Owen. Before he was recruited by John, Phil had been a street lawyer in south Philly. Got his law degree at night. Had a general practice for neighborhood clients. From what I've heard, no one here wanted him until Vince Fiore called around. Vince told us he was helping Phil's brothers open a savings bank that should provide some business. He also predicted a resurgence of Phil's sister's singing career."

Owen and Rick gave each other narrow eyed glances. Brock noticed. "Oh. You didn't know. Phil's sister is Franny Gentry, born Francine Giunta.

Barbara gasped. "Wow! Virginia and I loved Franny Gentry when we lived in Des Moines. What ever happened to her?"

"Well, Vince Fiore was wrong. Her career never revived. She does sing locally in those oldie but goodie reviews. But she hasn't made a record in years."

Barbara leaned expectantly toward Brock who bit his lower lip for a few seconds before continuing.

"A friend of mine who works at the Porter firm here in town grew up with Phil in St. Andrea's parish down on Second Street. He says being Franny Gentry's sister was Phil's only claim to fame. Phil always said he was going to be an entertainment lawyer, but he couldn't get into a full time law school. Ended up going at night. And when his sister's career tanked, so did his big dreams. He ended up with that small time practice in South Philly."

Owen could almost smell Gordon's cologne and realized Brock had not brought them up to date on Gordon's status.

"And what's happening with Gordon? Do you know where he is now?" He was hopeful that Brock would report that Gordon and Scalero were under arrest with their friend from the Social Club.

"No. He didn't show up for work today, which is not surprising. One of our partners who was an assistant DA talked to the white-collar crime division in the DA's office. They have police looking for Phil to bring him in for questioning. We'll make all our files available to them." He crossed his arms and shrugged as though that last bit wrapped everything up.

But Owen couldn't contain himself. He almost shouted.

"You're kidding me! White collar crime! What about the murder of Virginia Steele? And Marian McNeil? And almost me?"

Rick held up a hand to hush Owen. "Odee, Mr. Brock has no idea what you're talking about. He hasn't been told of your suspicions."

"They're no longer just suspicions, Rick. You heard Chet Odum." Owen leaned toward Brock.

"You should know that the circumstances of Virginia Steele's accident were suspicious, even to the police. I've had her car inspected and we learned this morning that it shows clear evidence that tampering caused the accident."

"And what has that got to do with Phil and John?" Brock's jaw dropped as he stared at Owen.

"Virginia and a woman at Brokers Title uncovered the Morris Estate scam and somehow that became known to Frazier and Gordon and a guy named Scalero who manages the Brokers Title office in Mt. Holly. Both Virginia and the other woman are dead, killed in two arranged accidents."

Brock said nothing as he clunked his elbows on the table and rested his head in his palms. Then he scratched his head with both hands. Rick and Barbara sat motionless. Owen felt a sheen of sweat on his forehead. Finally, Brock got up from his chair.

"Please, wait here while I discuss this with some of our partners. I'll send in coffee and something to eat."

The three of them sat in silence. Rick reached for a stack of papers in front of Brock's seat and began thumbing through them. Owen couldn't have cared less. He was worried about Barbara, afraid his blunt recital had picked at a fresh wound. He reached across the table and put his hand over hers. She turned her hand upward and squeezed his. Her eyes blinked and watered. Owen brushed away her tears with his finger. Rick looked over and smiled.

They waited a full hour with an array of paper plates, Styrofoam cups, a thermos of coffee and a tray of half eaten sandwiches spread out in front of them. They could have been a group of associates working through lunch to prepare work for a senior partner. But Brock arrived to report to them.

"We called the police again and told them your story. We all take your claims seriously, Owen. The police want you to go down to the Roundhouse and give them a statement. Meanwhile, they'll contact the New Jersey authorities and have re-assigned the case to homicide. They've also expanded their search to include Scalero."

• • •

At the Roundhouse, Philadelphia's central police headquarters, the call from a major law firm in the city made sure that Owen received the attention he thought he deserved. He even got an apology of sorts from Kopinski who, apparently, was one of the main men in the homicide division.

"Christ, Delaney, I was sure you were a nut job. Expected that if I let you go on, you'd have evidence that Elvis was poisoned, or something. My bad. Should have known better."

"No problem," Owen lied. He just wanted to get on with his story. And Kopinski did in fact look like the pro Commissioner Barnes said he was. He was anything but the burly and crude cop Owen had imagined over the phone. He could have worked at Fletcher & Rhoades. Maybe forty-five, close cropped graying hair and intelligent brown eyes that never blinked. Pin-striped suit and shoes ferociously spit shined.

Owen gave a full account of his adventure including the mugging at Dellasandro's, his belief that he had spotted the mugger at the Downtown Social Club on Snyder Avenue and his belief the unseen guy who had assisted Gordon and Scalero the night before was the selfsame mugger from the Social Club. Kopinski nodded and smirked at his interviewing partner when Owen mentioned the Social Club. Owen took that to be a good sign.

It was nearly three o'clock when he finished and he was exhausted. He returned to the waiting area where he'd left Rick and Barbara and found them asleep in their chairs.

"Hey, guys. Wake up." He gave Rick a punch on his shoulder but just rested his hand on Barbara's. Rick snapped himself upright in his chair. Barbara shifted her weight and tried to reposition herself before blinking her eyes open and smiling at Owen. Had Rick not been sitting next to her, Owen would have told her how beautiful she was when she was asleep. He had failed to tell her that when she awoke that morning. But, instead, he was all business.

"All done. They've added the Social Club to their search. All we have to do is wait till they're all brought in. What should we do now?"

Barbara was very clear about protecting Owen, suggesting that he come to New York with them and hide out until the bad guys were caught. Rick agreed.

So they headed for the Big Apple after stopping in Chestnut Hill to get Owen's pain pills, pack some clothes and push his car to a convenient hiding spot alongside the garage at the Jennings house. He was afraid to turn the ignition key until the car had been fully checked out.

Chapter 35

Barrett picked up a late edition of the Daily News at the corner store on his stroll to the Social Club the afternoon after the abortion at Frazier's farm. He read the news of John Frazier's suicide while he was sitting at the bar. There was no mention of any other dead—like, maybe, Delaney—at the scene. He hung his head in his hands.

"Problem, Al?" The bartender was an old guy from St. Andrea's.

"Afraid so."

Barrett's mind was racing. First off, he figured getting paid was now an issue. There was not gonna be a big payday for Nicky and Phil so, unless they would make good with their own cash, there was not gonna be a big payday for him either. And second, he was afraid the lid might blow off the whole gig. That kid knew too much and he knew that Phil and Nicky were involved. When they got picked up, they might talk about him. That is, if they were stupid, they might. Once they mentioned him, their own crimes go from embezzlement to murder.

The two girls were not the first time he'd used Boston Brakes. And none had ever been questioned in the past. If Nick and Phil just kept their mouths shut, everything would be fine. They could claim all they were guilty of was a failed attempt at the one big scam organized by that guy Frazier.

One thing Barrett liked about the Social Club was the ease with which you could have some pretty dicey conversations. Unless you spoke the words *kill* or *shoot* or *steal* or *burn down* in a voice that called attention to yourself, nobody heard nothin'. And no one gave a shit. In truth, most guys didn't even listen when you talked around the big issues with vague threats or promises. So he called Giunta right from the bar.

"Phil? Al. I guess you saw the news."

"Yeah. Think I'll stay in a motel for a few days. See what happens. Nicky wants to head for Miami. He's got a brother down there."

"He shouldn't do that. It was all that guy Frazier's doin'. You were just helpin' out. And nothing came of it anyway. So what's the big deal? No one's gonna connect the girls to your little scam."

"I don't know, Al. You never know where it might go. And this wasn't the first time."

"And that reminds me, you guys still owe me twenty five big ones. I assume you got plenty stashed away."

"Jesus, Al. It was all small stuff. No way you can get paid now. As they used to say down at St. Andrea's, *fahgettaboudit.*"

Barrett felt his body temperature rising. *fahgettaboudit, my ass.* From what Nicky had said, there should be enough around to pay him. Giunta wouldn't be so cool about the money if he was standing in striking range, not miles away on the phone. He'd be hemming and hawing and massaging his forehead faking deep thought about how he was gonna pay up. Barrett could almost see him shaking in front of him. But the further away he was, the more arrogant he got. He just couldn't take close up pressure. Barrett had an image of Phil laying his head on his arms in a police interrogation room, sobbing, when they pressed him about the deaths of those two girls. He was no Richie Caputo.

"Yeah, I'll fahgettaboudit."

SATURDAY, SUNDAY and MONDAY
October 29, 30 and 31

Chapter 36

Owen was pleased with the living arrangements in New York. Joanie moved in with Rick and Owen stayed in the girls' upper west-side apartment with Barbara. With a regular regime of pain medication, his side began to feel better and he and Barbara soaked up the city over the weekend, meandering around her neighborhood, dining at cozy bistros, seeing films and making relaxed love in Barbara's tiny bed.

On Monday morning, with Barbara already off to work, Owen was reading *The Times* at a corner café near Barbara's apartment when his cell phone rang.

"Owen, this is Carter Brock. The police just called. They received two separate reports on our boys. Last night, Phil Gordon was killed when his car hit an abutment on Interstate 95. And Scalero looks like he took his own life in his garage. Hose from his car's exhaust pipe." Brock was breathless. "The police think Phil's crash might have been a suicide too."

Owen knew better. It was now down to him and the raspy voice from the Social Club.

He called Kopinski immediately.

"Kopinski here."

Owen identified himself and Kopinski barked "Ah. I guess you heard the latest."

"I did, sir. Carter Brock told me you guys think both deaths were suicides. No way. They were both the work of that guy from the Social Club."

"Oh, yes. The mysterious guy from the Social Club."

Owen couldn't tell if he was being mocked. His face felt hot. But it cooled a bit as Kopinski continued.

"Well, Owen, we've got two problems. First is that we have to convince the Burlington County authorities in New Jersey that they have two unsolved murders on their hands. Technically, it's their case and they think Gordon and Scalero were the do-ers. And they're both dead."

Owen could see that problem; but Gordon had been killed on I95 down by the sports complex. That was a Philly case.

"But what about Gordon's murder? That's your jurisdiction."

Kopinski exhaled into the phone. "Yeah, but that brings us to the second problem. We don't just walk into that Social Club asking if they know anyone good with cars and explosives. As my old parish priest Father Osbahr would call it, that place is a den of iniquity. It's a gathering spot for much of the organized crime in that part of the city. With the right introduction and a little cash you can get just about anything you want in there. And it often serves as a clearing house for out of town specialists."

Kopinski went silent. Owen could imagine him shrugging his shoulders. Owen got the picture. It left much to be desired.

"But have you checked out Gordon's car for signs that his accident was . . ." Owen struggled for the correct word, " . . . pre-arranged?"

"That's being done as we speak. But even if we find signs of those Massachusetts Brakes, or whatever they're called, there's little we can do about it. You haven't even given us a decent description of the guy."

"It's Boston Brakes. And, I told you, the guy has a distinctive voice. Like Oscar the Grouch on Sesame Street. And he drives a red pickup, maybe"

"Not enough. Besides, the guy is probably from Pittsburgh or Detroit; and, if you've been reading the papers lately, you know it's not the only homicide we're investigating. But we'll keep trying."

Owen had indeed been reading the Philly papers up in New York, searching for details of the Frazier affair and its aftermath. Maybe if Fletcher & Rhoades hadn't done such a good job of hushing up the scam and suicide, the girls' deaths would be front-page news. But no. The headlines were all about a sniper who had terrorized the University area. He'd killed one and wounded several in the last few days.

When the call ended, Owen pressed a fist to his teeth as he realized the Virginia/Marian cases might be closed by the "suicides" of Gordon and Scalero; and the case against the mugger from the Social Club, who he had started to think of as "Oscar," might never even be opened for want of evidence that Scalero and Gordon were actually murdered. He shivered at the thought of Oscar roaming free, the invisible hand in the deaths of four people.

Owen decided he should help find the guy. He considered calling the Inquirer crime desk to tip them off about the entire story. News coverage might light a fire under Kopinski. But that would expose himself to the news spotlight. And who knew where that would lead? Maybe a sneak attack by Oscar.

But Owen couldn't just leave matters to drift and suppress the thought of Oscar possibly out to get him. He was feeling more like his old self and was no longer inclined to just bury such unpleasant thoughts. He'd had his fill of that, learned from his experience with

Colgrove that it didn't work. They found their way to the surface one way or another. Even if Oscar had no murderous intentions toward him, or had gone back to Pittsburgh or Detroit or whatever, Owen wouldn't be able to rest without the matter settled. He had to do something to find Oscar. He had no confidence that Kopinski would put in the needed effort.

Owen had one advantage in the search for Oscar. He knew that Oscar existed and Oscar didn't know he knew. Unless Oscar assumed Owen had been in the barn while he and the others searched for him, or assumed that Owen had connected his mugging to the other events of the past week, Oscar was probably feeling home free by now.

On the other hand, if Oscar were the suspicious or obsessive type and felt he had to tie up loose ends by getting rid of Owen, he had some advantages too. He knew who Owen was and where he lived. He knew the car he drove. And he had all those murderous skills.

Owen needed to find Oscar before Oscar found him.

Chapter 37

Barrett leaned back on his sofa and gave a contented sigh when he saw the TV news clip of Giunta's car mashed against the wall of the overpass on I95. He didn't typically know his victims, much less have the strong feelings about them that he had about Giunta. So he was surprised at the lightness in his chest as he recalled wiring Giunta's Lincoln and then following him on the Interstate until the perfect moment.

His self-congratulatory mood was snapped by an image of Nicky watching the same news clip. He had to call him to tell him not to worry. Not to talk and not to worry. Giunta was as much a personal matter as anything else. Nicky had nothing to fear from him.

A woman answered Nicky's phone. When he asked for Nicky, she sobbed into the phone. "Nicky's gone." Barrett swore to himself. Nicky's running to Miami would only get him in more trouble. He wished he'd reached out to him sooner.

"He didn't take his phone with him? I'm calling his cell phone. No?"

The woman sobbed more vigorously. "I meant he's dead. He killed himself in the garage this morning. He ran a hose . . ." The woman moaned and Barrett said "I'm so sorry to hear that" and hung up.

Barrett went into his bedroom to lie down.

Damn. Not only had he lost a sort of friend, but he'd also lost the last chance to get paid even a piece of what he was owed. This job was just one big fuck up, but in a way, he was glad it was all behind him—even if writing off his fee put retirement further onto a back burner. Fighting to rid his mind of an image of Nicky slumped over his steering wheel in a smoky garage, he tried to think about the next steps in the Chester County explosion that he was supposed to pull off within ten days.

But concentration was difficult. He kept circling back to that Delaney kid. With Phil and Nick and that old lawyer dead, he was the only one who could conceivably tie him to the girls. But he'd have to be a genius to connect his mugging to the rest of the story. And unless he did that, there was no way Delaney even knew he existed. He closed his eyes, folded his hands over his stomach and relaxed with a long, slow, noisy exhale.

Chapter 38

After concluding that Kopinski wasn't going to put in much effort finding Oscar the Grouch, Owen wrote a note for Barbara, packed his clothes, took a cab to Penn Station and then a Metroliner to Philly. He got to Chestnut Hill about five. Still afraid to use his car or stay in his own home, he took a room in a small hotel on Germantown Avenue and walked the few blocks to his house to get things he might need, including the envelope Colgrove had given him. He didn't notice any sign of an intruder; but that was little consolation at this point.

Back at the hotel, he ordered in Chinese from Shanghai Garden and picked at his food while he struggled to make a plan.

His planning didn't go well. The only thing he had to start with was a sense that Gordon, Scalero and Oscar had a relationship that went back many years, Something about the familiar way they'd all related during the evening at Frazier's. Gordon and Scalero argued like teens on a street corner. And Scalero knew all about Gordon's brothers. Oscar had called Scalero "Nicky" and had treated Gordon with a kind of long standing disdain. He should call Kopinski with that insight tomorrow. Hopefully, he hadn't yet put the Oscar file in his bottom drawer.

Taking a break, he switched on the TV and scanned the channels. A cable quiz show in which passengers in a cab won money by answering questions posed by the cabbie stopped him short. An idea came to him.

By the time he'd worked out a strategy, it was almost nine. He called Rick to get Brock's home number. Rick thought Owen's plan was crazy, but he reluctantly gave him the number.

Owen immediately called Brock. He was not at home and his wife was unwilling to give Owen a cell number, saying only that Brock was at the Union League making arrangements for John Frazier's memorial service scheduled for ten the following morning.

Owen adjusted his mental schedule to fit in Frazier's memorial service. He hoped Brock wasn't going to be too busy to talk.

TUESDAY and WEDNESDAY
November 1 and 2

Chapter 39

The next morning, Owen took the train into town and walked to the Union League. The scene was impressive. Scores of lawyer types milling around the sidewalk in front of the building and on its graceful staircase. Dark limos pulled up to the curb, and uniformed drivers opened their doors for the local politicos and celebrities who just had to be there. He recognized Commissioner Barnes in the mix. When Frazier's wife emerged from a Mercedes and walked through the somber crowd into the building, a silent procession followed.

There were no seats by the time Owen reached the large ballroom in which the service was to be held. He stood in the rear. Maybe three hundred people total, with a lectern and banks of flowers in the front of the room.

Brock was in charge. He welcomed everyone on behalf of Mrs. Frazier and the firm, gave a summary of John's career and introduced the speakers: the Director of the Art Museum, the President of the Orchestra and several lawyers who had known John for decades. At the end, the Episcopal Bishop gave a prayer for the repose of Frazier's soul. No one mentioned the suicide. As they say, it was all a celebration of a well-lived life.

When the Bishop finished, the mourners left through the doors at the rear of the hall. Owen bumped through the crowd, drifting up toward the front of the room where Brock had stayed, sitting next to Mrs. Frazier.

Frazier's widow wore a loose fitting black suit that disguised a somewhat pudgy but still athletic build. Owen could easily picture her swinging a golf club with authority. Her wavy silver hair curled at her neck in a no-nonsense senior style. He stopped when he was about ten feet to their side. He could smell the flowers behind the lectern to his left. Mrs. Frazier noticed him and whispered something to Brock.

Brock waved for Owen to come closer. Owen held up his hand to indicate he could wait. But Brock rose, walked over and took him by the elbow.

"Frances asked to speak with you."

Owen's heart sank. What could he possibly say? None of the speakers had even mentioned the suicide. He not only knew the details but the reasons as well.

As he and Brock stood in front of Frances Frazier, Brock spoke.

"Frances, this is Owen Delaney. His father worked with the firm for many years". Mrs. Frazier glanced up at Owen's hair.

"Yes. I remember Owen very well. From our picnics at the farm. That hair is impossible to forget." Her hazel eyes showed no sign of tears. She turned toward Brock. "Carter, I would like to speak privately with Owen, if you don't mind."

"Certainly, Frances. I'll be out in the hall." Brock picked up the notes for his speech, gave Owen a wide-eyed look, and left the way the others had gone. Owen and Frazier's wife were alone in the ballroom. She shifted in her chair so she could face Owen directly.

"Tell me, Owen, what really happened? I know you were there, but I don't know why. They told me that you were discussing a job with the firm. But then why were the police there? And where did John get a gun?"

Owen sat down next to her. He didn't know what to say. The firm had obviously tried to comfort her with a whitewash. But the truth was sure to come out eventually. Why not tell her now? She knew there was more to the story.

So he told her. In general terms, skipping the murder part, he told her. It took a few minutes. And after he finished with his guess that John had shot himself when he realized his stealing was going to be found out, Mrs. Frazier bowed her head. She sat motionless with her folded hands resting on her knees. Her calm reminded Owen of Barbara hearing Joanie tell the tale of the twins' troubled life in Iowa. After what seemed like forever, she lifted her head and took a deep breath.

"That makes so much more sense, Owen. I can't say that I'm surprised." She inhaled deeply. "You know, John's family money disappeared long ago. Even before his father died, the family fortune had shrunk. You're too young to remember the Penn Central bankruptcy, Owen. But John's father lost a lot of money in that. And other bad investments after he sold his banking firm. John didn't realize that he would be inheriting so little. When his parents died, he was shocked." She shifted in her seat and shook her head.

"But John was always about appearances. Do you know he would leave his firm paychecks uncashed for weeks so people there would think we didn't need the money?" She took a tissue from her purse.

"It was so difficult to continue living the way he insisted on living. Big contributions. Money to keep the farm just so." She buried her face in her hands. Then, with the slightest of sniffles, she lifted her head and sat upright again.

"And as his income from the firm dropped, it got worse. He was very angry. He hated the young lawyers who got paid so well. I got sick of him talking about the old days."

Owen felt he had done his duty. He wanted the conversation to end. But Frances wasn't finished.

"And then it all stopped. Somehow, suddenly, there was always enough money. John said he had given up and decided to put in more hours at the firm. But it didn't seem to me that he was working much harder. I guess that's when he started stealing."

She turned in her seat and faced the lectern, no longer looking at Owen. Owen rolled his eyes in relief and leaned back in his own chair. They both sat staring ahead for a few minutes. Then, Frances got up, straightened her skirt and turned toward Owen. "Thank you, Owen. You have been a big help."

When Owen stood, Frances took his arm. "We can go now."

When they reached the hall outside the ballroom, Owen could see Brock talking on his cell phone. Excusing himself from Mrs. Frazier, he approached Brock as he was hanging up from his call.

"Sir. Can I ask you a question before I leave?"

Brock didn't respond. Instead, he asked "What did Frances want? What did you tell her?"

"I'm afraid she pried most of the truth out of me, sir. She seems to have suspected something on her own. Though I didn't tell her about all of the mysterious deaths."

Brock turned and walked over to Frances. She was smiling. "Carter, young Owen was very comforting to me. Do not be angry with him."

The three of them walked out of the building to the Mercedes waiting for Frances. As Brock readied to close its door, Frances reached her arm out from the back seat to stop him.

"Remember, Carter, don't be angry with him."

"Don't worry, Frances. We will all be fine."

Owen was not sure whom they were talking about.

Frances Frazier's limo pulled away and Brock turned to Owen. "You had a question?"

"Yes, I did. I need the name of your friend at the Porter firm who went to school with Phil Gordon."

"His name is Dan DePre. Why do you need to know?"

"Just curious about some things. Do you think he'd talk to me if you asked him?

Brock cocked his head and frowned. Owen could feel a "Stay out of this, for your own good" lecture coming on. No news about the white-collar scandal at Fletcher & Rhoades had reached the media and Brock certainly wouldn't want Owen to undo their hard work. But maybe remembering the sweet words of Frances Frazier, Brock's face softened.

"If you promise not to mention the shenanigans he and Frazier were up to, I'll tell him you're working with me on a memorial service for Phil and we need some background."

"I promise. And Carter, I swear Mrs. Frazier *knew* there was something fishy about the story you guys told her." Owen had never before addressed Brock as Carter. He liked the feel of it.

Chapter 40

Dan DePre invited Owen to see him in his office at five, when he'd thought he'd be finished work for the day. His modestly sized office was cluttered with open files and his desk was a mess. Papers stacked in uneven piles that toppled over onto each other. Barely any room to work. Off to the side of his desk chair, his computer was festooned with Post-it notes. His suit coat was lumped over the guest chair. That chair, too, was piled with papers. The poor housekeeping reminded Owen of his room in Chestnut Hill.

But DePre was a jovial guy. A Pillsbury doughboy in suit pants, rumpled white shirt and wild, Hawaiian-print tie. His squeaky voice had laughter in it. His round face was constantly smiling. As Owen expected, he was in his early forties, about Gordon's, *or Giunta's,* age. His full head of brown hair was speckled with grey and its neat part was the only crisp thing about the man.

"Find a seat, Owen. I'm sure there's one in here someplace." DePre waved an open hand in the general direction of the guest chair. "I'm a tax attorney and never meet clients in my office. At least that's my excuse for the mess." He gave a squeaky laugh. "You've seen those bumper stickers on beat up old cars, *My Other Car is a Rolls*? Well, I'm having a door sign made for here saying *My Garage is as neat as a pin.*"

Owen folded DePre's suit coat over the back of the guest chair and gathered the papers from its seat and set them on the floor. He moved some files from the floor in front of the desk and set the chair into position to talk with DePre, who was parting the sea of paper on his desk as Owen did the rest of the housework.

DePre was the first to speak once they were ready. "So you want to know about Phil Giunta, eh?"

"Yes, sir."

"Call me Dan, Owen. You know, I once worked on a deal with your dad." DePre leaned back in his chair and Owen was afraid it would tip over backwards. But he had obviously done this before and he just rocked it as he continued.

"Big merger, with complicated tax issues for our client. He was a real professional, your dad." He let the chair fall back to its upright position. "But, anyway, about Phil."

DePre was a great storyteller. He had known Giunta since grade school at the Catholic school in St. Andrea's parish which, he said, was "deep in the heart of South Philly." It was a tough place. The typical guy from the neighborhood grew up to be a dockworker, a cop or a petty hood. As little kids, they were taught by experience to grab theirs before they grab yours.

"Vince Fiore grew up in our neighborhood. He was a few years older than us. But if you know anything about his career, you can see a lot of St. Andrea's in him." DePre leaned back again.

"The crowd that Phil ran with was tougher than most. I wasn't part of it. Always too fat to be a tough guy. There was a big kid named Nicky Scalero. Another guy named Rich Caputo. The Walsh brothers, Pat and Mike, and a guy named Al Barrett." DePre grabbed his computer stand for balance as he rocked.

"Truth is, Phil wanted in with the group more than they wanted him. His family was better off than the others, particularly by the time we entered Newman High. Hell, the Walshes' dad was in prison most of the time. But Phil's dad was a tobacco and candy wholesaler on Christian Street near the Italian Market. Phil's older brothers—they were probably ten years older than him—they worked in the business until their old man decided they needed to go to college. He could see that the convenience store chains were gonna kill the corner candy store, which was his bread and butter, and he didn't want his boys to take over a dying business. In their turn, the brothers insisted that Phil go to college too."

Owen scrambled for questions that would shift DePre's monologue to a reminiscence about Gordon's friends. But DePre wasn't even looking at him. He closed his eyes as he leaned back at an impossible angle and rocked himself with his arm still holding the computer stand.

"And then there was Francine. You know Phil's sister is Franny Gentry. She was maybe five years older than Phil. Always singing in school and parties. Like that. Then she was discovered by Lou Richards. You might remember his Sunday morning show on Channel Three. They broadcast it from Lauritano's restaurant. All local talent." DePre glided his chair back to upright and leaned over his desk toward Owen.

"The point is, with the family having a little money and his sister turned into a recording star, Phil sometimes thought he was hot shit."

Owen had already heard from Brock the story about Gordon's dream of being a big time entertainment lawyer and he drifted off as DePre described the tension between Phil and others in the neighborhood. But he refocused on his mission when DePre mentioned Giunta's cologne.

"Can you imagine that, a supposed street kid walking around the neighborhood in a suit and smelling like a flower shop?" DePre paused and Owen had his chance to speak.

"What ever happened to the other guys from the gang?"

To Owen's relief, DePre remained upright with his elbows on his desk. "Well, Rich Caputo ended up in jail by the time he was twenty-three or so, just after me and Phil graduated from Temple. He had been robbing houses in Society Hill. When he got out, he went straight. Got a job at a deli around Second and Shunk and, after maybe ten years, bought it from the owner who was retiring."

Owen hoped there weren't too many delis around Second and Shunk but didn't ask for specifics. Didn't think it was wise to suggest he would be doing follow up interviews. Meanwhile, DePre continued.

"Nicky Scalero? I have no clue. But I know the Walsh brothers work on the docks. Someone told me they make more on the side selling stolen cargo than they do from their union wages."

Owen was apprehensive about asking where the Walshes could be found. He'd ask Caputo. If he could find Caputo. DePre seemed to have forgotten Barrett. "And Barrett?"

"Oh, yeah. Barrett went into the military. Special Forces. But I heard he got kicked out. Always fighting. I have no idea where he is now."

Owen held his breath as DePre leaned back again, hands spread out in front of him in a gesture of finality.

"So Phil was the only one of his gang to make anything of himself. Maybe that's the theme of your story. But, truth be told, that was only because his brothers pushed him. They now have a law practice and a little bank on Snyder Avenue. And I guess, because Phil always hoped for a glamorous life riding his sister's coattails."

So far so good. DePre had finished up still assuming he'd merely given background for the firm's memorial tribute to Phil Gordon. Owen was reluctant to jeopardize the successful deception. But he had to ask.

"Just curious, Dan. Did any of those guys from the neighborhood have a distinctive voice? A raspy voice? Phil's secretary said he occasionally got calls from a guy who sounded like Oscar the Grouch. Said he was an old friend of Phil's." DePre had been so pleasant, Owen's throat went thick with guilt over the lie.

DePre didn't flinch. "Nope. I'm the only one with a funny voice. Like it stalled during puberty."

"Well thanks, Dan. You've been a great help." Owen got up and held out his hand to DePre. He wanted to get out of there quickly. They shook and he said he would find his way out. Not that he thought DePre was inclined to walk him to the elevator.

Chapter 41

Barrett could only case the Chester County meth lab in the late afternoon. The place was busy at night. So every other day, he'd drive through the rundown industrial park near US1 and Route 202 and figure out the best approach. Meth labs themselves were pretty volatile and once he got things started, his work would be obliterated. Particularly since once the cops saw what the place was, they'd assume the explosion was what they might call self-inflicted. With each trip, he'd bring a duffle bag full of supplies to the motel room on 202. With a week or so to go, he felt pretty comfortable with his plan. And, having done work for these clients before, he had no worries about payment.

But that disaster of a job for Giunta had taken a lot out of him and he regularly found himself daydreaming of a beach in Florida, or California, or maybe a cabin in Vermont. He was getting too old for this kind of life. One or two more good paydays to add to his army pension and he was done.

Chapter 42

When Owen left DePre it was about six, already dark now that daylight savings had ended. Owen walked to Suburban Station and took the train to Chestnut Hill. At the newsstand in Chestnut Hill he bought the local weekly and threw all of it away except the classifieds.

In his hotel room, over General Tso's chicken from Shanghai Garden, he scanned the classifieds for a cheap old car, made some phone calls and found one for sale by an owner who lived only a few blocks from the hotel. They agreed to meet at eight the next morning before the owner went to work.

When he finished his chicken, he went downstairs to the hotel computer and surfed around until he found a security shop in Roxborough that, from its website, looked like it could meet his needs. Then he spent $39.95 on his credit card for a year's subscription to Peoplesearch.com, and gave an hour's time in an effort to track down that old gang of Phil's.

By nine o'clock the next morning, Owen was waiting outside at the nearest motor vehicle service agency in the two thousand dollar junker he had purchased for cash, courtesy of old man Colgrove. He had a temporary registration and new tags on the car within a half hour after the agency opened for business.

The old junker ran well enough for his purposes. He filled it with gas and drove to the security shop in Roxborough. After a three-hour wait and one thousand more of Colgrove's cash he was ready.

Since speaking with DePre, Owen had known he'd focus first on Al Barrett. Special forces training. Hot tempered. But how would he find him? Peoplesearch.com had identified sixteen "Al Barretts" in Philadelphia, most of them in black neighborhoods. None in South Philly. So he figured that, before tracking down each one, he'd first go down to Second and Shunk and hope there weren't sixteen delis in the neighborhood.

Owen was in luck. Only two delis in the area. And one was named Caputo's. What was even better was the guy behind the counter, balding with a maybe too dirty apron over a middle aged gut, looked like he was probably the owner. Owen ordered a roast beef hoagie and asked the guy if he was Rich Caputo.

"The one and only." His whole face smiled: eyes, mouth, cheeks. His teeth were uneven but they gave his cheerful face a cockeyed happiness that almost made Owen laugh. When he finished using the meat slicer, Owen gave him a line about the Phil Giunta memorial. Told him Dan DePre had mentioned he had been a friend of Phil. For a street-smart guy who had served time, Caputo didn't show even a tiny bit of suspicion. Owen was grateful as Caputo talked while he was made the hoagie.

"That was a long time ago. Completely different lifetime. We were all smartasses back then. But Phil was lucky. He had a good family to keep him on the straight and narrow. College. Law school. Did you know his brothers own a bank? Me, I got into trouble and had to pay for it. Lucky to be where I'm at today. Shame about Phil, though. Read about it in the Daily News."

Owen let Caputo ramble on with the now familiar stories about Gordon's fancy clothes and high-fallutin' plans. When he paused to cut a hoagie roll, Owen spoke up.

"What about the rest of Phil's old buddies? Do you know what they're doing now?"

"Well, Pat Walsh is a regular customer here. He lives up Second Street if you want to find him. I don't know where Mike lives but Pat says they're both doin' fine. They bought a place at the shore, Wildwood, I think. From what I hear, though, they've been stealin' down at the docks. It'll catch up with them someday." Caputo had set out a piece of deli-wrap on the counter and was flattening out Owen's roll on it. He continued to talk while he worked.

"Nicky Scalero moved to Jersey and I haven't heard anything about him in years. You want oil, mayo or what?"

"A little bit of oil. Lettuce, tomato, onions, sweet peppers, salt, pepper and oregano." Like most Philadelphians, Owen had a definite taste in hoagies. But he was hungry only for more information.

"What about Al Barrett?"

"Oh. That guy. You don't want to contact him. Besides, I have no idea where he lives. I'd like to forget him, myself. But he comes in here every now and then. Just to say hello, he says. You said salt, pepper and oregano?"

"Right. So Barrett must still live in Philly?

"I guess so. But, like I said, I don't care for the guy. He was always a nasty dude. Truth is, I was afraid of him. He got me into a lot of trouble before he joined the service. I was scared of ratting on him, so I went to jail and he got into the Special Forces."

Caputo cut the open hoagie in half, closed it, and wrapped it in the deli-paper, finally taping it tight with a short strip of tape from his dispenser.

"Since he got his voice box broke in a fight, he sounds as nasty as he really is. No. You don't want to interview him."

Owen's heart began to race. He had his man. And he was from Philly. Not an import from Pittsburgh or Detroit. Owen couldn't wait to start the hunt.

"Well, Rich, you have been helpful. I may try to reach Pat Walsh, too. How much for the hoagie?"

"It's on me. For Phil."

Owen thanked Caputo and almost ran out to the junker.

He grabbed the print out from Peoplesearch.com from the passenger seat. Most of the Al Barretts on the list lived in areas of the city where Owen was pretty sure that a white guy from St. Andrea's was not going to end up. That left only a few possibles. But even though there were no Al Barretts listed anywhere in South Philly, Owen assumed from Caputo's story that Barrett still lived there. The list was probably incomplete. It would be more productive to spend most of his time in South Philly.

Chapter 43

Owen hit pay dirt in three days. He had made one or two forays each morning to other white sections of the city to check out Al Barretts on the Peoplesearch list before spending his afternoons cruising the vicinity of the Social Club. All he had to show for his Peoplesearch labor was a rabbi in the Northeast and community college professor named Al Barrett who lived in East Falls. But on the third afternoon he spotted a figure dressed like the Dellasandro's mugger walking toward him on Fourth Street. He drove past him and made an illegal U at the corner of Fourth and McKean, then backtracked at a walker's pace. Fortunately, there was not much traffic to honk him forward at a faster speed. A few blocks down Fourth Street, Barrett—Owen had already started thinking of him as Barrett—entered a row house with a red pickup parked in front.

Ka-ching!

Owen called Kopinski. He was out. Owen told the wheezing Detective Cooper who answered that he had found Oscar.

"Oscar who?"

"Just tell Kopinski that Owen Delaney called to say he found Oscar. It's important."

"O . . . kay." Cooper yawned.

"When do you expect him back?"

"Hard to say. He's out on that university sniper thing."

"Well, leave him a big note then. Please."

"Sure. I'll do that. *Oscar*, you said?"

"Right. Owen gave his cell phone number and hung up.

Owen began a stake out immediately, afraid Barrett might flee before Kopinski got back to him. From the junker parked along the street or from a pizza shop about a hundred feet down, he watched the row house all morning. Kopinski never called.

He saw Barrett leave about noon carrying a duffle bag which he fastened with bungee cords in the bed of his pickup. Owen stayed in place when the pickup drove off, afraid that tailing Barrett on the road required skills he didn't have. But he found himself pounding his steering wheel when Barrett hadn't returned by six-thirty. Owen left for Chestnut Hill hoping he hadn't lost Barrett for good, that the duffle bag wasn't stuff he needed for a getaway.

• • •

First thing the next morning, from his hotel room in Chestnut Hill, he called Kopinski again. Still out. A woman with a high-pitched voice answered the line.

"We don't expect him in today. He did a double shift on the sniper case yesterday and he's off today."

"Is there a message on his desk from Owen Delaney? About finding Oscar?"

"I'll look." Owen could hear the phone clunk on Kopinski's desk and the shuffling of papers.

"Don't see anything. Want me to write one?"

"Yes, please. Write that Owen Delaney has found Oscar. Use big letters." He gave her his cell number and asked her to repeat it to prove she had at least written something down.

He drove the junker back to South Philly and almost screamed when he saw the red pickup parked in front of a hydrant on Barrett's block. He sat and waited all day in an illegal space about fifty feet away, occasionally running into a nearby pizza shop for a slice or two and a quick pee.

At about five, Barrett left for a walk. But this time Owen followed. On foot. Barrett went to the Social Club. Owen alternated his watch time among two pizza shops on the block, ordering a slice at a time until he was stuffed and he was sure the proprietors were suspicious. Barrett emerged about eleven and walked back home. Owen snuck to his car and drove back to Chestnut Hill.

• • •

In the morning, Kopinski called while Owen was having an early breakfast in the coffee shop next to his hotel.

"Delaney? I got your message. Hope he's the right guy. But I'm tied up with the sniper business and have to hand the Oscar matter over to Detective Cooper. He's nearing retirement, but he's still pretty good. He'll call you as soon as he can."

"I'm sure I got the right guy. His name's Al Barrett. When will Cooper call?"

"He's not in yet. It's only seven thirty. But I left the file on his desk with a note to call you. Should be this morning."

Shit, Owen thought. Cooper didn't even bother to write down his message for Kopinski. Owen figured it was best to head back down to Barrett's house again.

He got there about nine and waited in the junker. No movement by Barrett. About noon, he took out his phone to call Cooper but realized Kopinski had not given him Cooper's number. He called Kopinski's line instead. No answer. Didn't anyone stay there during lunch? The thought of calling the Inquirer popped into his head again. Or maybe calling Carter Brock would be safer. He decided to give Cooper more time.

But Cooper never called, and two more calls to Kopinski's line got nothing but promises from that same high voiced woman to leave a message for Cooper. She sounded pissed that he kept calling.

That evening, after a long day of seeing nothing of Barrett except another afternoon excursion with that duffle bag in his pickup and his early evening stroll to the Social Club, Owen called Barbara while he waited in his car up the block from the club. When he told her where he was and what he planned to do, she screamed at him.

"No! No! That's crazy. You'll get yourself hurt! Or worse."

"Calm down, Barb. I don't intend to be on my own. I've called the police and I'm just waiting to hear from them."

After a litany of promises by Owen to be careful and not do anything without the police, they chatted pleasantly about all sorts of other things until the charge on his phone ran out, a few minutes before Barrett left the Social Club.

Barrett left alone and walked home along the same route he'd taken the previous night.

In the morning Owen saw on his fully charged phone that he had received a voicemail about eleven the previous evening. From Cooper. Finally.

Owen could hear a TV blaring in the background of Cooper's message, and Cooper stopped talking several times, apparently to pay more attention to the show. By the time the message had played out, Owen's gut was churning. Cooper was going to be off the next two days but had "just wanted to touch base about this Oscar thing" before he went down the shore to close up his beach house. Sorry he missed Owen.

Damn. How could this be happening? It was Kafkaesque. He closed his eyes and pressed the heels of his hands to his temples until it hurt.

Promise to Barbara or not, he decided to execute his plan on his own. If he played it right, he'd be safe enough.

Chapter 44

That night was cold, the first real cold one of the fall. Owen could see his breath as he sat in the junker with the engine off, glad he'd bought a watchmen's cap that morning at a stall in the Italian Market. He had stopped there for a sandwich, fruit and a fill-up of a coffee thermos in preparation for his long day of sitting and watching. As usual, Barrett had taken his duffle bag somewhere during the afternoon, and returned in time for what must be dinner at the Social Club. At about nine forty five, Owen left his spot near the Social Club and parked on Fourth Street, under a streetlight near where Barrett habitually crossed to reach his home. He rolled his window down and hoped the light was good enough.

At about ten fifteen, he saw Barrett coming down Fourth Street, dressed in his usual outfit, hood up against the cold. Like most people Owen had noticed walking by themselves over the past few days, Barrett faced straight ahead and did not look around until it came time for him to cross the street.

There was no traffic and Barrett stepped off the curb about fifteen feet in front of the junker and started to cross to the side on which Owen was parked. Owen took a deep breath and called out.

"Hey Al. Al Barrett."

Barrett stopped in the middle of the street. *Now* he looked around, taking in the empty rowhouse stoops up and down the block and squinting into the cars parked in Owen's vicinity. He apparently saw nothing to concern him and approached Owen's open window. His hands were in his oversized pockets. That worried Owen. Owen had to be quick. Before Barrett reached him, he flashed a brown envelope out the car window.

"Three thousand dollars. There's more to come if you agree to leave me alone."

"Who the fuck are you? I've never seen you before in my life." Barrett grabbed the envelope and snuck a peek inside as he bent down for a closer look at Owen. Owen pulled off the watchcap.

"Maybe now you remember."

He thought Barrett registered a flicker of recognition. He was sure when he rasped "Why would I want to hurt *you*?"

"Let's just say I've been worried, okay? I'll bring you some more in a few days." Owen faced forward, ready to pull away, but Barrett reached through the window and grabbed his jacket. Owen took his foot off the gas, felt his knee quiver, but told himself he could always speed away if he had to.

"Get out of the car." Barrett's thick voice was conversational but firm. Owen didn't move. Then Barrett yelled. "Get out of the damn car before I pull you through the fuckin' window."

Owen hoped someone would hear the commotion but the street was deserted. So he stayed where he was. Barrett leaned in the window and began patting Owen's chest with his free hand.

"If you got a fuckin wire on you, I'm gonna beat you senseless, shithead."

Owen understood and was barely able to control the impulse to sneak a peek at the tiny video recorder clipped to the passenger side sun visor.

"If that's all you're worried about, let me out. No problem."

Barrett yanked open the door and stepped back as Owen twisted out of the car and stood eye to eye with him.

"Turn around. Hands on the roof. Spread your legs." Barrett had obviously done this before.

Owen did as he was told and the search was over in seconds. Barrett relaxed. Owen shook himself off before speaking.

"Satisfied? All I want to do is buy a little peace of mind."

Though he felt like puking, Owen was proud of the calm he projected. He got back into the junker and rolled up the window. Barrett glared at him and he glared back, he hoped for long enough to suggest he wasn't afraid. Then he pulled away, leaving Barrett standing in the light from the lamppost, staring blankly at his taillights.

He pulled over next to a fire hydrant a few blocks down Fourth Street. He had barely breathed during the short drive. The tremor in his hands, even as they held the steering wheel, reminded him of the old folks he had visited for a community service project in high school. Suddenly, his simple plan was no longer so simple. He should have assumed Barrett would take the offensive in some way. And he might again. On the other hand, while Barrett was no amateur, his skill set might be a bit outdated. He hadn't even considered the possibility of a hidden camera in Owen's car.

Owen wondered if he should go back to the shop in Roxborough and replace his NanoCamHD camcorder with one of the mini recorders they sold embedded in a Coke can. Or maybe the one built into a pair of eyeglasses. But the guy had said that the picture quality with the NanoCamHD was the best. And that was key. Besides, Barrett would probably be more lax next time.

Chapter 45

Barrett dropped Delaney's cash on his kitchen table, grabbed a beer from the fridge and sat down to think. It was obviously not a good sign that the kid had found him. How the fuck he did that, he couldn't even guess. Hell, when he called him over, he had no clue who the kid was until he took off his hat. But unfortunately, now that he knew, it meant there was more *neutralizing* to be done.

He took a long swig of his beer and rocked on his chair, remembering the kid had said he'd be back with more. For a guy smart enough to find him, the kid had a pretty stupid take on how to protect himself. Delaney'd been better off using the money to get someone to neutralize *him*. But if he is that stupid, it would make sense to milk him for all he can before putting him down. Make up for the failed payday from Giunta. God knows the kid must be rich, from the looks of his house.

Barrett felt his heartbeat quicken as he imagined using his picks on the Delaney back door once again and searching for a hidden wad of cash. Speed up the transfer of funds. Skip the installment plan.

He smiled and took another long swig. Then it occurred to him that Delaney was the type to keep his money in the bank. Rich kids like him used credit cards and checks. He probably thought there was some reason he had to withdraw his cash in small amounts so it wouldn't look funny, or something. Asshole. He thunked his beer on the table and chewed on the inside of his cheek.

Okay, so he'd wait and play the kid's game.

Chapter 46

Owen drove up to New York and stayed with Barbara that night. She was already asleep when he called enroute. But since his previous visit she was, often as not, without a roommate. Joanie had even moved a few of her things into Rick's place.

In the morning, when he told her what he'd done the night before, Barbara gasped.

"Owen! You promised!"

"I know, Barb. I know. But I just didn't know what to do. The cops are either overworked or not interested. Leaving it up to them feels stupid. My plan is the only way. Without it, all I've got is a weird voice and a red pickup. On his face alone, I couldn't even be sure Barrett was the guy who stabbed me."

They had been having an early morning coffee at a Starbucks on Fifty Ninth Street near the stop for Barbara's bus. Had they not been in a public place and had Owen not been keenly aware that he and Barbara had never before argued, he'd have raised his voice. As it was, he spoke more rapidly than Barb was used to.

"And besides, even if I could prove he was the guy after me, that doesn't tie him to the four murders he committed." He reached out and touched her hand.

"If the cops don't do something soon, I'm going to keep going. Believe me, I'll be safe."

Barbara took a sip of her coffee and looked over the rim of the cup directly into Owen's eyes. Without seeing her full face, Owen had a hard time guessing what she was thinking. In the short time he'd known her, Owen had developed a respect for her self-discipline and the firmness of her opinions. So his stomach churned and he prayed that she wasn't going to give him an ultimatum.

She put the cup down, pulled her hand away from his and folded her two hands together on the edge of their table. She said nothing and nervously tapped her thumbs together. Owen held his breath. Finally she sighed and almost whispered.

"I don't agree, Owen. But I guess I understand." Her lower lip quivered and she put a hand to her mouth. "If something happened to you after Virginia, I'd have a hard time living with myself."

"I promise I won't take any crazy chances." Owen reached out and grabbed her hand again. They sat in silence until the bus arrived. Owen remembered that one of the minicams came inside a thermos.

Owen neither called nor heard from anyone in the Philly police department all day. At dinner with Barbara that night, Owen could almost believe things were back to normal. But he occasionally found himself thinking of a book he had read about George Mallory, the first Englishman to try to climb Mt. Everest. He failed on his first attempt. Several years later, in the days and weeks leading up to his second excursion, he was ecstatic with anticipation, keen to finally make it to the mountain's peak. But his wife, who put on a show of support, was filled with dread and unspoken anger.

George Mallory died in that second attempt.

Chapter 43

Over coffee at Starbucks the next morning, Owen buried himself in *The Times*, rising up occasionally to report tidbits of the news to Barbara who was checking emails on her cell phone. All very domestic. As the time for her bus to Sterling and Moss drew near, Owen stood up.

"I heard nothing from Cooper or Kopinski yesterday. I'm sick of waiting. I'm going to try to meet with Barrett again tonight. He's wondered about me long enough."

Barbara moved toward him and gave him a peck on the cheek and a squeeze of his shoulder. Without saying a word, she turned and walked to the bus stop.

When he finished his coffee, Owen called the Roundhouse in Philly and actually got through to Cooper who confessed that he hadn't yet read the case file. Then Owen tried in vain to reach Kopinski to ask that the case be transferred to someone else.

Owen made several more unsuccessful attempts to reach Kopinski while he drove to Philly. So by mid-afternoon, jaw sore from a day-long clench, he set himself up in a coffee shop along Barrett's route to the Social Club. When he spotted Barrett walking toward the Club with a buddy a little after five, he assumed the routine was set for the rest of the night; and he drove to the Oregon Diner and picked at salad and lasagna before driving back to Fourth Street. He had to wait up the block for a long while before the spot under the streetlight at the corner was free. It was not a legal spot, but that didn't seem to matter in South Philly.

At about ten fifteen, Barrett came strolling down Fourth Street, again paying little attention to his surroundings. Owen could not be sure, but it looked to him like Barrett was a little unsteady on his feet.

Barrett got to the corner and looked both ways without giving any indication that he'd noticed Owen or his junker. When Owen hollered to him this time, the brown envelope was already dangling out the open window.

Barrett approached without the caution he'd shown the last time. A good sign. When he was a few feet away, Owen pulled the envelope back inside the car.

"I still need your word that I'm going to be safe." When he heard what he had just said, a bad line delivered with without conviction, he thought Barrett might laugh at him. But he didn't. Maybe he *was* a little tipsy. At any rate, it got the conversation started.

"Why would I want to hurt you, kid?" Barrett's speech was lightly slurred.

"Oh. Just to clean up loose ends. If Nicky and Phil were disposable, I certainly should be." Owen flipped the envelope to Barrett.

"I'll see you soon." He drove off before Barrett had any chance to react.

Owen hoped that the prospect of easy cash would keep Barrett on the string; but he knew mentioning Gordon and Scalero was raising the ante.

Chapter 47

At his kitchen table again, Barrett counted the money he'd gotten from Delaney. Eight thousand total. Not twenty-five by a long shot, but it was at least something for all his work.

His body felt heavy and he grimaced slightly when he thought about the ballsy question the kid had asked. Was the kid just guessing? Or did it mean he was still trying to figure out where he stood himself? And why the fuck didn't he just go to the police if he had suspicions? Crazy.

The more he thought about it, the less he liked dealing with a crazy. No telling what could happen. It would be better to end this thing quick. Get on with the meth lab job and, if he didn't have enough to retire, maybe he could get a legit job with a demolition company.

Chapter 48

Guessing he'd pushed the right button by essentially accusing Barrett of murdering Gordon and Scalero, Owen's heart was still pounding an hour later as he stretched out on the bed in his hotel room. Hands laced on the pillow under his head, he tried to put himself in Barrett's shoes. Would the lure of easy money trump his instinct to deal with his accuser in his usual way? What would he do when he thought he'd milked Owen for all he could get? And when would that be?

In the morning, after a nearly sleepless night, he walked to the street where he lived and staked out his own house from the still idle construction site across the way. About eleven, as he had imagined in one of his Barrett ruminations, the red pickup cruised by and then, on a second pass up his street, drove in his driveway to the rear parking area.

Barrett got out and went to the back door. How he opened it, Owen could only guess. But he stayed for about an hour. Had he planted a bomb? Just searched the place for cash? Or was he just waiting for Owen?

When Barrett left, Owen called Kopinski's line. He had seen on the news that the university sniper had been caught. Hopefully that meant Kopinski could focus on Barrett. But no. Kopinski was meeting with the DA all day and Cooper had taken another personal day off. So he returned to his hotel room and lay down on the bed again, rehearsing his act for that evening. Fuck the cops. He was going do what he had to do and hoped that Barrett would be surprised being visited two nights in a row.

• • •

That night, Owen picked a different spot, about two blocks closer to the Social Club. He wanted to catch Barrett off guard. As Barrett walked up Fourth toward his home, Owen coasted alongside him and called out from the middle of the street.

"Hey Barrett, I got more money." He stopped the car and waggled another envelope as Barrett approached.

Barrett smiled and nodded, keeping his hands loose at his sides. That comforted Owen. As Barrett got to conversational distance, Owen snatched the envelope back into the car.

"One question for you first." He kept his voice low.

Barrett bent down to get a better look at Owen and maybe to hear him better. His face was framed perfectly by the open window and Owen could smell alcohol on his breath. Owen continued in a tone he hoped was believably casual.

"Actually, two questions."

Barrett grunted. Owen took it to be a non-committal invitation to go ahead and ask.

"Just wondering. How could you be sure those girls would die? People have lived through worse."

"And what's your second question?" Barrett's face hardened. Owen tensed, but pushed on.

"Nicky Scalero. Wasn't it hard? You two went way back."

"Shit, kid. You got that all wrong. Nicky did that to himself. I would never have hurt him." Barrett moved closer, his head almost through the open window. "But once he knew I got to that wuss

Giunta . . ." He stopped and made a face that looked like he was sniffing raw sewage.

"No one ever trusted that fucker. Nicky must have figured it was me or the cops. He was always a big bear with a chicken heart."

"I still wonder what would've happened if those girls had lived." Owen worried he was pushing his luck. Barrett almost took the bait but promptly spit it out.

"Well they didn't, did they?"

Barrett now had both hands in the open window and was shifting his weight foot to foot. Owen decided to get out of there before he exploded. He handed him the envelope.

"I'll see you again when I get some more."

Barrett was still leaning into the car as he pried open the flap of the envelope. After peaking at the cash he raised his gaze up to Owen and noticed the minicam on the visor just beyond Owen's head.

"What's that?" He pointed with his chin.

Owen hadn't planned for this.

"Speed trap detector" was all he could think to say. Barrett squinted.

"I don't think so. Gimme it."

"No. I spent good money for that. I'm not givin' it away."

Barrett stuffed the money envelope in his pocket and grabbed Owen with both hands, yanking him toward the window and screaming in his face.

"You sneaky bastard."

Barrett let go with his right hand and reached down for the door handle. As the door latch clicked, Owen gently pressed down the accelerator. Barrett couldn't open the door against the forward momentum of the vehicle, so he started to jog alongside. Owen picked up speed but Barrett ran faster, now tugging on Owen's jacket with both hands again.

Though steering was difficult, Owen decided to accelerate wildly and let Barrett land where he may. But scanning the street in front of him, he saw a car stopped about eighty yards ahead in the middle of the narrow, one-way street, letting out some happy passengers.

He veered to the left hoping he could knock Barrett off him by pinching him between his car and those parked along the street. But squeamish about the idea, he performed the move too slowly and Barrett let go without getting hurt. He slid behind Owen's car as it neared the line of parked vehicles. Now Owen was between the group of revelers in front and Barrett in back.

He tooted his horn as he quickened his pace toward the car up ahead. Two of the passengers were still chatting with others in the car. A third gave him the finger as he honked and drew closer. Barrett walked calmly up the street behind him. Owen rolled up his window and locked the door.

One more honk and it became clear that the group ahead was pissed enough to spite him. Two of them now stood staring him down with their arms folded across their chests. Barrett moved closer.

Owen then did the only thing he could do. Putting the car in reverse, he turned to look out the rear window and accelerated, steering with his left arm. The position stretched out his still tender knife wound. But that was the least of his worries. He barreled down the street at Barrett who was forced to jump away when Owen got about five feet from him. He tried but failed to grab the door handle as Owen passed, then ran after the car trying to hop on its hood. Owen hoped he could avoid hitting parked cars as he weaved down Fourth Street with Barrett chasing him. And he hoped no cars would turn on to the one-way street as he backed out of it.

His luck held and he exited on McKean with a panting Barrett still fifty feet away.

He drove the junker to the Roundhouse on Franklin Square where Kopinski had interviewed him. It was unlikely that Kopinski would be on duty at that hour, but it was important that he show his evidence to the police before Barrett fled. He explained himself to the sergeant on duty who called Kopinski. Owen spoke to Kopinski and filled him in quickly on his self-help adventure.

While they waited for Kopinski to come in to headquarters, Owen connected the video adapter to a computer, inserted the card from the NanoCamHD and, in minutes, was reliving his meetings with Barrett. The quality of the video was fantastic, every bit as good as that taxi cab quiz show, despite the limited light. Every word spoken was intelligible. Kopinski would love it.

And love it Kopinski did. Despite calling Owen an asshole for confronting Barrett, Kopinski did admit that the video together with Owen's prior testimony was more than enough to take Barrett in. He did that right away, finding Owen's law school diploma and about five thousand dollars of his money in the process. The judge denied bail, and the DA indicated he expected to get life imprisonment for Barrett.

At Owen's request, Kopinski had Owen's Highlander and his house inspected for explosives. The car was clean: but they did find a powerful device wired to the thermostat in the family room.

Barbara had requested—and with Rick's help been given—a few days off to travel down to Philly to be with Owen. He loved having her in the house and she said she couldn't get over how relaxed she felt with so much space and no work pressures tormenting her. She was even able to call her Aunt Donna to share the upsetting details of Virginia's death. And Aunt Donna had her own news for Barbara. Hated stepfather Bruce had remarried. To that one old friend of Ginny's. It had to have been the news of her engagement that sent Ginny into her tailspin.

A few days after Barbara returned to New York, Owen received a call from Fran Resnick. Once Resnick had learned the details of Virginia's murder, he tracked down Owen through the Rancocas police and wanted to apologize and offer thanks. Owen was pleased with his own graciousness, but still wondered whether Marian had any life insurance.

And finally, cleaning out his junk email folder, Owen noticed a series of old emails captioned "Popeye". Most of the girls he'd self-importantly emailed about their online stalker had answered to say everyone at the complex knew Roman's little hobby and just played along, but thanks anyway.

EPILOGUE
One Year Later

"Trust me, Owen. It will all be fine."

They were already in West Virginia and Owen was still unhappy that he'd agreed to go. But Barbara had been determined from the moment she read about the memorial service in *The Times*. First, she had asked for a few days off at the Porter firm and, as usual, found that Philadelphia firms were more easygoing on these matters than those in New York. They had been great about the wedding. Then she had called Owen who was at the university library working on a paper due for his class in contemporary American lit. Owen had initially refused to go.

"Why would I want to do that?" The idea seemed truly outlandish to Owen.

"Because you need closure, that's why."

It occurred to Owen that he might someday do a paper about the over-emphasis on the sappy concept of closure in literature and, for that matter, in the lives of everyday people. Indeed, the first image that occurred to him when Barbara told him Colgrove had died suddenly was of himself, alone at Colgrove's lonely grave surrounded by leafless trees, spilling his seed onto the fresh turned earth. That was the kind of angry closure he envisioned.

But he had given in and agreed to drive with Barb to Kentucky for the service at Southern Kentucky University.

As they approached the university, Barbara pulled *The Times* obituary from her bag and reread it.

"His career was quite impressive, you know."

"Uh huh." As they got closer to the town, the memories of his Christmas time visit almost two years before became more clear and surprisingly painful. He did not want to talk about Colgrove.

"It says here that he married his current wife only seven years ago. His first wife died back in '96. She was the one he was married to when he knew your mom." Barbara read in silence for a few moments before resuming her commentary.

"Looks like you had a half-sister who died as a teenager. Neither Colgrove nor the second wife ever had any other children." She folded the paper and put it away.

"You're all that's left, buddy. Hard to believe he treated you the way he did."

"Yeah." Owen was holding back a huge sob.

As they pulled through the main gates to the university and followed the directions of student traffic guides to the hall where the service was to be held, the tightening in Owen's chest became a full-blown seizure and breathing became difficult. A crew cut young man in an orange poncho directed him to a parking spot. As he pulled into it, Barbara put a hand on his shoulder. At her touch, he began an uncontrollable cry. He had thought he was over Colgrove. Maybe he did need some sort of closure.

They sat in the car for a few minutes before joining the other attendees walking from the parking lot and collecting into a line in front of a gothic stone building that was apparently the university's original convocation center. Looking around, Owen guessed that he was the only mourner arriving in tears. If they only knew.

The service itself was predictable and lasted about an hour. Reminded him a lot of the service for Frazier. Except that, when it was finished, Colgrove's wife was the first to leave, followed by a procession of faculty members in their academic gowns.

Heroically, the widow Colgrove waited in the vestibule of the building to thank everyone who had come to remember her husband. She was in her sixties, a pleasant looking woman with neatly coiffed grey hair and a trim figure set off well by her black mourning dress. As Barbara pulled Owen towards the woman—he had been trying to avoid the perfunctory meeting—Owen could see that her exchanges with those greeting her were more than perfunctory. She seemed to know them all and lit up for each new face that greeted her. Her eyes twinkled and, despite the circumstances, she smiled throughout and often laughed. Owen imagined that his own mom would have looked like her had she lived to her sixties.

Owen and Barb had sat in the rear of the hall and were among the last to file toward Mrs. Colgrove. Owen was grateful that Barbara took it upon herself to speak when they were finally standing in front of her.

"Hello, Mrs. Colgrove. I'm Barbara Delaney and this is my husband, Owen. From Philadelphia. We are very sorry for your loss."

Apparently not recognizing either Barbara or Owen, the light in the woman's face dimmed for a second before she asked "And how did you know George?"

Owen spoke up, probably too coldly. "We really didn't. I only met him once. Two Christmases ago. As Barbara said, we are sorry for your loss." He took Barbara by the elbow and tried to move along. But the woman squeezed Owen's arm.

"Wait." She looked up at Owen's hair. "Are you by chance the young man whose mother sent you to George? As she was dying?"

Owen froze, overcome with a weird sense that he was looking at himself and Barbara and Mrs. Colgrove from afar. He did not respond until Barbara nudged him with her elbow.

"Ah. Yes, ma'am. I am"

"Oh, you poor boy. George told me all about it." She lowered her voice and moved closer to them.

"He told me he needed to go to the office that day for a meeting though he'd promised to take Christmas week off. Your meeting disturbed him enough for me to notice when he got home. I pressed him but he didn't want to talk about it. When I became angry, thinking he had met with an old flame, he decided to tell me everything. Everything but your name. He was afraid I'd try to contact you." She reached out and took hold of Owen's shoulders.

"I was so mad at him for how he treated you. And me. Never having any children myself, I so much wanted to meet you. But he refused. We didn't speak for days."

Her grip on his shoulders shifted to a big maternal hug.

"Dear boy. Please stay here. Visit with me. We have to get to know each other."

Owen smiled as she ran her hand over his hair.

The End

Acknowledgements

It's very likely that every first time novelist cringes at passages in that first work that he just couldn't seem to get exactly right. Needless to say, that is the case with me and *Shock Treatment*. However, there would have been many more cringe-worthy passages and plot elements had I not benefited from the input of a host of early readers who gently maneuvered me toward the version I am willing to foist on the reading public. Janet Benton, Carol Gaskin and Philip Newey each did me a great service with full blown critiques; and Mary Ellen Caffrey, Roseanne Potter, Bill McCarthy, Brian Baxter, Peter Lapham, Carol Moehrke, Cathy Holzmann, Rhonda Dix-Norris, Harry Conry, Doug Huron, Jennifer Cohen, Tamara Jaron and George Rennie all made helpful suggestions which improved the work—and my work—immensely.

About the Author

Gene Caffrey is a retired Philadelphia lawyer and real estate investor
who has had a life-long love of sports and the novels of Dick Francis.
He has been married for nearly 50 years and is the father of two
grown children. His familiarity with the gritty streets of Philadelphia
and his near total recall of its characters informs his writing with a
refreshing authenticity. He now divides his time between
Philadelphia, Sarasota (FL) and his farm in New Jersey.

47350954R00180

Made in the USA
Lexington, KY
04 December 2015